The POWER OF Love

CLARK SELBY

The Power of Love
Copyright © 2025 by Clark Selby

Library of Congress Control Number: 2025916503

ISBN
979-8-89641-094-2 (Paperback)
979-8-89641-095-9 (eBook)
979-8-89641-093-5 (Hardcover)

TABLE OF CONTENTS

1

Phone Call from Home

It was seven o'clock in the morning on July 9, 1999, in Seoul, Korea, when Chance heard a ringing noise in his head: what was it? As he tried to wake up, he couldn't remember where he was and what that awful ringing noise was in his head.

Finally, he awoke enough to remember he was in his apartment in Seoul and the ringing noise was his damn telephone. Who would be calling him this early in the morning?

He got up from his bed and made his way carefully across the bedroom to where his telephone was located on the dresser.

Chance was having trouble picking up the phone but eventually got the phone up to his ear and said, "This is Chance Clark."

The voice on the other end of the line said, "Dad, it's Chase and Shane. Mom was taken by ambulance to St. John's Hospital in Springfield, Missouri, today."

"What's wrong with her?"

"She went to the doctor this morning and he sent her to the hospital. They did an MRI and found she had a large aneurysm in her carotid artery and a small aneurysm on the left side of her brain.

"The doctors in Big Springs were afraid the large one in the carotid artery might rupture any time and they didn't have doctors in Big Springs who could handle it if did, so they sent her to St. John's Hospital in Springfield."

"Where are you and Shane?"

"We're in my car outside St. John's Hospital." "Have you seen a doctor in Springfield yet?" "Yes, we have."

"What did he say?"

"He said he needed to do an angiogram and to do it they have to insert a device like the ones they use to look at the heart. They have to go up through her neck into the carotid artery to see how bad the rupture is.

"Dad, he said it may kill her to do the procedure, but because the aneurysm is so large he doesn't know if she can live without doing something with it."

"Have you seen Mom since she got to St. John's?"

"We have, for only a few minutes. She's in an intensive care unit, so we can only see her a few minutes every couple of hours."

"How is she feeling?"

"Bad, she's hurting a lot and can't talk much and when she does talk she's hard to understand."

"OK, Chase, I'll see if I can get a flight out of Seoul this afternoon and be there as soon as I can. I'll call you back to let you know my flight schedule as soon as I know it."

After Chance got his reservations for his flights home he called Chase on his cell phone and told him his flight would leave Seoul at 3:00 p.m. for Los Angeles, then his next flight would take him to St. Louis, and then he would take another flight on to Springfield.

He said he should be there by around eight or nine o'clock the next night.

Chase told his dad that Shane and he would stay and keep checking on Mom as often as they could. He said the doctor told them he would do the angiogram sometime that night.

Chance began to get himself ready for a very long day. After he was dressed, he started packing clothes and tried to think of everything he thought he would need to take home.

He didn't have any idea how long it might be before he was back in Korea, so he didn't know how much he should pack.

He decided to pack his one large suitcase and take his briefcase with him.

His driver was scheduled to pick him up at eight forty-five this morning to take him to the office. He thought he would go to the office and talk to World Star Parking System's Korean partner and his country manager before going to Kimpo Airport.

Chance had a meeting with their Korean partner, Jimmy Kim, and his country manager, Charles Lorenzan, and told them what was going on with Ann and that he had made arrangements to fly home that afternoon.

They were both sorry to hear about Ann because they knew and liked Ann and said they would keep her in their prayers and that they would go with him to the airport.

Chance appreciated their prayers, as he was trying to keep his mind busy while he continued sending prayers to God for Ann to be all right.

Making their way through Seoul traffic was always an adventure; he was certainly pleased he didn't have to drive in Korea.

He had an excellent driver who made his way through Seoul traffic like an Indy 500 driver in a Memorial Day race.

Chance always thought the North Koreans could never invade Seoul since all the South Korean drivers would have to do was to get out of their vehicles, leave them parked on this eight-lane expressway, and block their tanks from ever getting through.

Arriving at the airport, Chance checked in for his flight and found he had enough time to have lunch with Jimmy and Charles. Conversation over lunch was light, as each of the three men was lost in their thought in some way about what Ann was going through.

Charles's thoughts turned to all the health problems his wife had been going through and since Jimmy was so fond of Ann and Chance, he hoped it would turn out well.

Chance couldn't stop thinking about what if she couldn't make it through the angiogram tonight. He wouldn't even have a chance to be with her and tell her how much he loved her.

After lunch Chance hugged both Jimmy and Charles as they were leaving to go back to the office.

Chance asked Charles to e-mail World Star Parking's main office in Washington, D.C. and tell them about Ann and that he was flying home to be with her.

He promised he would call them after he knew how Ann was doing.

After his friends left, he cleared security, immigration, and customs and went to the business lounge to wait for his flight.

Two hours later they announced his flight was boarding, so he picked up his briefcase and went to the gate to board his plane.

Arriving at the gate, he didn't have much time to board the plane and find his business-class seat.

By the time he settled in his seat, a flight attendant asked if he would like to have something to drink before they took off.

He asked her for a diet coke, since he finally had made the switch from regular coke to diet coke a few months ago to save a few calories.

The flight attendant quickly came back with his diet coke and asked if he would like anything else before taking off, and he told her no, thank you.

Before he had a chance to finish his diet coke and eat the ice, the announcement was made to fasten their seat belts, followed by the usual safety information required on every flight he had ever been on.

He had heard it so many times that he could do the safety information announcement without referring to a written copy of it.

He knew he had probably flown somewhere between five to six million miles; he knew for sure he had flown almost two million miles on TWA and American, which didn't count any of the miles flown on more than forty other airlines.

None of that made much difference right now, but the mind works in strange ways; it jumps from one thing to another, sometimes without really thinking about any one thing.

Maybe it did just to take his mind off the only thing that mattered at this moment in his life: Would Ann still be alive by the time he got to Springfield?

As the plane streaked its way across the Pacific Ocean, Chance thought back to all the illnesses and broken bones Ann had been through during her life.

Chance then took out a copy of Ann's medical history which he carried in his briefcase and looked it over to review all her problems; he felt like it looked more like a medical textbook than someone's medical history:

1961-1962: She had ITP (idiopathic thrombocytopenic purpura), resulting in having her spleen removed.

1963: Benign cystic disease of the ovaries, removal of left ovary and partial removal of right ovary.

1971: Small bone broken in left leg in a fall.

1974: Cystic tumors, hysterectomy, and bladder repair.

1980: Cystic fibroid breast disease in both breasts, tracked with annual mammograms to be sure it wasn't cancer.

1982: Fracture of right radius and ulna of the wrist in a fall.

1984: Lyme disease resulting in heart arrhythmia, fatigue, and chronic joint pain.

1990: Congenital defect of her left kidney requiring repair by surgery in 1995.

1993: Large hiatal hernia to be treated with drugs for the rest of her life.

Fractured left radius and ulna of the wrist and the twelfth vertebrae and pelvis in a fall.

Hospitalized with low blood count: dizziness, fatigue, joint pain, and dry mouth. Diagnosis: Lupus and Sjogren's syndrome.

Chance wondered how Ann was able to go through all the pain and suffering she went through over the years because he knew he would never have been able to stand it.

As his 747 continued flying across the Pacific Ocean, Chance thought back to when he and Ann first met in Algebra class in South

Webster Junior High School in Webster, Kansas. They had been fourteen years old and they had been together ever since.

They talked their parents into letting them get married when they were both sixteen years old. Their parents knew them well enough to know they were both determined to get married and be together. They thought if they didn't let them marry, they would just run away.

Their parents wanted to be involved in their lives and didn't want them to be going off and not even knowing where they were or if they were all right. So they finally gave in and let them get married.

On December 22, they would be married forty-seven years and they had never regretted the decision they made to get married so many years ago.

Like most couples, they had their share of good times and bad times, but they never felt like they had made a mistake getting married so young.

Chance thought about all the changes Ann had to endure with him being transferred so many times and changing jobs. Ann would have liked to have lived in the same town, the same state, and the same country.

Chance loved change and he knew Ann hated change.

They went through several years where they moved to a different city and state every thirteen months.

Ann would just get her house fixed up the way she wanted it and then she had to sell it and move somewhere else and go through the same thing all over again.

Chance knew she had to really love him to make all those moves as bad as she hated to make changes.

Chance couldn't imagine life without Ann. She had to be all right; she just had to be!

Eight hours later they landed in Los Angeles. Chance gathered his things, retrieved his bag from baggage claim, cleared customs and immigration, rechecked his bag, and went to find the gate for his flight to St. Louis.

After finding his way to his new gate, he called Chase and told him he was in Los Angeles and was waiting for his flight to St. Louis.

Although he was almost afraid to ask, he asked if they had done the angiogram on Ann yet. Chase answered no, they planned to do it the next day.

Then Chance asked, "How is Mom doing?"

Chase said, "Because of her pain she's pretty well out of it. They have her doped up so much she can hardly talk."

"The next time you see her, tell her I'm on my way home and I love her."

"OK, Dad, I will. I love you." "I love you, too."

As Chance hung up the phone he felt tears trickle down his face. He took a tissue from his pocket and wiped the tears from his face.

It seemed like it was hours before his next flight was called, but finally his flight was ready to leave. So far everything on his trip was going smoothly and his flight from Seoul had left right on time and landed in Los Angeles exactly on time.

The hours dragged by from Los Angeles to St. Louis.

Chance could see they were going to be landing on time in St. Louis and he was right, because just then the captain announced they were ready to land.

The captain said, "Please fasten your seat belts because we have a lot of weather in the St. Louis area and it's going to be a rough landing."

The captain didn't lie; Chance was being tossed around like he was on some kind of a carnival ride.

When the wheels hit the runway, all the passengers and crew were relieved that the plane was on the ground and rolling straight down the runway. The captain turned the plane onto a ramp and soon had the plane parked at a gate.

Chance grabbed his briefcase, got off the plane, and checked the monitor to see which gate his flight to Springfield was leaving from.

He found the gate number for his flight and saw the monitor indicated his flight was delayed due to weather.

He walked directly to the gate for his next flight and found a large crowd of people milling around waiting for the flight.

Chance went to the counter and spoke to an airline clerk who was working the flight and asked if they knew how long the flight would be delayed.

The answer he received wasn't what he wanted to hear.

The clerk told him they didn't have any idea how long it was going to be, since the flight scheduled earlier this evening for Springfield had already been canceled.

Chance asked if that was why there were so many people waiting at this gate.

The reply: Yes, it was.

Then Chance asked if he would be able to get on the flight when it was ready to leave. He was assured he would be on his flight.

Chance called Chase again and told him what was going on with the flight from St. Louis to Springfield.

Chance asked if they had done the angiogram yet; the answer was still no, and it still hadn't been scheduled, but the hospital staff expected the doctor would still do it sometime that night.

Chase told his dad they were having a violent storm in Springfield at the moment.

After they finished their telephone call, Chance tried to sit down and wait in the gate area but was having a very hard time doing it.

The longer he waited the more concerned he got that they were never going to get this flight off and that the flight would be cancelled.

Finally, at eleven o'clock, the gate agent announced the flight had been cancelled and the passengers had a choice of several different flights the next morning.

The airline had made arrangements for lodging for the night for the inconvenienced passengers, including transportation to and from the hotel and breakfast in the morning.

Chance couldn't wait until tomorrow so as soon as the announcement was made he went directly to the Hertz rental car counter.

After securing a car, he called Chase again to tell him his flight had been cancelled until the next morning and that he had rented a car and was on his way to Springfield.

Chase told him the decision had been made not to do the angiogram until the next day and his mother was asleep after they gave her enough meds to put her to sleep.

Chase told his dad he and Shane had a room at the Hampton Inn on South Glenstone and they had gotten him a room there, too. They had the keycard for his room.

Chance suggested to Chase that they leave his keycard at the front desk and he would get it when he got to Springfield. He wanted his sons to be able to get some rest and not have to stay up waiting for his arrival.

Chase told his dad, "Shane and I are normally up at this time of night anyway so call me when you get here."

Chance drove through torrential rain all the way to Springfield; it quit raining just as he pulled into the Hampton Inn's parking lot in Springfield at two forty-five on the morning of July 9.

Chance called Chase as soon as he turned off the car's engine. Chase told his dad they would be right down to help him get his things into his room.

Both of Chance's sons were quickly down to the parking lot. It was easy for them to find him since his car was the only vehicle in the parking lot with its lights on.

Chance got out of the car and gave a Shane a big hug and then it was Chase's turn for a hug.

They were really glad to see him and to be there for Mom so he could help her make decisions on things that might have to be done for her.

Since Chase was the oldest, he thought he would have to help his mom make decisions so he was relieved his dad was home to do it.

The three of them talked for an hour before Chance said, "I have to get a shower and lie down for a few hours before we go to the hospital this morning."

The boys left his room and each gave him another hug and told him they would see him soon.

2

WHAT'S NEXT FOR ANN

Chance woke up at 6:00 a.m. and took the shower he had planned to take before he went to bed but was just too tried to do. He planned to meet his sons at seven to go to breakfast and then go to St. John's to see how Ann was doing.

After he made himself ready for the day he called his sons' room, and Shane answered the phone.

Chance asked how they were doing and if they were about ready to go. He found they were both ready to go.

They decided to go to Aunt Martha's Pancake House, a well- known restaurant in Springfield, for breakfast.

After breakfast Chase drove them to the hospital to see what was happening with Ann.

Arriving at the hospital they found Ann had been moved from the intensive care unit into a private room during the night so they could see Ann any time they wanted to.

They made their way to her new room and Chance had the opportunity to met Dr. Michaels, her neurologist, who was with her when they arrived.

He told them he wanted to do her angiogram this morning but he needed Ann's signature to give him permission to do the procedure.

Chance walked past the doctor and leaned down and gave Ann a kiss and said, "Hello, love. What are you doing here?"

Ann was happy to see him; even though she couldn't say so, he could see it in her eyes.

Chance introduced himself to the doctor and asked the doctor to explain what he actually was trying to accomplish by doing an angiogram.

The doctor explained they needed to see how large the aneurysm was in her carotid artery and if they thought it would soon rupture. He needed Ann's signature on the permission surgery form before he could do the angiogram.

Ann made herself understood well enough for all of them to understand she wanted to talk to her husband before she agreed to sign anything.

Hearing what Ann said, the doctor, nurse, and Ann's two sons left the room so Ann could talk with Chance.

Chance asked, "Honey, why don't you want to do the procedure? I understood the doctors thought they needed the information from an angiogram to know how to treat you."

Ann perked up enough with Chance being with her that she said, "The doctor said I might die from doing the angiogram."

"Ann, you have been through so many surgeries before that you could have died from. Why does this one scare you?"

"They are going up in my brain. What if something goes wrong? I might not even know who I am."

"Let's ask the doctor to come back in and talk with us again about how they do an angiogram, OK?"

"All right, see if you can get him to come back to talk to you about it."

"OK, honey, I'll ask him to come back to talk with us."

Chance left the room to find a nurse to see if she could get the doctor to come back to talk with them.

When Chase and Shane saw their dad coming out of Ann's room they followed him as he walked down the hospital hallway.

Shane asked his dad, "What did Mom decide to do about the angiogram?"

"She hasn't decided yet. She wants me to hear what the doctor has to say about the angiogram."

Just then they met the nurse who had been in the room with the doctor and Chance asked if she could ask the doctor to come back to the room to talk with them.

The nurse told Chance she would get the doctor right away and meet them back in Ann's room.

Chance, Chase, and Shane went back to Ann's room and told her the doctor would be coming to talk with them again in a few minutes.

Chance sat down next to Ann's bed and without anything being said he began holding her hand waiting for the doctor to return.

About ten minutes later the doctor and the nurse returned to Ann's room.

Chance continued to hold Ann's hand and asked, "Doctor, can you explain what you have to do to perform the angiogram?

Although the doctor had explained the procedure before to Ann, Chase, and Shane, he began explaining it to them again so Chance could hear it.

He said, "The first thing we will do is to give Ann some medication, here in her room, to relax her, then we will move her to an operating room and give her an anesthesia to put her to sleep. Next, we will cut a small opening in her neck in order to insert a small device with a lens into the artery in her neck slowly pushing the lens up into the carotid artery to see how and what the aneurysm looks like.

"We will be continually taking pictures as the device travels through the artery just like when we do a heart. When we have this information recorded, we will know what we need to do to treat Ann.

"I'm just the doctor getting the information for the neurosurgeon. He will be the one to decide what needs to be done. "After we finish getting this information, we will remove the device from her artery and close the opening we used to insert the device, and then Ann would go to the recovery room. She should be back in her room in two to three hours."

Chance asked, "How much of a risk is there doing this procedure?"

"It has risk and depends somewhat how bad the aneurysm is. I have done several of these procedures and each one is different."

Chance asked, "If you had to guess, based on your past experience, do you think Ann has a chance of dying if you do the procedure?"

"Based on what I can tell by looking at her MRI again, she could die, but I would say she has an 80 percent chance of doing just fine with the procedure. We need to have the results from the angiogram to know how to treat her for her aneurysm."

Ann said, "OK, I'll sign the form."

The doctor said, "Good, I'll get everything ready to do the procedure and see you all after we are through."

The nurse raised Ann's bed up so she could sign the form to have the procedure. Ann signed the form and the nurse left to help get things ready for Ann.

Only a few minutes passed before the nurse returned with a shot to help Ann to relax before she went into the operating room. After the nurse left, Chance sat down again and held Ann's hand, and her two sons stood next to her to give her all the support they could.

Some twenty minutes passed before two orderlies came into Ann's room and picked her up and placed her on a gurney to take her to surgery.

One of the orderlies told them they could come with Ann to the doors of the operating rooms.

Chance, Chase, and Shane followed along behind Ann's cart, and Chance heard one of the wheels on the gurney squeaking angrily giving a haunting sound to the scene.

Arriving at the entrance to the operating room the orderlies stopped and asked Chance if he wanted to give his wife a kiss before she went in.

Chance did; he leaned down and gave Ann a long kiss and said, "OK, Annie, we'll be waiting for you as soon as you wake up. I love you and I'll see you pretty soon. You will be OK, my love."

Chance stood up and moved away from the gurney, and the orderlies took Ann through the operating room doors.

Chance, Chase, and Shane made their way to the surgical waiting room and found several people waiting there for news about their loved ones having surgery.

An attendant sitting behind a desk in the waiting room asked Chance whom he had in surgery and Chance replied, "My wife, Ann Clark, she having an angiogram."

"I will let you know as soon as I hear anything about how things are going in the operating room," the attendant told him.

"Thank you."

Chance and his sons found three chairs together and took a seat. Before long Chase said, "I need to call Marie and let her know what's going on with Mom."

Chase got up and left to go out to his car to call his wife, Marie, so she knew what was happening with his mother and to be sure everything was all right at their trout fishing resort.

Soon after Chase left, Shane told his dad that he should go call his wife, Jan, to tell her what was happening with his mother.

Chance agreed, so Shane left to call his wife.

Now Chance was left alone and he kept very busy praying for Ann to be all right and for the medical team doing her procedure to do it perfectly.

An hour went by and his sons hadn't returned and he had heard nothing about Ann from the attendant.

One thing Chance knew from his past experience waiting in hospitals was that minutes passed by like hours, days like weeks, weeks like months, and months like years.

A few more minutes passed and both of his sons returned and Shane asked, "Have you heard anything about Mom yet?"

"No, I haven't. How are your wives doing while you two are sitting around waiting in the hospital?"

Shane replied first saying, "Jan said everything was OK in Fayetteville."

Chase said, "Marie was worrying about Mom but everything at The Trout's Inn is OK."

Chase and Shane sat back down and began waiting with Chance for news on their mother.

Another hour passed when the waiting room attendant answered another one of her many telephone calls and then said, "Mr. Clark."

Chance jumped up from his chair and went over to the attendant's desk with Chase and Shane following right behind him. When they arrived at the desk the attendant said, "Mr. Clark, your wife is doing fine and is now in the recovery room and will be there for about an hour. Her doctor will be out to talk with you in a few minutes."

"Thank you, we appreciate your help."

The three of them went back to their chairs and sat back down to wait to hear from Ann's doctor.

Chance said out loud, "Thank you, Lord, for being with Ann and her doctors during her procedure."

A few of the people in the waiting room turned to see who had said that but most of the folks in the waiting room were too concerned about their own loved ones to even hear what Chance said.

Another ten minutes passed before the doctor came into the waiting room to talk with them.

Dr. Michaels said, "Everything went fine and Ann is in the recovery room and should be back in her room in about another hour. She shouldn't have any problems recovering from the procedure.

"The information from the angiogram has been sent to her neurosurgeon, Dr. Bellman, and he will be in to see her later tonight after he has time to study her angiogram."

"Thank you, Doctor," Chance replied.

The doctor turned and left them in the waiting room and Chance said, "I think we might as well go down to the cafeteria and have some lunch and then we can go back to Mom's room."

Chase and Shane agreed.

As they left the waiting room Chance stopped at the attendant's desk and thanked her for her help.

After lunch the three of them went back to Ann's room and waited for Ann to be brought back to her room.

Chance said, "I don't think you two have to stay here anymore after you get a chance to see Mom.

"You know, I can call you both and let you know what Dr.

Bellman has to say after he comes in tonight."

Both of them agreed they would go home after they saw their mother, now that their dad was there to stay with her.

The orderlies returned with Ann about 2:30 p.m., and they lifted her off the gurney and placed her back on her bed.

One of the orderlies said, "You did very well, Mrs. Clark.

You are back in your room and your family is here."

Ann opened her eyes and saw Chance standing next to her bed and asked, "Where are my boys?"

"They are right here, Annie." Chase said, "We're here, Mom."

Shane replied, "Yes, Mom, we are both here."

Her nurse came in and asked Ann how she was feeling. Ann replied, "I don't know. I guess I'm OK."

The nurse asked, "Would you like something to eat? You haven't had anything to eat or drink yet today."

Ann said, "I'm really thirsty. Can I have something to drink?" "Would you like to start with some water?"

"Yes, water would be good."

The nurse told her she would be right back with her water pitcher and a glass.

Chance moved over next to Ann's bed and reached down and touched her forehead because he thought she looked hot. Then he just left the back of his hand against her forehead and stroked it gently back and forth against her skin.

The nurse returned with Ann's pitcher, filled with ice and water, and a clean glass for her drink.

The nurse asked, "Honey, do you want me to help you with a drink?"

"Yes, I would, or Chance could do it if you don't have time." "I've got time to get you a cold drink of water."

The nurse filled the water glass full of water and placed a straw in the glass and tried not to get too much ice in the glass so it wouldn't be too cold for Ann.

The nurse moved up the head of Ann's bed so Ann could take a drink. She moved the bedside table next to Ann's bed and took the glass from the table and held the straw up to Ann's lips and Ann slowly began to suck the water from the glass until the glass was empty.

After Ann finished the glass of water she asked for another one.

Ann drank two full glasses of water before she told the nurse she had enough water for now.

The nurse asked Ann if she would like to have something to eat and Ann said, "I think I need to rest. Maybe I can have something to eat later."

The nurse told Ann she was getting ready to go home and she would see her in the morning.

The nurse turned around and was walking to the door when she said, "Honey, if you need anything just push your call button." Shane made his way next to Ann's bed and said, "Mom, I'm really glad you got that test over with and that you're doing all right."

"From what the doctor said yesterday I thought I wouldn't make it through the procedure."

Chase said, "They said you did really well, Mom." "I don't like that doctor."

Chance replied, "Honey, I guess you don't have to like him, since from what he said you don't have to have him anymore."

"Good."

Chance, Chase, and Shane could only smile at Ann's attitude toward Dr. Michaels.

Chance knew Dr. Michaels really scared Ann yesterday about her dying during the angiogram and he could hardly blame her.

Chance understood from what his sons said that the doctor said it in such a way that it would have scared anybody, including both of his sons.

Chase and Shane told their mother they were going to go home now and they were glad her procedure was over and she was doing all right.

They said they needed to get back to work.

Before leaving, each of them gave their mother a kiss and a hug and told her they loved her.

Ann told them both she was sorry they had to be gone from home because of her.

After they left, Chance sat down in the chair next to Ann's bed and reached over and touched her on the shoulder. She closed her eyes and went to sleep.

Ann didn't wake up until the aide brought in her supper tray. The aide asked Ann if she could feed herself and Ann told her she could.

The aide removed the cover off the dinner plate and poured some ice tea in a glass for Ann. Then the aide asked if she could do anything else and Ann told her she could handle it.

Ann raised the head of her bed up so she could eat her turkey and dressing. She was really hungry, since she hadn't had anything to eat yesterday or today.

Ann's tray had a small salad, turkey and dressing, corn roll and butter, and a small piece of lemon pie. It didn't take long before she had finished eating everything on her tray, as well as two glasses of ice tea.

When Ann finished her supper she asked Chance if he shouldn't go down to the cafeteria to get something to eat before they closed.

He told her yes, he did need to eat something before they closed, since he hadn't eaten much for a couple of days because he had been so worried about her.

He said, "I think I'll be able to eat something now since I know you are doing OK."

"Well, I don't think I'm OK, but I'm better, just knowing you're here with me. Please go eat something before the cafeteria closes."

"OK, love, I'm going, but I'll be right back." Chance leaned over and kissed Ann before he left.

After Chance returned to Ann's room he found that she had company, a doctor and a nurse he hadn't seen before.

The doctor turned around when Chance came into the room and said, "I'm Dr. Bellman. You must be Ann's husband— Chance. Ann told me you came from Korea."

Chance said, "How do you do, doctor? Yes, I'm Ann's husband, Chance Clark, and I did just return from Korea."

Dr. Bellman extended his hand to Chance and the two men shook hands.

Dr. Bellman said, "I was telling Ann that after I studied all the information from her MRIs and her angiogram. I believe the best thing we can do at this time is to do nothing.

"The location of the aneurysm is in her asymptomatic right cavernous carotid artery and it is in such a position that it is completely within the cavernous sinus and doesn't pose a risk of rupturing.

"I suggest we wait five months and have a follow-up MRI in December. It's my thought it would be more of a risk to Ann if we tried to operate than to do nothing.

"Do either of you have any questions? If so, I'll try to answer them. Otherwise, we will keep Ann here for a few days to see if we can get her feeling better before we release her to go home."

Ann and Chance were shocked to hear what Dr. Bellman had to say after the dire prognosis they had yesterday.

No, they didn't have any questions they could ask right now, but they had a thousand questions going through their minds.

Since they didn't ask any questions, Dr. Bellman said, "Ann, I will look in on you tomorrow and see how you are doing."

Chance said, "Thank you, Dr. Bellman, for your information."

Dr. Bellman and his nurse left Ann's room and Chance reached for Ann and held her as close as he could with her on her bed and him leaning over her.

After a few minutes passed, Chance told Ann, "That's great news. I need to call the boys and let them know what Dr. Bellman said."

Ann agreed and Chance telephoned Chase and Shane and they were both as shocked as Ann and Chance were.

Ann was released from St. John's Hospital on July 13, to return home to Big Springs, Arkansas.

After Ann was safely home, Chance went to meet with Ann's primary doctor, Dr. Caye.

Chance told Dr. Caye that Ann and he were concerned with what they had been told by Dr. Bellman and thought they should seek a second opinion about what should be done about Ann's aneurysm.

Dr. Caye suggested Chance should take Ann to Mayo Clinic in Rochester to see if they agreed with the diagnosis of Dr. Bellman.

Chance agreed with Dr. Caye and asked him to make an appointment for Ann at Mayo Clinic in Rochester, Minnesota. The doctor said he would see if he could get an appointment at Mayo for her.

The following day, Dr. Caye's nurse telephoned and advised Chance that Ann had an appointment at Mayo Clinic on Tuesday, July 20, at twelve noon.

Chance thanked her for her help and told Ann she had an appointment at Mayo now.

The nurse told Chance he needed to get copies of all the X-rays and MRIs from St. John's Hospital to take with them to Mayo Clinic.

Saturday, July 17, Chance and Ann drove to Springfield to pick up copies of all her X-rays, MRIs, and medical records from St. John's to take with them to Mayo.

On Sunday, July 18, Ann and Chance drove from Big Springs to Des Moines, Iowa, and spent the night at the Sheraton Four Points Hotel. The following day they drove on to Rochester, Minnesota, and checked in at the Holiday Inn next to Mayo Clinic.

Ann's first appointment at Mayo was at noon on July 20, and her appointments and tests continued until Friday, July 23.

After all her tests and a review of the information brought from Big Springs and St. John's, Mayo agreed the best thing to do at this time for her aneurysm was to do nothing but to keep checking on her aneurysm every five or six months.

Mayo's confirmation of Dr. Bellman's decision certainly made both Ann and Chance feel better about Dr. Bellman, and Ann would continue seeing him instead of making trips to Mayo.

Mayo also confirmed that Ann had a whole lot of other health problems including indeterminate visual scotomata, mixed connective tissue disease, hypertension, idiopathic thrombocytopenic purpura, osteoarthritis, kyphosis, static/ dynamic upper back pain, postural myalgia, lupus, possible rheumatoid arthritis, and fibromyalgia.

Neither Chance nor Ann had much of an idea about what most of this meant but they were sure the information about their findings would be sent directly to Dr. Caye and he would be able to deal with it for Ann.

Ann and Chance were very impressed by the efficiency and organization of the staff at Mayo Clinic. They found it unbelievable the time the doctors took with her to explain everything about the conditions they found and what she should do to treat them.

Although Mayo had thousands of patients going through daily, each one of her doctors seemed to be fully engaged with her care.

When all of Ann's test and appointments were finished, even checking out of the clinic was quick and easy.

Friday, July 23, Chance and Ann left Rochester right after they had lunch. Their plan was to stay in Des Moines that night.

However, arriving in Des Moines they found the Iowa State Fair was going on and there were no rooms to be had in Des Moines.

So they decided to drive all the way to Big Springs and arrived home at 12:30 a.m. on Saturday, July 24.

What an incredible seventeen days they had just lived through—the emotions, the lows and highs, the stress and worry, and in the end they knew God had looked after them.

3

LIFE, WORK, AND TRAVEL GOES ON

Thursday, August 12, Chance and Ann flew from Springfield to St. Louis and from St. Louis to Anchorage, Alaska, where they checked into the Marriott Courtyard Hotel.

On Friday, they spent time looking around in Anchorage and did some shopping. Ann bought a new coat that she liked very much.

Saturday, they took an Alaska Train from Anchorage to Whittier; then they boarded the ship *Emerald Sea* for a cruise of Prince William Sound.

They enjoyed the opportunity to view glacier calving, which as explained to them, meant that large chunks of the glacier's ice, which looked so blue in color, broke away and fell into the bay.

It was a sight and sound like no other either of them had experienced before. It was so beautiful.

After the train ride back to Anchorage, they had an early dinner in order to get up at 2:30 a.m. to repack and get to the airport for their 5:30 a.m. flight to Seoul.

If you looked at their arrival time of 7:15 a.m. in Seoul, you would think it was a very short flight; however, if you understood that it was 7:15 a.m. on Monday morning you would understand it took them a little longer than about two hours to fly from Anchorage to Seoul, Korea.

They had to cross the International Date Line and several time zones, so it was more like eight hours of flying to get to Seoul.

Arriving in Seoul, they soon cleared customs and immigration without any problems, retrieved their luggage, found a taxi, and went directly to their apartment in Seoul.

Chance had only rented and moved into the apartment on the first of July so when they arrived at the apartment, Chance had his first opportunity to show Ann around their two rooms.

Although it wasn't a very large apartment, it would work well for them. It had a combination living-dining and kitchen in one room and a bedroom with adequate- sized closets for their clothes and plenty of drawers for their underwear.

The apartment had a large bathroom with a washer and shower, and of most importance to the Clarks, it had a westernstyle toilet, not just a hole in the floor, the Korean style of toilet.

Their kitchen included a device that they neither of them had any idea of what it could be used for. Later, when Jimmy Kim, their company's Korean partner, was at their apartment, Chance asked him if he knew what the device was for and Jimmy explained it was a built-in rice cooker. They never used it, but at least they knew what it was for.

For the next forty-eight days Chance and his team worked at preparing a proposal to establish an on-street parking system for the city of Seoul. After they finished preparing the proposal they hand-delivered it to the mayor of Seoul.

After the proposal was delivered to the mayor, Chance's work was finished in Korea.

Ann and Chance left Seoul on October 3, 1999.

In November 1999, World Star Parking System won a contract to collect revenue from the parking meters in Milwaukee, Wisconsin, and

Chance was busy setting up the new system they had described in their proposal.

While Chance was working to get the parking meter collection operation set up, he got a call from Ann who told him that she had been to the Big Springs Hospital for a test for breast cancer and they had found a lump in her right breast and planned to do surgery the next week.

Chance left as soon as he could get a flight out of Milwaukee to Springfield to be with Ann.

After spending several days with Ann in the hospital, Chance had to return to Milwaukee to begin the collection service of their parking meters as required by their contract with the city and was scheduled to begin on Monday, November 29.

The takeover turned out to be a disaster! The foreman he had hired quit at the end of the first day and so Chance had to go back to his second choice for a foreman and hire him.

Chance was so sorry he had to leave Ann to face her surgery by herself. On Monday, November 29, Ann had her breast surgery. Later that night Chance called Ann to check on her after her surgery and was so happy to hear that the lump removed from her breast was benign. Thank God, it was not cancer.

This would be the only good news he would have this week.

Ann had another appointment with Dr. Bellman, her neurosurgeon, in Springfield on Friday, December 3, and he continued to tell her there was no change in her aneurysm and they had no plans to do anything about it.

By the end of the first week of their new operation in Milwaukee, they were behind collecting by more than a thousand meters. Not good news, his people had to get better and faster with the collections.

Saturday, December 4, was Ann's sixty-third birthday, and where was Chance? Not with her for her birthday, again. She would be home by herself on her birthday again, while he was off working somewhere.

With all of Ann's health problems, he should never be away from her; he needed to be home to help take care of her all the time.

By Friday of the second week, they were able to get all the meters collected that they were required to collect.

His new foreman, as the cowboys would say, took the bit between his teeth, and knew what had to be done and how it had to be done, so Chance felt comfortable enough leaving the job in his hands.

When Chance returned home the next day he found Ann was still having a lot of pain in her breast. Her doctors told her they needed to continue checking her breast for several more months because she had several hard spots in her breasts.

Ann finished out her medical tests for 1999 by having a chemical stress test on her heart on December 15, at St. John's Hospital, leaving them enough time to do their Christmas shopping.

Throughout 2000, Ann continued to have too many health problems and more and more tests for a variety of things, and her doctors continued to follow up on checking the hard spots in her breasts.

They finally concluded it was scar tissue, so she didn't have to continue with that anymore. At least that was one less health problem Ann and Chance didn't have to worry about anymore.

In June, she was having a lot of problems breathing and went through lots of test again at St. John's Hospital in Springfield.

The conclusion was she had a mild obstructive lung defect and the decision was to have her do physical therapy to see if it would improve her air flow.

In September, Dr. Bellman had an MRI done to check on Ann's aneurysm.

During an appointment with Dr. Bellman on October 3, he told Ann he didn't need to see her anymore because there wasn't any change in the aneurysm, but she was to continue seeing Dr. Michaels.

Chance guessed this was one more health problem he didn't have to worry about with Ann.

Ann fell twice in November, once while doing therapy at the hospital and then again while she was trying to get back in bed after going to the bathroom in the middle of the night. Neither of these falls resulted in any broken bones, but plenty of pain and bruises.

After having an MRI in December, Dr. Michaels confirmed she had had a number of small strokes and asked her to follow up with Dr. Caye to see if she should change some of her meds to be sure one of them wasn't causing this problem.

On January 3, 2001, Dr. Caye took Ann off several of her medications to see if she would begin feeling better.

Dr. Caye saw Ann again on January 9 and had her admitted to Big Springs Hospital. She continued to lose weight, lost her appetite, had no energy, and felt sick all the time.

After several days in the hospital and many tests later, Dr. Caye told Ann and Chance that her stomach was not functioning correctly because it had no motility, and he planned to call the doctors at Mayo Clinic to see what they might suggest for the problem.

The decision was to give her a drug called Raglan, to be taken thirty minutes before mealtimes and one at bedtime.

Ann continued to stay in the Big Springs Hospital with IVs and bed rest until Dr. Caye released her to go home on January 16.

January 23, Ann had been resting on a couch in the family room and got up to take her medication and fell on the carpeted floor and broke two small bones in her left foot which required wearing a removable cast for eight weeks before the bones healed.

In March 2001, World Star won a major contract in New Orleans. Chance and Ann drove there so Chance could get everything set up to take over the new parking meter system.

Chance and Ann arrived in New Orleans on March 20, so Chance could sign the contract to take over New Orleans' parking system and give him the opportunity to locate an office and shop for the new operations. It took him a few days to locate a suitable location for their office and shop, but he found one and rented it.

After Chance finished doing everything he could do at this time in New Orleans, he and Ann drove on to Washington, D.C. to attend a meeting in World Star's home office. They were there only for a few days before heading back to Big Springs.

As Chance and Ann were driving back from Washington, D.C. to Big Springs, and while they were traveling through Kentucky, they received a cell phone call from Ann's sister Lee Roberts.

Lee told Ann their mother had died at twelve forty-five that afternoon in Lee's home in Dallas. Plans were being made to have her body taken from Dallas back to Webster for her funeral.

Lee and her family would be in Webster Tuesday night and Ann told her they would be there at the same time.

Ma Harris's funeral was held on April 5, and all the family was there to say good-bye. It was a hard time for everyone, as she had been a rock for the family since their father died so many years before.

Her body was laid to rest next to her husband, Jack, who had died in 1957. It was hard to believe she had been alone for forty- four years.

They stayed in Webster until Saturday, visiting with their family, and then drove home to Big Springs later that day.

Chance had to get back to New Orleans as soon as he could, so he and Ann arrived back in New Orleans on April 11.

His project manager, Tracy Johnson, arrived in New Orleans two days later and began working with a local contractor laying out all the parking spaces in the central business district to accommodate their new parking meter installation.

Things seemed to be going well: they had hired some people to work with them, the city officials were working to help them get things organized, a fleet of vehicles were purchased, and it appeared they were making very good progress on all fronts.

The rest of April and most of May, Chance and Ann remained in New Orleans.

Chance and his crew continued to get the equipment installed and in operation.

In June, Chance and Ann returned home to Big Springs, Arkansas, to keep a scheduled appointment for Ann with her urologist on June 13.

Ann was having so many problems with incontinence that she wanted to see her urologist to see if he could suggest something which could help her. The urologist had done a sling bladder repair surgery for her in 1999.

She told him that leakage from her bladder had become much worse in the last few weeks.

After an exam and review of her general health, her urologist suggested that since she had a past relationship with Mayo Clinic, he thought she should go there to see if they could provide a better solution for her problem than he could.

Dr. Caye, Ann's primary doctor, contacted Mayo and asked for an appointment for Ann to see about her incontinence. They would schedule an appointment for her.

Chance and Ann returned to New Orleans, and Chance continued working on the project, getting everything ready to complete the installation of the new parking meter system while waiting for an appointment with Mayo Clinic for Ann.

On July 17, Ann had her appointment at Mayo Clinic to see about her bladder problem, and as always when you were a patient at Mayo, you received extensive tests on your overall health.

They found she was having problems not only with her bladder but she had problems walking, with balance and her gait. Their conclusion about these problems suggested that she may have Parkinson's disease, or symptoms of Parkinson's, which may have been caused by her taking the medication Raglan.

She was advised to stop taking Fosamax and Premarin, as well as Raglan.

The problems with her bladder would not require surgery, but because she couldn't totally empty her bladder when she urinated, that was causing her leakage.

Their recommendation to her was to have her do selfcatheterization three times a day to stop the problem. In addition, she was told to take 50 mg of Macrobid daily to help prevent infections. They had an appointment with a nurse who would teach Ann how to do her catheterization. The nurse told them in great detail on how to do the catheterization. So both Ann and Chance learned how to do the catheterizations.

On July 30, Ann saw her primary care doctor, Dr. Caye, and he agreed to take her off Fosamax and Premarin and to have her stop taking Raglan to see if she could do without it and still be able to eat. He also gave Ann a prescription for 100 mg of Macrobid since they didn't make 50 mg of the drug as the doctor at Mayo had suggested. On July 31, Ann quit taking Raglan and was sick almost all day but was able to eat some.

4

ANN'S HEALTH–FROM BAD TO WORSE

Chance and Ann returned to New Orleans on August 3, and Chance went back to work on the parking meter project.

On August 7, Chance and Ann were waiting in line at Poncho's Mexican Buffet to have dinner when Chance saw Ann's eyes suddenly roll back and that she was in the process of passing out and falling down. Chance reached out and caught her and slowly and gently let her go down onto the floor.

Since she didn't fall on the floor or hit her head, Chance didn't think she had broken anything.

One of the people in line with them told Chance that she was a nurse and checked Ann's pulse and her breathing, and another person in line called 911 for an ambulance.

The nurse asked for someone to get her a cold, wet washcloth or a towel or something. It took about ten minutes before Ann came to and asked what happened. The nurse told Ann she had fainted and told Chance to keep her lying on the floor until the ambulance came.

Chance kept his arm under Ann's head until the ambulance arrived and before the ambulance attendants tried to move her, they checked Ann out as much as possible to be sure she was in a stable condition.

Before they put her on a stretcher they started her on oxygen and again checked her heart rate and pulse. They decided she was OK to lift up and they placed her on the stretcher and loaded her in the ambulance.

One of the ambulance attendants told Chance they were taking her to East Jefferson Hospital and explained how to get there.

Chance thanked all the people who had helped Ann and left to go to East Jefferson Hospital.

By the time Chance arrived at the hospital, Ann was already out of the ambulance and was in the process of having blood tests, X-rays, and cardiac monitoring, and they had her on an IV.

The hours dragged by as the emergency room doctors put Ann through every test they could think of and couldn't really determine why Ann had blacked out.

After five hours of testing they released Ann from the hospital and the doctors told them they believed Ann was dehydrated, causing her to pass out.

On August 9, Ann contacted Dr. Caye and told him what was going on with her. Dr. Caye told her to start taking her Raglan again four times a day since she continued to be sick after passing out two nights previously.

Chance came back to their long-stay hotel room every day to have lunch with Ann to be sure she was all right.

Things were progressing very slowly, and some days Chance thought they would never finish the installation. It took them until August 24 to complete the new parking meter system for the City of New Orleans.

Chance and Ann left New Orleans the same day to return home to Big Springs, Arkansas, and arrived home on Sunday, August 26.

Because Ann had numbness in her left leg and foot, she went to see Dr. Caye on August 30, 2001, and he scheduled an MRI to be sure she didn't have a tumor in her spine causing this problem.

Ann had a MRI in Mountain Home, Arkansas, on September 6 and got the results from Dr. Caye on September 11. He was happy to tell her she didn't have a tumor in her spine.

Next, he had her have an electromyography test on her legs at the Big Springs Hospital.

On September 13, Dr. Caye's office called and asked Ann and Chance to come in to discuss the results from the electromyography test. He concluded the numbness was much worse compared from when the same test was performed at Mayo Clinic on July 23.

His conclusion was that she had peripheral neuropathy and he put her on 10 mg of Prednisone three times a day for ten days to see if her stomach could tolerate taking it.

He also took her off Macrobid because he thought this might be contributing to her leg problems.

On September 11, 2001, all of Ann's health problems paled at the sight on TV of the Twin Towers going down in New York City and the destruction of the Pentagon in Arlington, Virginia.

Later they heard an airplane had crashed in Pennsylvania, also caused by terrorists.

It was beyond every American's belief. These acts shook every fiber of what it meant to be an *American* these things simply couldn't have happened here, no way.

Ann had an appointment with Dr. Michaels, her neurologist, on October 1, to tell him about the problems she was having with the numbness in her legs and feet.

After seeing her, he ordered a complete MRI of her spine and told her after he had studied the MRI he would contact her and Dr. Caye.

On October 5, Ann received a call from Dr. Michaels and he told her he had read her MRI and didn't find anything significantly wrong with her spine. He did tell her he would send Dr. Caye a letter suggesting some recommendations for some future treatments for her. October 19, Ann had an appointment with Dr. Caye to see about following through on a recommendation Mayo Clinic had made about her having physical therapy.

Ann told Dr. Caye that she was feeling worse every day and wondered if he had received a letter from Dr. Michaels with some suggestions for new treatments. The answer was no, he hadn't received anything from Dr. Michaels.

Dr. Caye made arrangements for Ann to begin physical therapy beginning on Monday, October 22.

On October 20, Ann fell at home while going from the master bathroom to their bedroom, no more than three steps.

She wasn't seriously injured, but she couldn't get up without Chance helping her. She told Chance her left knee just gave away and she wasn't able to get up without help.

On October 22, Chance took Ann to her physical therapy appointment. He had to help Ann out of their van to get her into the hospital where her physical therapy was to be conducted.

Joyce Thomas was a nice young woman who would be her therapist and she spent time making an evaluation of Ann's strength and general overall physical capabilities.

Joyce suggested Ann come three times a week beginning on the following Wednesday.

Chance took Ann back to the hospital on Wednesday to start her therapy and after less than ten minutes, Joyce said, "Ann, I'm sorry but you just don't have the strength and are not in good enough condition to do this type of therapy.

"I'll talk to Dr. Caye and suggest he have home care come to your home to see what kind of therapy you might be able to do."

Chance helped Ann back into their van and drove back home without saying anything.

Arriving home, Ann said, "Chance, I'm sorry I couldn't do the things Joyce was asking me to do."

"I'm sorry, too. I was hoping the therapy would help you build up your strength and help you walk better. We'll just have to wait and see what Dr. Caye thinks."

"Chance, I'm really tired of being sick all the time."

"I know, honey, but I guess we don't get choices about what happens to us. All we can do is the best we can. If I could, I'd be willing to share some of your health problems."

"Don't say that, Chance. You don't want to be sick like I am." "No, I don't, but I sure wish I could do something more to help you."

"You're doing too much already, I love you."

Chance helped Ann get into her favorite chair and she turned on the TV to take her mind off her problems.

November 1, 2001, Ann woke up at 3:00 a.m. and tried to turn over in bed to get up to go to the bathroom but she couldn't do it.

She was lying on her left side, with her right leg on top of her left leg and she couldn't get her right leg off her left leg.

She woke Chance and told him her problem. Chance got up and moved her right leg off the left one and helped Ann into the bathroom.

After she finished urinating, she was able to get up from their high toilet stool and slowly made it back into bed.

Chance got up around seven thirty the next morning, went to the bathroom, made coffee, and came back into the bedroom.

Ann said, "Chance, I can't get out of bed." Chance replied, "It's OK, I'll help you."

Chance pulled the cover off Ann and turned her over toward the right side of the bed, helped her up to a sitting position, and proceeded to lift her to a standing position.

However, she couldn't stand even with Chance holding her.

He sat Ann back down on the bed and turned her on her side and laid her back down on the bed.

Chance said, "I think we better get you to the hospital to see what's happened to you."

Ann agreed.

Chance asked, "Ann, what do you want to wear?"

"Pick out one of the blue slacks and the blue blouse with the white stars on the collar."

Chance helped her put on her panties, bra, slacks, and blouse and then asked, "What kind of shoes do you want?"

"A pair of blue loafers, they are down on the closet floor."

Chance found the shoes she wanted and put them on without any stockings.

Chance got his office chair with arms and wheels, picked Ann up, and put her in his chair to get her into the garage and into the van to take her to the hospital.

It was a good idea because Chance couldn't have carried Ann all the way from their master bedroom to the garage.

He only had one problem: When he got to the garage he would have to pick Ann up and carry her to the van because there was one step down from the house into the garage.

Arriving at the garage Chance got in front of Ann's chair, opened the door, and stepped down into the garage; he had Ann hold on to the door frame as Chance prepared to take Ann out of the chair and carry her to the van.

Before Chance tried to pick Ann up off the chair he went to the van and opened the passenger-side front door.

Then he went back to the door; and he had Ann let loose of the door frame; he turned her chair so she was now sitting with her feet facing the hinged door frame so she would come off the chair with his right arm under her butt and she would be able to put her arms around his neck as he picked her up off the chair.

Chance managed to do it all in one motion; he had Ann in his arms and was making his way over to the van, and then Chance slid Ann onto the front right seat of the van.

When he first started carrying Ann to the van he didn't know if he would be able to make it that far or if Ann was going to pull his neck off, as hard as she was holding onto him. He knew she was afraid that he was going to drop her so he said nothing.

Chance put on Ann's seat belt and pulled it up tight to keep Ann from sliding off the seat as they made their way to the Big Springs Hospital.

Arriving at the hospital, Chance drove into the emergency entrance drive and went inside the hospital emergency section and told the first person he saw that he needed a wheelchair to get a patient into the hospital.

An aide quickly grabbed a wheelchair and followed Chance out to the van. When they got to the van's passenger-side door, Chance opened the door and unfastened Ann's seat belt as the aide positioned the wheelchair near the van door. Chance slid Ann into his arms and she put her arms around his neck to hold on.

Chance set Ann into the wheelchair as the aide stood behind the chair and told Chance he would take the lady inside while he parked his van out of the emergency drive.

They soon found out Dr. Caye was out of town until November 12 and his associate, Dr. Chelsea, would be over to see Ann later in the evening.

In the meantime, they started doing X-rays, blood tests, and several other tests to see what was wrong with her, and admitted her to the hospital.

The next day an orthopedic doctor came to see Ann and told her he looked over her X-rays and bone scans and told her she didn't have any broken bones in her back and hips, so there wasn't anything he could really do to help her.

He also said they would keep her in the hospital for a few days and see if the physical therapists would be able to help her to stand and walk.

After six days of trying to work with the physical therapists, Ann still couldn't walk or stand by herself.

So where do we go from here?

Dr. Chelsea met with Ann and Chance late morning on November 8 and said, "I've tried to contact your neurologist in Springfield—Dr. Michaels, and haven't been able to talk with him about what's happened to you.

"Ann, I talked with a neurologist in Mountain Home—Dr. Robertson, and he's agreed to work with you.

"We are going to transfer you by ambulance from Big Springs to the hospital in Mountain Home today.

"Chance, Dr. Robertson asked you bring copies with you of all of Ann's MRIs that they did here."

Chance replied, "OK, I'll make arrangements to get the MRIs and take them with me. What did you say the doctor's name was?" Both Ann and Dr. Chelsea answered at the same time, "Dr. Robertson!"

"OK, I think I got it."

Dr. Chelsea said, "Good luck, Ann."

Chance stayed with Ann until the ambulance crew came to Ann's room to transfer her from Big Springs Hospital to the hospital in Mountain Home.

After they placed Ann on a gurney, Chance leaned over and kissed her and said, "OK, sweetheart, I'll see you in Mountain Home as soon as I can get some things from home to take with me to be able to stay over there with you."

"Don't forget the MRIs."

"No, I'll get them before I leave the hospital, OK?"

"OK."

The ambulance crew took Ann out of her room and directly to an elevator to go down to the ground floor to load her into their ambulance.

As Chance watched his wife being moved down the hospital hallway he thought she looked like a very sick little girl and tears formed in his eyes.

5

WHY DOESN'T ANYONE HAVE AN ANSWER?

Chance waited a long time before he could get the MRIs from the Big Springs Hospital to be able to take them to the hospital in Mountain Home. He wondered what they thought he was going to do with them, sell them out on the street?

Chance knew hospitals had to protect their patient records but sometimes he thought they really overdid it.

Finally, he signed the papers as Ann's representative and received the MRI film to take to the Mountain Home Hospital with him. It took over an hour to lay his hands on them. Unbelievable!

Before he left Big Springs, Chance stopped by home and packed a suitcase with enough clothes for him to be able to stay for four or five days.

On his way to Mountain Home he called his office in Washington to let his company know what was going on with Ann and that he didn't know when he would be able to get back to work.

His boss, the chairman of the board of directors, was so sorry to hear about what was going on with Ann and told Chance, "Of course, your family has to come first. Just keep us informed of what's happening with Ann."

Chance promised to do that.

Since The Trout's Inn was on the way to Mountain Home, he stopped to let his son Chase and his wife, Marie, know what was going on with Ann.

They were surprised Mom was been moved to the Mountain Home Hospital, but Chase was pleased because he was sure the hospital in Mountain Home was better than the one in Big Springs. Chase said to his dad, "Instead of getting a room over in Mountain Home, why don't you stay here?"

Chance agreed that he could save a little money and have family to talk with. He could certainly use the support with the way things were going with Ann.

Chance would have liked to stay a lot longer instead of going to another hospital but he knew how insecure Ann was when he wasn't with her.

Before Chance left The Trout's Inn, Chase told his dad he would call Shane and his aunt Lee to let them know what was happening with Mom.

Chance thanked him for doing this. Anyway, Chase thought he was the official family news provider.

Arriving at the Mountain Home Hospital he asked for Ann's room number and was told she was in Room 432.

A nurse was with Ann when he arrived at her room and she was telling Ann all the things they expected Ann to do while she was there.

One thing Chance never thought about was that they would want her to get fully dressed every day.

Before Chance could say anything, Ann said, "I can't get dressed."

The nurse said, "Don't worry, we'll help you dress."

After the nurse left Ann said, "I don't like this hospital. They want me to be dressed every day and to go to the dining room for all my meals."

Chance replied, "Honey, give them a chance. Have you seen your doctor yet? He may have entirely different ideas about what you will do and may write totally different orders for your stay here."

"I can't feed myself very well. I can't cut up my food and I don't like people staring at me while I'm trying to eat. Besides, it takes me forever to eat a meal.

"These people don't know how much I'm hurting and they won't give me anything for pain until the doctor writes some orders for my pain pills. I don't know how much more I can stand."

Chance said, "Ann, I'll go talk to the supervising nurse to see if she can call the doctor to see if she can't get you something for pain, OK?"

"OK, but I've got to have something for this pain."

Chance left Ann's room and went to the nurse's station and asked if the supervisor for this floor was available. He was told by a nurse that she was in her office and she would ask her to come to Ann's room and talk to him.

Chance went back to Ann's room and before he got in the door he could hear Ann softly moaning in pain.

As Chance entered the room he pulled the door of Ann's room closed.

Chance said, "I talked to one of the nurses, and she said she would have the supervisor come to see us."

Ann didn't reply; she only began moaning a little louder than she had been before he came into the room.

"Honey, I'm sorry, we'll get you something for your pain very soon, I hope."

Just then Chance heard a soft knock on the door and said, "Come in."

The door opened and the floor supervisor came in and said, "I understand you wanted to see me."

Chance answered, "Yes, I'm Chance Clark and this is my wife, Ann. She is in a lot of pain since she hasn't had any pain meds since she left the Big Springs Hospital and she's really hurting."

Ann said nothing; she just continued to softly moan.

The supervisor asked, "Do you know what kind of pain medication she was on when she was in the hospital in Big Springs? Chance replied, "No, I don't remember the name of it, but I have a copy of the meds she was on. It's in the file folder I brought from the Big Springs Hospital. I gave it to the nurse at the desk when I came in."

The supervisor replied, "OK, I'll go find out what she was taking for pain over there and call Dr. Robertson and get his OK to give it to her. We sure don't want her in this much pain.

"I hope I can catch him before he leaves the office since it's almost five o'clock. He usually comes to the hospital sometime after seven to check on his patients."

"Thank you, I know Ann appreciates your help as much or more than I do."

The supervisor left Ann's room and about twenty minutes later she returned with Ann's pain medication.

She gave Ann the pills and had to hold the water glass for Ann to drink enough water with a straw to swallow her pills.

Ann said, "Thank you, I hope I can get some relief from this pain.

The supervisor replied, "I hope you do. We don't want you in so much pain. I'm sure after Dr. Robertson is here tonight he will get all of your orders written so we have everything we need to help you."

The nurse who had been talking with Ann earlier when Chance arrived came in and said, "Since you are still in your hospital gown from Big Springs, we'll have your dinner brought in here tonight."

Ann didn't answer her, but Chance did and said, "I'm sure Ann will appreciate it."

An aide brought in a tray with a light meal and a glass of ice tea for Ann.

The aide asked, "May I help you with your dinner?"

Ann said, "No, it's all right, if I need some help, my husband can help me."

The aide left and Ann put her bed up so she could eat a few bites of her dinner but she didn't have a lot of luck getting down more than a couple of bites.

Ann simply was hurting too much to eat. She knew she had taken a pain pill but it wasn't working fast enough to ease her pain. Her pain was all through her lower body and she didn't know how she was going to be able to cope with this much pain.

Ann kept thinking, Why doesn't someone understand what's happening to me? Why?

She managed to drink some of her tea after Chance put some Sweet'N Low in it for her. It felt good in her mouth and her throat, her mouth and eyes were dry all the time.

Dr. Robertson finally showed up around 8:30 p.m. and introduced himself to Ann and Chance.

He explained they would be doing several tests on Ann to see if they could determine what was causing Ann's problem with standing and walking.

He said, "What I've seen so far on your X-rays and MRIs doesn't seem to indicate any type of structural damage or disease of your spine."

Chance replied, "That's good, don't you think, Doctor?" "Well, it's good, but it doesn't explain why Ann can't stand or walk. I will be doing a lot more studying of her X-rays and MRIs and looking over her medical history to see if I can get any clue about what's happening with Ann.

"I'll see you in the morning, Ann. Is there anything I can do for you tonight?"

"You could make me stop hurting."

"I doubt that I can do that, but I'll be sure you get your pain medication given to you on a regular schedule to help ease some of the pain. I'm going to have them start you on an IV to get some more fluids in you. Good night."

Dr. Robertson turned and was out of the room in a flash.

Chance said, "When he finishes talking, he can sure get out of a room in a hurry."

Even as bad as Ann was hurting, she gave the slightest smile at what Chance said. He could always make her laugh.

A few minutes passed before a nurse came in with equipment to put an IV in for Ann.

Chance thought this was always fun for Ann while they tried to find a vein to insert a needle in for her IV.

For once, the nurse found a vein that looked good enough to make the insertion of the needle, only to have the vein roll away from the needle causing Ann to utter a little sound of pain.

The nurse said, "Ann, I'm sorry I hurt you."

"It's OK. I know it's hard to find a vein you can use in my arms."

The nurse replied, "I'll look again to find a vein I can use and try not to let it roll away from the needle this time."

The nurse then took a long look at both of Ann's arms before settling on a vein in Ann's left arm. This time the nurse moved the needle in slowly and, eureka, the needle went into the vein.

Chance wasn't sure if Ann or the nurse was happier about getting the needle in the vein.

After the nurse had the IV going and working well, she told Ann she would be back in with some more pain meds in a few minutes.

Chance said, "I do think your nurse was as happy about being able to get the needle in a vein as you were. It really upset her when your vein rolled away from the needle and I know it hurt you."

"I'm just glad she found one she could use."

"Ann, I'm going to go over to Chase's to spend the night, and then I'll be back early in the morning in time to help you get dressed.

"Will you be OK if I go?"

"I won't like it, but I'll be all right. I know you need some rest.

Chance leaned over Ann and, putting his right arm around her shoulders, lifted her up and gave her a goodnight kiss and said, "Good night, I'll see you in the morning."

Chance eased Ann back down on her bed and turned to go when he said, "I love you."

"I love you too, Chance."

Chance didn't turn around to see Ann; he didn't want her to see the tears in his eyes.

Chance certainly didn't want Ann seeing him crying.

Arriving at The Trout's Inn, Chance brought Chase and Marie up-to-date on what went on at the Mountain Home Hospital and told them he had to go to bed because he would be going back to the hospital early in the morning and it was already past midnight.

Chance left them and went over to unit number eleven and went to bed.

It was good Chance's body didn't require a lot of sleep because it was soon five thirty and Chance was up, dressed, and on his way back to Mountain Home.

By 6:30 a.m. Chance was in Ann's room.

Ann was awake and waiting for him to come back.

Chance knew she didn't like him being away from her due to the condition she was in now. She was afraid of everything, since she couldn't understand what was happening to her.

Chance had become her security blanket.

She knew he would take care of her and she never wanted him out of her sight.

Chance said, "Good morning, love. How are you this morning?" "I'm here."

"Well, love, that's a good way to start the day. Did you get any sleep last night?"

"Some."

The nurse came into the room and asked, "How are you this morning, Ann? Are you hurting as much as you were yesterday?"

"No, getting my pain pills on schedule has helped my pain." "Good, we didn't like it when you were having so much pain." "Neither did I."

After Ann's breakfast was brought in, she tried to eat some of it, but again she could only get a little bit of it down.

An aide came in and took Ann's tray and filled out a chart of how much Ann had eaten. She told Ann she would be back in a few minutes to help her get dressed.

Sure enough, a few minutes later the aide came in and asked where her clothes were, and Chance showed her he had put the few clothes she had with her in a closet.

The only clothes she had here were the ones Chance had brought to the hospital in Big Springs to wear in case she was released from the hospital. Chance had put her bra and panties in a drawer in the closet.

The aide took out the panties and Ann's bra and told Ann, "You should put your panties on first."

Ann gave her aide a puzzled look and asked, "How do you think I can do that?"

"Well, if you can't do it lying on bed, we will just have to have you stand up at the edge of the bed so you can get your panties on."

"I can't do that, I can't stand up. I can't even move my legs to be able to put on my panties."

The aide then said, "I'll help you while you're in bed," and she pulled the cover off Ann and took her panties and put them over her feet and began pulling them up over her ankles and said, "Just roll over on your right side so I can pull your panties up."

Ann made an attempt to turn over by pulling with her arm on the left side of the bed's safety rails but she didn't move, except her upper body turned a little.

"I can't do that either."

The aide then went ahead and pulled Ann's panties up over her butt by turning Ann's body side to side to get the panties on.

Next, the aide got Ann's slacks and proceeded to put them on the same way as she had put on her panties.

Chance handed Ann's bra to the aide as the aide asked Ann to raise the head of her bed up.

Next, she told Ann to go ahead and put on her bra.

Ann said, "I can't put my bra on. I can't get the straps over my shoulder and reach back and fasten it."

The aide asked her to try and Ann tried and she did manage to get the straps over her shoulders, but when she tried to fasten the bra behind her back, she almost fell forward on the bed.

The aide caught Ann just before she fell, face down on the bed.

The aide said, "OK, I'll fasten your bra for you. We can't have you falling off the bed."

Next, the aide got Ann's blouse and handed it to Ann and told her to go ahead and put it on.

Ann struggled for a little while before the aide said, "It's OK, honey, I'll help you get it on."

"Thank you."

After the aide finished putting on Ann's blouse, she told Ann, "I'll get you your comb and a toothbrush and you can get your hair combed and your teeth brushed. Then you should be ready to go to therapy."

Neither Chance nor Ann realized what was going on when the aide asked Ann to get dressed by herself. It was all about her doctor wanting to find out how much Ann could do to take care of herself.

They soon found out she could do very little to dress herself.

The aide observed Ann was able to comb her hair and brush her teeth.

Ann finished these two tasks and the aide said, "I'll get a wheelchair and take you to therapy. I'll be right back."

After her aide left the room Ann said, "I don't feel like going to therapy."

Chance didn't say anything and before he could have said anything the aide returned with the wheelchair.

The aide positioned the wheelchair at the top of the right side of the bed, locked the brakes, turned Ann around, put her arms under Ann's, slid Ann off the bed, and set her into the wheelchair.

Once the aide had Ann in the wheelchair, she put a seat belt around her so she didn't slide out of the chair.

The aide began pushing the wheelchair out of Ann's room, but stopped before she went out the door and turned around to address Chance. "Mr. Clark, if you want to, you can wait here. Ann should be back in her room in about an hour, or maybe you would like to go downstairs and have a cup of coffee in the cafeteria."

"Thank you, I may do that. Either way I'll see you two back here in an hour."

Chance did go down for coffee and returned to Ann's room in less than an hour to be sure he was there before Ann returned.

It was a little longer than an hour since Ann left her room when the aide returned with her and put her back into bed.

Chance asked Ann, "So how did it go with your therapy, Ann?" "Chance, they told me they expected me to start walking. They took me out of the wheelchair and two therapists held me up between a couple of rails, put my hands on the rails, and had me try to hold myself up. I couldn't do it.

"Then they worked at exercising my legs and it hurt like hell. The last thing they had me do was working on some hand weights to help build up the strength in my arms. I did that until

I thought my arms were going to fall off.

"Then they told me they would be back in at three o'clock for my next round of therapy. I don't know why these people don't understand, I can't move my legs! Believe me if I could I'd be doing it without them telling me to."

Chance was standing next to Ann's bed touching her arm and said, "Annie, you are going to have to keep trying to see if they can help you."

"I'm really hurting and trying to do those things is just making me hurt worse. I just want to go home."

"Sorry, love, we need to stay here and see if they can help you."

Dr. Robertson came to see Ann every day and sometimes twice a day and on November 13, Dr. Robertson came in late in the evening and told Ann and Chance he wanted to do a spinal tap to draw fluid from her spine.

The doctor tried to find a nurse to help him but they were all busy working with other patients so he asked Chance if he could help him draw the spinal fluid.

Chance told the doctor he would help him but he would have to tell him what he wanted him to do.

Dr. Robertson said, "I need you to help turn Ann over on her right side and keep her lying in that position without moving, while I draw the fluid from her spine."

Chance turned Ann over on her right side and placed her left leg over her right leg to help keep Ann from moving during the procedure.

Dr. Robertson had several vials to draw the fluid into with by using a very long needle, the longest needle Chance had ever seen.

The doctor asked Chance if he was ready and he nodded his head to indicate he was.

Chance kept his hands steady on Ann's body to be sure she didn't move when the doctor put the needle into Ann's spine.

The doctor placed the needle into Ann's spine and began filling the vials with a clear-looking fluid and he continued drawing fluid until he had filled several of the vials.

After the doctor finished drawing the fluid he cleaned the area of the spine with an alcohol pad and placed a Band-Aid on the place where he had inserted the needle into Ann's spine.

Dr. Robertson thanked Chance for his help.

Then Chance turned Ann back over onto her back.

The doctor said, "We will send the spinal fluid off for analysis and see if that can help us get a better understanding of what's going on with you, Ann."

The only thing Ann and Chance ever heard about the results of the spinal fluid test was that there were eleven white blood cells and two red blood cells in her spinal fluid, without any explanation as to what that meant.

Ann went to therapy twice a day, five or six days a week. Chance didn't know if it was doing anything to help her or not.

Ann had been in the Mountain Home Hospital for three weeks and every Friday afternoon it became a fight with the insurance company to be able to keep Ann in the hospital.

They wanted to send Ann home because they didn't believe she was making enough progress to warrant her staying in the hospital any longer.

They demanded to see something showing Ann's condition was actually improving. It became a weekly battle to keep Ann in the hospital to allow her to be able to do her therapy.

Ann's birthday, on December 4, would soon be here and she was still in the Mountain Home Hospital and she really wanted to be home for her birthday.

Chance talked to Ann's sister Lee, who lived in Dallas, at least once a week to keep her up-to-date on Ann's condition as he had been doing since Ann had been in the hospital.

Lee had been ten years old when Chance and Ann got married, so she was like a little sister to Chance.

Lee had married Dean Roberts, who had worked with Chance in Webster on the city's parking meters.

Dean also left the city to work as a service engineer for Superior Parking Meter Company, like Chance, and later became a sales representative for the company.

Dean and Lee had six children, four girls and two boys.

Lee told Chance she was planning on coming to Mountain Home to be with Ann for her birthday.

Chance knew Ann would be very happy to see her.

Chance would see if he could arrange to get Ann released from the hospital long enough for her to go to a Mexican restaurant for her birthday.

He knew it would please Ann more than any present he might be able to give her. Ann loved Mexican food and they certainly didn't serve her any in the hospital.

Chance talked with Dr. Robertson about letting Ann out of the hospital for a couple of hours on her birthday so she could have her Mexican dinner.

The doctor told Chance it would be all right, and he would write a note for the floor supervisor, allowing Ann to go out to dinner on her birthday.

The day before Lee was planning to come to Mountain Home, one of the therapists asked Chance to come down to therapy to see how Ann was doing.

Chance followed Ann and the therapist to the therapy facility and was able to watch through a window as they got Ann out of her wheelchair and helped her up to the two railings.

Ann had told him about those rails after her first session of therapy. She put her hands down on the railings and she began to take a step by holding on to the rails.

Chance was surprised, since Ann had never told him she had been able to take a step.

Ann only took maybe five or six steps before turning herself around on the rails and starting back to where she began. Before she took the last step back to where she started, she took both hands off the rails and took the last step without holding on.

Chance was shocked, pleased, and was so proud of Ann!

On Ann's birthday, her sister Lee and one of her twin daughters, Lynn, arrived from Dallas early in the afternoon, bringing Ann several birthday presents.

Chance made a trip home to Big Springs to pick up one of Ann's pantsuits that she loved to wear, to go out for her Mexican dinner. He arrived at the hospital after Lee and Lynn arrived.

Ann wasn't the only one who was pleased to see Lee and Lynn. He gave both women a big hug and a kiss, while telling them how happy he was to see them.

He couldn't wait to tell them about Ann taking a step yesterday without holding on to her rails. They were both surprised and pleased to hear Ann was making progress.

A couple of hours later, Chase, Marie, Shane, and Jan arrived at the hospital to celebrate Ann's sixty-fifth birthday and bearing birthday gifts for her.

Ann's room now looked very festive with brightly colored balloons, lovely wrapped birthday presents, and lots of smiling people; perhaps the person with the biggest smile of all was the birthday girl.

Chance thought it had been a long time since he'd seen Ann smile.

Her aide came to help Ann get dressed into the pantsuit Chance brought from home for Ann to wear for her birthday party. They all moved out into a small waiting room a little ways down the hall from Ann's room while the aide got Ann's clothing changed. It didn't take long before Ann was changed and ready to go to dinner.

A problem with the nurses arose as they were ready to leave the hospital for Ann's birthday dinner. The nurses didn't have the permission note from the doctor allowing Ann to leave the hospital. Some period of time passed while the nurses searched for the permission note and couldn't find it.

Chance mentioned Dr. Robertson said he would leave a note with the floor supervisor. A quick search in the supervisor's office was made and the note from the doctor was found on her desk.

Chase knew a Mexican restaurant in Mountain Home where they could have Ann's birthday party.

Chance brought Ann down in a wheelchair to their Chrysler Van and put Ann in the right front seat, and Lee and Lynn got into the back seats.

Chase, Marie, Shane, and Jan went in Chase's SUV since he was leading them to the restaurant.

Arriving at the restaurant, Chance got Ann out of the van and into her wheelchair while the rest of the family followed behind her wheelchair into the restaurant.

Shane opened the restaurant door and held the door open, allowing his dad to push Mom's wheelchair in first, with the rest of the family following.

It took a little while for the restaurant staff to put together a large enough table for all of them to sit together.

The food was very good, so the choice of this Mexican restaurant for Ann's party turned out to be good one and the restaurant's staff made a big fuss over Ann, which made Chance feel good.

Ann ate more food at this meal than she had had in six meals at the hospital.

Jan made Ann a birthday cake and asked the restaurant staff to serve it along with ice cream, but before cutting the cake, Ann had to blow out the two candles on the cake; one candle was a six and the second candle was a five.

After Ann blew out the two candles, everyone sang "Happy Birthday" to her. Some of the restaurant staff sang along, some in English and some in Spanish.

It brought a smile on Ann's face worth a million dollars to Chance.

When they returned to the hospital Ann got to open all her presents and she enjoyed them all but she had to have Chance help opening most of them for her.

All too soon the party was over and after getting hugs and kisses from all the visitors, it was time to get Ann into bed for the night.

Chance helped the aide change Ann into her nightgown and then he gave her a huge hug and a very long kiss goodnight before telling her he would see her in the morning.

Ann was soon fast asleep; it had been a very busy day.

The next day, Lee and Lynn stayed visiting with Ann and Chance almost all day.

Finally, they left around five o'clock, telling Ann they were staying the night with Chase and Marie at The Trout's Inn before going home to Dallas in the morning.

Ann had been thinking they might be driving back to Dallas that night, so she was happy they would be staying with Chase and Marie.

On December 15, 2001, Ann was released from the Mountain Home Hospital to return home.

Chance didn't know who was happier: Ann, Chance, or Blue Cross.

They were never told by the doctor what caused Ann not to be able to stand or walk. She was just to continue taking therapy with the Big Springs Hospital beginning the next week.

Chance thought to himself that the doctor didn't give them a reason for Ann's condition because the doctor himself didn't know what was wrong with Ann either.

6

THE ROAD CONTINUES FOR ANN

On December 18, Chance took Ann to the rehab department at Big Springs Hospital to continue her therapy. Arriving at the hospital he unloaded the wheelchair and carefully took Ann out of the right front seat of the van, and he had a very hard time doing it.

It didn't seem like Ann could help as much as she had been able to in the past.

After an evaluation of Ann's condition was made by the therapist, the therapist decided it was much too difficult for Chance to transfer Ann in and out of their vehicle.

She called the county health department and made arrangements for them to come to the house to do Ann's therapy.

It was a big relief to Chance because he could see he wasn't going to be strong enough to keep lifting Ann in and out of the van very much longer.

After a visit the next day from a nurse from the county health department, she concurred with the hospital's therapist that Ann should have her therapy at home.

They would have a therapist come to Ann's home twice a week to work with her.

From December 20 to January 11, 2002, a therapist came to Ann's home twice a week to work with her.

However, during that period Ann continued to get sicker with each passing day and was no longer able to move either of her legs. Nor could she help do a pivotal transfer any longer to help Chance get her in and out of her wheelchair.

In order for Chance to be able to keep taking care of Ann at home by himself he bought a lot of equipment to help him including bed rails, a larger wheelchair, a freestanding trapeze to let Ann pull herself up in bed, a bedside commode, a shower seat with a slide transfer board, a small reclining chair for the family room, and a used Chevy handicap van with a lift system.

Ann had an appointment, made in October, to see Dr. Michaels in Springfield on January 14, so Chance decided to take Ann to see him to see what he thought about Ann's problems.

After seeing Ann for only a few minutes, the doctor was shocked to see how bad she was now and immediately admitted her to St. John's Hospital.

His nurse took Ann, in her wheelchair, and Chance through a tunnel from his office building directly into the hospital and by the time they arrived, the hospital had a room ready for Ann.

Dr. Michaels ordered an MRI, a spinal tap, blood work, and several other tests for Ann, including another evaluation by the hospital's physical therapist team.

Dr. Michaels was determined to find out what had happened to her since he saw her on October 1 of last year.

The other reason Chance thought the doctor was so concerned was when Dr. Chelsea, Dr. Caye's associate in Big Springs, tried to get Dr. Michaels to see Ann prior to sending Ann to Mountain Home Hospital, he was told Dr. Michaels didn't have time to see her.

Later that same evening Dr. Michaels came to see Ann, and when he found she hadn't had her spinal tap yet, he decided to do it himself.

For the second time when the doctor wanted to do a spinal tap on Ann, the doctor couldn't find a nurse to help him, so he asked Chance to assist him.

By now, Chance knew what he had to do to help the doctor since he had done it once before helping the doctor in Mountain Home.

Chance concluded nurses didn't like being around when spinal taps were being done.

On January 17 Dr. Michaels started Ann on a five-day treatment of Methylprednisolone SOD SOCC 500 mg and sodium chloride 0.9 percent 100 mg twice a day.

The next day, Dr. Michaels told Chance he had found two spots on Ann's spinal cord and some small spots in her brain.

He said he thought the spots on her brain were caused by small strokes or blockages, but he did not think they would be the source of her problems standing and walking. He also told Chance he didn't have the results back from her spinal tap test yet.

Hearing that didn't surprise Chance much, since he didn't think the doctor in Mountain Home ever got back all the information from the spinal tap he did on Ann.

On January 19 Dr. Michaels asked Dr. Smithson of physical medicine to examine Ann to design a program to help improve Ann's trunk control and for her transfers in and out of her wheelchair.

Chance had rented a room in one of the long-term motels where he could pay a weekly rate that was much cheaper than staying in a regular motel room.

Ann finished her five-day treatment of Methylprednisolone SOD SOCC on January 21 but would continue to receive Prednisone by mouth for several more days.

Taking all of this potent medicine was causing her lots of problems having bowel movements. They had tried to give her several things to help her with this problem without any results.

The doctor told her night nurse to do a digital bowel movement for Ann before her bowels became totally impacted. The night nurse on duty was an older nurse, one of the only nurses in this huge hospital who still wore a stiffly starched white uniform, white stockings, white shoes, and a cap with her pin from her nursing school. Chance liked her a lot and was happy to see one nurse who still looked like she was a professional nurse working in this huge hospital.

He could understand why the other nurses wore the type of uniforms they wore. He was certain the new uniforms were much easier to take care of and more comfortable to wear.

Just the same, Chance still appreciated seeing a nurse who looked like a nurse.

The older nurse quickly showed Chance how to do a digital bowel movement for Ann.

The nurse told him, "If you're going to keep taking care of Ann, you're going to have to learn how to do this, because it may be the only way Ann will ever be able to have a bowel movement in the future."

She was right, because from that time on it was the only way for Ann to have a bowel movement.

On January 24, Ann was moved from the critical care floor to a transitional care unit inside the hospital. She continued to have severe pain in her legs and spine.

They began giving her shots for her pain in between the time she was scheduled to take her pain pills.

The night of January 28, 2002, in a private meeting with Dr. Michaels, the doctor confirmed to Chance for the first time that Ann had an autoimmune disease called Central Nervous System Vasculitis.

Dr. Michaels said Ann had had an inflammatory change in her thoracic spinal cord and CNSV was a life-threatening disease because it keeps damaging parts of the brain.

Dr. Michaels left after he delivered his news to Chance on Ann's disease and her outlook, and Chance was left standing out in the hallway outside Ann's room.

Chance needed to gather up all his courage to go back into Ann's room and do all the things he did for her every night without breaking down in front of her.

Chance thought he did a pretty good job of not showing the emotions he was feeling right then.

As Ann was finishing up doing her thing, a nurse came in with all of her nighttime pills. When Ann finished taking her pills, she was ready to go to sleep, and Chance kissed her goodnight and told her he would see her in the morning.

Ann managed to say she loved him before he left her room.

Chance went back to his motel room and got down on his knees, as he had been doing almost every night since Ann had been so sick, and said his prayers asking God to help Ann get better.

Chance didn't know what he would do without Ann: she had been his life. What would he do without her?

A few days later the doctor had an ultrasound test done on Ann's legs and they found a blood clot in her right femoral deep vein. A few hours later they placed a Simon-Nitinol Cava Filter in the inferior vena cava.

Ann did well during and after the procedure.

The therapy department personnel designed a special wheelchair for Ann, with help from a wheelchair supplier, but were told it wouldn't be available for about four months. In the meantime, they would outfit one of their wheelchairs as close to being like the one being made for her as they could, and she could use it until her chair was ready.

Ann and Chance's best friends, Doc and Susan Schmidt came from their home in Wichita, Kansas, to see Ann and spent a couple of days visiting with them. Ann was so thankful they could come and be with her while she was in the hospital.

Ann and Susan had several long talks, while Doc and Chance talked about the parking business. Years ago, Chance had gotten Doc into this crazy business and they had worked together for several years both at Superior and World Star.

Chance told Doc while they were out of Ann's room that he wouldn't be going back to work with World Star because he would be taking care of Ann for the rest of her life.

Chance told Doc confidentially what the doctor had told him about Ann's Central Nervous System Vasculitis being a lifethreatening disease.

Ann's sons and daughters-in-law were up to see Ann as often as they could while running businesses.

Chance and Ann were visited by their friend Susan O'Hara who now lived in Springfield, several times during Ann's long confinement in St. John's Hospital.

Susan's visits were always an uplifting time for both of them. She was such a good friend, and of course, she sent cards to Ann all the time when she was in the hospital.

On February 13, they weighed Ann and she had lost sixteen pounds since she had been in St. John's Hospital. Chance certainly wouldn't recommend getting Ann's condition as a way to lose weight.

After a thirty-two day stay at St. John's Hospital, Ann was sent home on February 15, 2002, by ambulance.

The nurse at St. John's Hospital contacted the Big Springs Hospital home care unit to come to Ann's house to make arrangements to help Chance take care of Ann.

The hospital's folks from Big Springs Hospital came the day after Ann was home from St. John's.

They made plans to come to the house three times a week to help with Ann's bathing and give her physical therapy, as well as with having a nurse come once a week to check on how Ann was doing.

This schedule didn't last long. When the aide arrived at four o'clock in the afternoon to give Ann a bath, Chance had already given her a bath at nine in the morning. Chance dispensed with their services.

During a visit by Ann's home health care nurse, as she was going out the front door she said, "Mr. Clark, why don't you contact hospice and have them help you with Ann?"

Chance said, "I understood hospice was designed to provide service to help with people who were dying soon."

"Hospice doesn't have a time limit as to how long they help. I've worked with patients who have had hospice care for more than two years and they are still working with them."

"I didn't know they did that. Besides, her doctors haven't ever told me Ann was dying."

The nurse said, "She is very ill."

"Yes, I know that. What I would like to do is to find someone who could come and stay with Ann while I run errands and to buy groceries, things like that. Maybe I could find someone who had some medical experience to stay with Ann if I had to be away from home."

"How many hours a day would you like to have someone help you?"

"I don't know, maybe three or four hours a day during the week."

"I may have someone who would be willing to help you. I have a friend who has been helping to care for a lady who passed away a few weeks ago. She worked at the hospital for over twenty-five years and retired from the hospital not too long ago.

"If you think you might be interested in trying to work something out with her, I'd be happy to call her to see if she would still like to do some work part-time."

"I would appreciate it if you would give her a call. I would like to talk with her."

"OK, I'll give her a call and have her call you. Her name is Genell Thomason."

A few hours later the same day Chance received a call from Ms. Thomason and they made arrangements to meet the next day.

When Chance and Genell met the very next afternoon, Chance introduced her to Ann and told Ann that he was talking to Genell about coming to stay with her sometimes while he went shopping.

Ann didn't have any reaction to the news at all. She was generally in so much pain she didn't always comprehend what was being said to her.

Chance hired Genell to work four hours a day five days a week and to start beginning the following Monday at 1:00 p.m.

By February 28, Ann was not doing well. She was very sick to her stomach and was having problems speaking. After talking with Dr. Caye's nurse on the phone, she advised Chance to call 911 and have an ambulance take Ann to the hospital.

Ann stayed in the Big Springs Hospital until March 8 before Dr. Caye released her to go home by ambulance. He had kept her on IVs for several days and changed several of her medications during her hospital stay to see if anything could help her.

In April, Dr. Caye put her on oxygen and Chance called American Home Patient Care Company to set up an oxygen system in their home.

Chance had the oxygen system machine set up in his office, which was next to their master bedroom, to keep down the noise in their bedroom from the running machine.

They ran an oxygen supply line through the wall between the rooms and Chance had another very long line set up so he could take the line into the family room for Ann if she needed it there.

Chance also talked to Dr. Caye about taking Ann to Springfield to see Dr. Michaels again, considering how Ann was doing now. Dr. Caye felt it would be better to cancel the appointment instead of having her ride that many miles to and from Springfield, so Chance canceled her appointment.

By May 21, Ann was back in the Big Springs Hospital due to swelling of her left thigh and open bedsores on her heels.

While Ann was in the hospital, Dr. Caye had an ultrasound test done on her legs and they found two blood clots in her common femoral and superficial femoral veins.

Dr. Caye continued treating Ann for her various conditions. After Ann had been in the Big Springs Hospital for more than a week and continued to be very ill, not showing any improvement, Chance decided to go to Dr. Caye's office and talk with him by himself.

Although Dr. Caye's office was always very busy and even though he worked with two nurses and had patients in six rooms at a time, he came to meet with Chance in his office a few minutes after he arrived.

Chance said, "Dr. Caye, I'm really worried about Ann. She doesn't seem to be getting any better. Do you have any suggestion of what we could do to help her?"

"Chance, she's not getting better. She is getting worse every day and I don't know anything to help with her Central Nervous System Vasculitis."

"Do you have any idea of somewhere we might take her to see if they could do anything to help her?"

"It would have to be somewhere that could try some experimental treatment, like Boston Hospital, Cleveland Clinic, Stanford University, John Hopkins, maybe Mayo Clinic, or Barnes Jewish Hospital in St. Louis."

"I don't know how I could get her to most of these places. I certainly would like to take her back to Mayo, but I don't think she could survive the trip in our van."

"No, she couldn't survive the trip in your van. You could have her flown to Mayo, but it would cost more than $10,000 and your insurance wouldn't pay anything on it."

"What about Barnes in St. Louis? Do you think you could get her in there, and if you could get her in there, how could we get her there?"

"I will make a telephone call to talk to someone in their neurology department to see if they would take Ann. If they would agree to take her, we can have one of the Big Springs Hospital ambulances transport her there and your insurance will at least pay something on the transportation cost."

"Do you think they might be able to help her?"

"Barnes has ties with Washington University and they have some great doctors on the staff there. She can't get any better staying here."

Chance thanked Dr. Caye and gave him a hug and said, "Thank you, Charles, I really appreciate all you have done for Ann." The Clarks had been patients of Dr. Charles Caye for more than twenty years and had become very close friends over the years. The days dragged by with no word from Barnes Jewish Hospital yet about whether they would accept Ann as a patient.

Since Ann had been in the Big Springs Hospital, Chance was staying with Ann all the time. Sleeping in her room, either in a hospital bed or on the floor, he only went home to shower, change clothes, check the mail, and pay the bills.

Staying with Ann also allowed him to hear what her doctors had to say to Ann and about her. Many of the doctors came in to see their patients very early in the morning.

As one nurse told him, Dr. Caye came in a little past dark thirty. Chance wasn't sure what time that was, but he knew Dr. Caye was seeing his hospital patients not long after 5:00 a.m.

So if you wanted to be at the hospital to see the doctor, you either had to come in very early or stay overnight. Chance preferred staying overnight.

He became the one who did most of the caregiving for Ann while she was in the hospital. He did all of her catheterizations, her bowels, gave her daily baths, and even gave medications to her, since Dr. Caye wrote orders for Chance to give Ann her meds.

Ann got to the point where she wouldn't eat any of the meals the hospital supplied, so Chance went to restaurants and brought food to her or he went home and made something for her. At least he got her to eat something that way.

She liked McDonald's biscuits and gravy with an extra sausage patty for breakfast and the favorite thing she liked for him to make at home and bring to her was *Crab Louie.*

The first time she ever had it was at the Broadmore Hotel in Colorado Springs, and Chance learned how to make it for her.

In different hospitals, if the doctor didn't set it up for Chance to give Ann her meds, then most of the nurses would, because Ann had to take each pill with a spoonful of applesauce and she had a very large handful of pills to take four times a day.

Chance bought a small refrigerator that he took to the hospitals to keep Ann's applesauce cold, and it could operate both on their van's electrical power system and the normal 110 volt electric found in most homes and hospitals in America.

Chance learned one thing being in the hospitals with Ann, and that was to be sure he watched everything they did for Ann while she was there. He found sometimes they were trying to give her the wrong medications and it happened more than once. Sometimes they tried to take her for tests the doctors hadn't ordered for her and then found they were in the wrong room.

Not only had Chance became Ann's full-time caregiver, he was also her patient advocate, making sure everything that could be done to help Ann get better was being done and seeing to it they kept her from hurting as much as possible.

He kept records of the everyday care he did for Ann, plus records of all the tests given to her in or out of hospitals, a record of every doctor's appointment and what was discussed with the doctor, all her medications, and all the changes the doctors made to her medications.

Chance updated Ann's medical history every day and he kept copies of it with him to give to every new doctor she saw.

Chance saw Dr. Caye the morning of June 4 and the doctor told him he spoke with Barnes the day before, and they agreed to take Ann with a hospital-to-hospital transfer. Apparently, hospitals were not very fond of doing this.

Dr. Caye said, "They will let us know when they have a room available on the neurology floor, and then we can have Ann transferred there.

"The good news is that I spoke with the head of neurology and he told me they had blocked the next room available on the floor for Ann and he thought maybe they can help Ann with her condition."

In a choking voice, Chance replied, "Thank you, Dr. Caye, we appreciate you so much."

"Chance, I hope they can really do something to help Ann." After Dr. Caye left, Chance said, "Ann, we're going to go to

St. Louis to the Barnes Jewish Hospital very soon to see if they can help you get to feeling better."

Ann didn't reply; she didn't understand what Chance said, she was in too much pain to care.

On June 5 Chance was told by a lady from the hospital's business office that Ann was going to be moved by one of their ambulances to St. Louis to the Barnes Jewish Hospital. She said they were working right now to get two drivers to take Ann to St. Louis and drive the ambulance back to Big Springs today.

Chance began packing up Ann's things to send with her in the ambulance. He packed everything he had brought to the hospital from home for Ann and what he would need for himself, plus all of Ann's supplies and her fridge to take with him in Ann's van.

After he had Ann's things packed up and all of the other things he brought to the hospital for her, Chance got his clothes and kit bag packed and loaded everything in the van.

He had the van fueled and was now ready to go, just waiting for the hospital to find the two drivers they needed for the ambulance.

Around 10:00 a.m., the ambulance drivers came into Ann's room and began loading all of the things of Ann's they would be taking with her in the ambulance.

They already had all the paperwork with them that they needed to make the hospital-to-hospital transfer.

Because Ann was so afraid when Chance wasn't with her he brought her cell phone from home to take with her, and since she couldn't work the phone now, he showed the attendant who would be riding with Ann on the trip to St. Louis how to work the phone and how to answer it.

Chance told the attendant if Ann became too upset, to call him on her cell phone and Chance thought he would be able to calm her down by talking on the phone with her. If not, maybe they could stop and let him talk with her.

The attendant told Chance he understood how to answer the cell phone and how to call him by just pushing Chance's preprogrammed number. No problem.

The attendants transferred Ann from her hospital bed onto the gurney and started to their ambulance as Chance was getting into Ann's van. Before Chance could get out of the parking lot, he saw the ambulance already going down the street.

Chance pulled out of the drive intending to follow close behind them. At the first intersection they came to, the ambulance made the light and Chance had to stop for the red light. That was the last time he saw the ambulance carrying his love.

After the traffic light turned green and Chance could go, he thought when he got out on the highway he would catch up with the ambulance.

Chance was now on the highway and driving seventy miles an hour in a fifty-five miles an hour speed limit zone, and the ambulance was nowhere in sight.

When Chance got into Missouri and on a sixty-five miles an hour speed limit, four-lane highway, he was now driving seventy-five miles an hour, he still wasn't catching up with the ambulance.

Just before he got to Springfield, Chance got a call on his cell phone and he heard the ambulance attendant say, "Your wife wants to talk to you."

The attendant gave the phone to Ann and she said, "Chance, where are you?"

"I'm in your van somewhere behind you, but I don't know how far I am behind your ambulance. I'm trying to catch up with you."

"I don't like this ambulance. It hurts my back." "Ann, let me talk with the ambulance attendant."

Ann tried to give the cell phone to the attendant but he dropped it and when he tried to pick it up, he turned the phone off.

Chance kept trying to call Ann back and although the phone sounded like it was ringing it kept going to Ann's voice mail.

Chance was getting madder with every mile. Now he was now on Interstate 44, driving between eighty-five and ninety- five miles an hour.

He finally saw an ambulance in front of him, but when he got up close to it, he could see it was from some town in Missouri transporting some other patient somewhere.

Chance kept driving way over the speed limit and finally had to stop to make a potty stop and buy more fuel just a few miles outside of St. Louis.

When Chance arrived at Barnes Jewish Hospital and found a parking place, he had to stop at the information desk to see what floor Ann had been taken to and if they had a room number for her yet.

The information desk clerk told him what her room number was and Chance found a bank of elevators to take him up to the floor.

Arriving on the floor where Ann's room was, he made his way to a nurse's station and asked if his wife, Ann Clark, had arrived yet. He was told she had just been taken to her room.

The nurse took him directly to Ann's room and there she was. He saw the Big Springs ambulance attendants walking out the door of Ann's room. Chance was doing everything he could to control his temper because he was so upset with these guys he could hardly see straight.

He must have tried to call Ann on her cell phone twenty-five or thirty times on the long ride from Big Springs to St. Louis. He had been so worried about Ann during the trip and about how she was and if she needed him to talk with him.

He thought he had found the perfect way to keep her calm during the trip and this guy had no idea of how to operate a cell phone. Instead of saying anything bad or nasty to the attendants, Chance just said, "Thank you for bringing my wife here safely."

Chance went directly over to Ann and took her hand in his hand leaned over and kissed her and said, "Hi, Annie, I didn't think I was ever going to catch up with you. Are you all right?"

"I guess I'm all right. Just don't leave me again. I'm afraid when you're not with me. I need you with me all the time."

"I'll try not to leave you alone again, my love."

65

7

THE BARNES JEWISH HOSPITAL EXPERIENCE

The day before Ann left the Big Springs Hospital, Dr. Caye asked a surgeon to put a port into Ann's chest in order to be able to draw blood and to give her IVs and other medications without sticking her over and over.

However, as was typical with Ann, the veins in her chest wouldn't cooperate and after four tries, two on each side of her chest, the surgeon put the port into Ann's left jugular vein. She looked like she might be Frankenstein's Monster's sister with a port sticking out of the left side of her neck.

Her lead doctor at Barnes was Dr. Glenn from Washington University and the first time he came in to see Ann on her arrival, he brought in seven new neurologists who were doing their residency training with him at Barnes.

Chance would soon find out all of the doctors working at Barnes Jewish Hospital were from Washington University at St. Louis.

Dr. Glenn went over all the information they had about Ann's medical history and her current condition. He explained she was referred

66

to Barnes to see if they could determine exactly what was causing Ann's problems and to treat the problem, or to see if they could develop a treatment for her condition if one didn't exist.

Each of the new neurologists did a short exam of Ann and each one of them took a pin and stuck it into various places on Ann's lower body asking her if she felt anything. The answer was always the same from Ann; no, she didn't feel a thing.

Then several of them asked Dr. Glenn questions about a variety of things about Ann's condition.

After spending almost an hour in Ann's room, Dr. Glenn said, "I'm writing orders for tests I want done tomorrow on Mrs. Clark. They include new MRIs, extensive blood tests, and a spinal tap."

Dr. Glenn said, "Mrs. Clark, I promise not to bring as many doctors with me each time I come to see you."

Ann didn't reply to Dr. Glenn; she was too tired from her trip from Big Springs to speak but she did almost manage a smile.

True to Dr. Glenn's words, Ann was kept busy all day with MRIs and blood taken from her new port, which was a real blessing instead of hunting for a vein they could use to get blood from Ann. Later that night one of the doctors, Dr. Farmer, who was with Dr. Glenn the night before came in to do her spinal tap. Dr. Farmer called the nurse's desk from Ann's room and asked for a nurse or an aide to assist him with Ann's spinal tap.

The doctor was told that everyone was busy with other patients, and some of the staff were off the floor having dinner and wouldn't be back for another thirty minutes. Dr. Farmer asked Chance if he might be able to help him for a few minutes.

Chance couldn't believe it; this was the third time at three different hospitals in the past six weeks he would be helping a doctor with a spinal tap on his wife. Of course, Chance would help and he told the doctor he already had experience helping do a spinal tap on his wife.

Chance was concerned about Dr. Farmer, who was only in his residency, doing a spinal tap on Ann and wondered if he had enough training to do a spinal tap without causing damage to his wife. Chance found out later that Dr. Farmer was finishing his residency in a couple of weeks so the doctor was well trained to perform the spinal tap.

Chance immediately saw Dr. Farmer was very accomplished at doing spinal taps. He did the spinal tap in just a few minutes and had drawn seven vials of fluid from Ann's spine for their tests. Chance remembered at the two other hospitals they only took two vials of fluid so Barnes was very serious about the tests they were doing.

Later Dr. Glenn came in to see Ann with only three other doctors with him and said, "See, Ann? I only have three doctors with me tonight. I have several things to go over with you and with the results of the test we did today.

"We have studied the MRI of your spine and found you don't have any indication that you have any inflammation there. We've looked over the MRI and the angiogram of your brain. We found your brain has lesions in the right side and in a few other locations scattered in some other parts of the brain.

"Tomorrow we want to do an ultrasound of your heart to make sure your heart is not releasing plaque into the brain causing the lesions. If this test proves negative, then next week I want you to have a biopsy of your brain.

"This is the only way for us to know for sure if you have Central Nervous System Vasculitis or if you have some type of brain degeneration. If it turns out to be degeneration, then we have no way of treating it.

"However, if it is one of the two types of Vasculitis that we think it is, we can begin an aggressive treatment plan to stop the disease from progressing."

Chance thought Dr. Glenn had certainly said a lot in a few minutes to let them hope or to worry about. Chance couldn't decide which one they should do.

After Dr. Glenn delivered his mouthful of information, he and his entourage left Ann's room.

Chance said, "Well, that was more information than we received about your condition and the results from your tests after being at Barnes for two days than we've gotten in months from any place you've been."

"Chance, they're talking about doing a brain biopsy on me and I don't want to let them."

"Honey, you may have to do it so they can help you get better."
"No, I don't want it."

"OK, we don't have to talk about it right now. I need to get you ready for some sleep. These hospitals are ruining our sleeping time with their early morning starts."

After Chance had completed all the regular nighttime things for Ann, he made his bed on the floor next to Ann's bed. Chance lay down on his pallet and said to Ann, "Goodnight, my love, I'll see you in the morning." She was already sleeping and never answered him.

On June 7 Ann had the ultrasound test on her heart and the doctor who performed the test told her he didn't see anything that would indicate the heart was throwing off plaque. He also said the test indicated she had a small hole between her two heart chambers. Nothing else was ever said about this problem while they were at Barnes. The same doctor told Ann he studied her MRI and confirmed he found she had a lesion in the area of T7 in her spine. Later in the evening Dr. Garber, head of surgery for the neurology department came to talk to Ann about doing her brain biopsy. Dr. Garber was a very accomplished brain surgeon and was the hospital's leading teacher, specializing in teaching all types of brain surgery to other surgeons.

He carefully explained to them the risk involved with brain surgery and how he would do the biopsy. He told them he would first have a stealth MRI done to pinpoint the area of the brain where the lesions were shown on her previous MRIs.

Next, they would mark the area and shave off a small amount of her hair, then saw out a small piece of her skull, about the size of a quarter. They would remove a small amount of tissue from the brain in the area of the lesions. The next step was to save the tissue and send it to the lab for study. The quarter-size portion of the skull which had been removed would be replaced and stapled into place. The doctor said, "Ann, then you would be taken to a recovery area, where you would remain for about twenty-four hours before being brought back to your room. By the time you're back in your room we should have the results from your biopsy, and Dr. Glenn and I would be able to tell you the type of treatment we would start for you.

"Ann, I don't want to put pressure on you, but in order for me to do your biopsy next Tuesday, I need to know if you are willing to do it and if you will sign the consent form for the surgery by tomorrow morning.

"The reason I need to know by tomorrow morning is that I have to schedule the operating room and schedule the staff I need to help me with your surgery.

"In your condition, Dr. Glenn and I think it's necessary to get you started on treatment as soon as possible."

Ann said, "Doctor Garber, I'll let you know in the morning if I will agree to go through with this surgery."

"OK, Ann, I'll see you tomorrow morning."

After Dr. Garber left Chance said, "Ann, you know you're going to have to let them do this biopsy if they have any chance of treating you."

"No, I don't have to. The way I feel right now, I don't know if I want any more treatments."

"Annie, you know I need you with me. Think about it before give up.

The next morning came and by then Ann decided to have the biopsy, and it made both Dr. Garber and Chance very happy.

Ann signed the form and Dr. Garber said, "Ann, we will do everything possible to get you through this and get you feeling better."

"Thank you, Doctor."

Sunday afternoon Ann's sister, Lee, flew to St. Louis from Dallas to be with Ann and Chance during Ann's surgery.

On Monday, June 10, Dr. Glenn talked to Ann and Chance about the biopsy and told Ann it was the right thing to do so they could get started with a plan to start treating her. The doctor also told them he spent some additional time reviewing Ann's MRIs and confirmed she did have two lesions in her spinal cord, between T7 and T8.

Although neither Chance nor Ann had any idea of what that meant, they assumed it was important to the doctors who would be developing a plan to treat her.

They didn't take Ann down to do her stealth MRI until around two thirty Tuesday afternoon, just before they took Ann into the area where they would be doing her MRI and surgery. The attendant who brought Ann to surgery told Chance, "You better give your wife a kiss because you won't be able to see her again until sometime tomorrow."

Both Chance and Lee gave Ann a kiss and told her they loved her.

Then the attendant pushed Ann through the door to the surgery rooms.

Chance swallowed hard the big lump he felt in his throat and hoped Ann would make it through surgery all right. Then he said a silent prayer for her doctors to do a skillful job and for Ann to be all right.

After the doors of the operating rooms squeaked closed and they could no longer see Ann's attendant or the gurney she was on, Chance said, "I've got to go back to Ann's room and take out all of our things while she is in surgery and recovery. Her nurse told me they needed Ann's room for another patient who was coming in this afternoon."

Lee replied, "That's kind of bad, don't you think?"

"I think it's bad because I have to take everything out to the car and keep it until she gets back to a room. I've got a lot of things up there to move out and to move back in. I also have to find someplace to stay tonight, since I've just been staying with Ann in her room."

Lee said, "I'll help you get everything out of the room but can't promise to help move it back since I have to go home on Thursday." "Thanks, Lee, let's go get everything out of the room so we can go to the surgery waiting room and we can hear how Ann is doing." Chance and Lee took two trips to collect everything from

Ann's room and take it down to the car.

As soon as they finished moving things out of Ann's room they returned to the surgery waiting room. They found a couple of places to sit while they waited for any information on what was happening with Ann.

The waiting room had a couple of large TV monitors with information on all of the patients currently in surgery. Each patient's name was listed and gave the status of each patient such as: waiting to be moved to surgery, in surgery, in recovery room, and ready to be moved to a room.

Ann's name was on the monitor indicating she was waiting to be moved to surgery. As Chance and Lee continued to watch, the monitor didn't change until sometime after 4:00 p.m. when the monitor showed she was in surgery.

If the minutes were creeping by before, now they were creeping through molasses on the coldest day of the coldest winter on record in Siberia.

Chance and Lee continued to stare at the monitor until they thought their eyes might bore a hole through the screen. Finally, the monitor information changed next to Ann's name to show Ann was now in recovery.

Chance's prayers had been directed to heaven ever since they said good-bye to Ann outside the entrance to the operating room.

After several more minutes passed, the lady working at the desk in the waiting room paged, "Mr. Chance Clark, please come to the desk for a message."

Chance approached the desk and said, "I'm Chance Clark."

The desk attendant said, "Mr. Clark, Dr. Garber wanted to tell you he would be out to speak with you in about ten minutes."

"Thank you."

Chance went back to where Lee was sitting and told her that Dr. Garber would be out to talk with them in about ten minutes.

Chance sat back down next to Lee to wait for Dr. Garber. In less than ten minutes Dr. Garber appeared at a door marked "Private." Chance got up from his chair and seeing Chance getting up Lee followed suit. When Chance and Lee got to where Dr. Garber was waiting, Chance introduced Lee to Dr. Garber.

Dr. Garber asked them to come with him and he took them to a small family room where he could talk with them. Dr. Graber invited them to sit down and he began by saying, "Ann did fine during the operation. She is now in the recovery unit where it's likely she will remain until sometime tomorrow.

"You will not be able to see her in the recovery unit until the doctors there feel she is doing all right enough for you to visit her. When they feel she's doing OK, they will let you know by contacting the waiting room.

"I was able to get the tissues we wanted for the biopsy and it is being tested even as we speak. By the time Ann is back in her room tomorrow, we should be able to tell you the results of the biopsy.

"Do you have any questions for me?"

Chance said, "I only have one question. How long do you think it will take Ann to heal from the surgery?"

"I would say it shouldn't take longer than three or four weeks before the skull begins to knit back together."

Lee asked, "Doctor, will Ann have any loss of memory or lose any of her mental abilities by having the surgery?"

"No, the area of the brain we were in has to do with motor skills so she certainly shouldn't have any loss of memory or her ability to think."

"Thank you, Dr. Graber, we appreciate everything you've done," Chance said.

After Dr. Graber left them Chance said, "Maybe I should take you over to your hotel so you can make your dinner with Dean's sister and her husband."

Lee agreed so when they left the family conference room Chance drove Lee over to her hotel, and Chance told her he was going to go in with her to see if he could get a room in her hotel.

Arriving at the hotel, Chance and Lee went into the lobby and Chance asked at the desk if he could get a room for the night.

The desk clerk said, "I'm sorry, but we don't have any rooms available for the next three nights."

Chance replied, "Business must be really good."

"Business is beyond good this week in St. Louis. There is a large national convention going on in town. I've been getting calls ever since I came on duty, from every hotel around here checking to see if we had any rooms.

"Frankly, sir, I think you would have to go over fifty miles away from St. Louis to find a hotel room tonight. I'm sorry I can't help you."

"Thanks for the information."

Lee told Chance, "You can stay with me in my room."

Chance told Lee he thought he would just go back to the hospital and stay in the surgery waiting room in case they let him see Ann later tonight. He wouldn't want her to wake up and him not be there.

True to his word, Chance spent the night in the waiting room hoping to get to see Ann. When he first went back to the waiting room there was an attendant working at the desk and lots of people still waiting to hear about loved ones in surgery.

Some of the folks waiting there had someone who had been in an accident and some who had emergency surgery. It was a very busy place.

One by one people left the waiting room until they were all gone except the desk attendant who went off duty at midnight. Before he left, Chance asked him if it was all right if he stayed in the waiting room and was told it wouldn't be any problem until about four in the morning when a cleaning crew would be in and then he would have to leave until they were finished cleaning the room.

Chance lay down on the floor and tried to sleep. Maybe he got an hour or so of sleep before the cleaning crew came in and asked him to leave so they could mop the floor.

Chance didn't go very far away from the waiting room. He went into the bathroom located just outside of the waiting room door.

He went out to his car and got his kit bag and a towel and washcloth and washed himself up as much as one can with a washcloth and his towel; he shaved and changed his clothes. So he was as ready for a new day as he was going to be.

He took his dirty clothes: towel, washcloth, and kit bag back out to his car and returned to the waiting room to see that it was still closed. Chance decided to stand outside the door and wait until the maintenance crew finished their work.

He was soon rewarded for his wait as the cleaning crew began removing their various cleaning equipment and supplies out of the surgery waiting room.

As soon as the last of their things left the room, they opened the door for Chance to return to the place he had spent the night.

One thing he had learned from his experience the night before was that marble floors would never make a good substitute for his nice, comfortable, warm bed.

Chance checked the monitor for any new information on Ann and saw the monitor continued to show she was in recovery. The hours continued to drag as Chance waited to see something new on the monitor about Ann.

A little after 6:00 a.m. a new lady came to work at the waiting room information desk. After she had had a little time to get settled in her chair, Chance made his way to the desk and asked if she had any new information on his wife, Ann Clark.

She checked her monitor and told him no, there wasn't anything new since last night's posting. Then she asked if he would like her to call a nurse in recovery to see what they could tell her about his wife.

Chance said he would certainly like her to do that. She called and spoke with one of the nurses working in recovery. The nurse told the attendant Ann was still in recovery and she was doing OK. She thought sometime later in the morning or maybe early in the afternoon she would be ready to see her family.

Chance thanked the attendant and told her how much he appreciated her getting the information for him. As he was turning away from her desk he saw Lee coming into the waiting room and quickly went over to her to tell her the news he had just gotten from a nurse in recovery.

After getting this information both Chance and Lee felt a little better knowing Ann was doing OK and that they would be able to see her in a few hours.

Chance asked Lee if she had anything for breakfast yet and she said no, she didn't want to take the time to eat because she wanted to get back to the hospital as soon as she could.

Chance said, "Good, let's go have something to eat. I don't remember if I had dinner last night. Anyway, I'm really hungry."

The two of them made their way to the hospital cafeteria for breakfast and attempted to talk about something besides Ann and found it wasn't possible.

After they filled their plates and sat down at a table, Chance said with visible tears in his eyes, "Lee, I don't know if Ann's going to make it through all of this or not.

"I don't know if she will even be able to make it to December for our fiftieth wedding anniversary. Hell, I'm not sure she's going to make it to next week."

Lee responded, "I know it doesn't look very good, but maybe the doctors here can make her a lot better."

"Yeah, I know, we just have to pray and wait. It's so hard to watch her every day with all of her pain and be helpless to help make the pain stop.

"Lee, I never had a chance to tell you, but our doctor in Big Springs told me she only has a chance of making it if these doctors at Barnes can help her.

"Dr. Caye could only suggest a few places he thought might be able to help Ann. He said we needed to take her to either Mayo Clinic, Cleveland Clinic, Harvard Medical, Stanford Medical, or Barnes, with their Washington University doctors.

"We didn't have any way of getting her to any of these other facilities and, besides, with her condition she couldn't have traveled that far anyway. So here we are, praying they can do something to help Ann survive and that's as much as we can do."

They finished their breakfast without anything else being said and went directly back to the surgery waiting room to wait for news of Ann.

At twelve forty-five on the afternoon of June 12 the attendant at the desk paged, "Family of Ann Clark, please come to the attendant's desk."

Both Chance and Ann rushed to the attendant's desk and were told they could now go in to see Ann and she gave them her number, west wing, unit 478. She told them to go through the door out in the hall marked "Recovery Entrance" and they would see signs directing them to either the east wing or the west wing.

When they got to the west wing, they should ask one of the people working there to direct them to Ann's unit.

They quickly went out of the waiting room and through the door to the recovery wings and when they passed through the door they saw the sign directing them to the west wing.

Arriving at the west wing of the recovery facility, they were surprised to see an area that looked to be the size of a huge gym with small curtained cubicles on both sides of the large area, and there must have been over a hundred cubicles in total in this wing.

A nurse came up to them and asked them whom they wanted to see and Chance told her, Ann Clark. The nurse told them to follow her and she would take them to see Mrs. Clark.

As they were going back to Ann's cubicle, they passed the nurse's station where Chance saw there were all types of monitoring devices. He thought they must be connected to patients or the cubicles they were in. Chance thought it looked like the cockpit of a space craft.

Finally, they arrived at Ann's cubicle and they could see she was attached to a lot of different devices located in the cubicle as well as the ones back at the nurse's station.

Ann appeared to be asleep when they arrived and the nurse said, "Ann, wake up. You've got company."

Ann didn't open her eyes or try to respond to the nurse. The nurse tried again, "Ann, Ann Clark, can you open your eyes to see who's here to see you?"

Still Ann didn't respond.

The nurse shrugged her shoulders and said, "She's been awake and she's doing OK. Maybe she's not receiving company yet today." Since there was only one chair in the cubicle, the nurse brought over another chair for both of them to be able to sit down and wait to talk with Ann. The nurse left them because she had been called to attend to another patient.

After the nurse left them, Chance and Lee stood on each side of Ann's bed, looking at all the wires and hoses she was attached to. They could see the bandage on Ann's head; it covered all of her head.

Chance said, "If they only removed a piece of Ann's skull the size of a quarter, she sure has a huge bandage."

Lee replied, "It's probably that big because they wouldn't want her to be able to touch or scratch it."

Hearing Chance and Lee's voices, Ann began to slowly open her eyes.

Chance said as he put his hand on Ann's, "We didn't think you wanted to see us today, sweetheart. How are you doing?"

Ann struggled to speak and managed to say, "I don't know." Lee asked, "Is there something we can do for you?"

"You can make me stop hurting."

Chance asked, "Where are you hurting, Annie?" "Everywhere!"

Then Ann began trying to move her hands but couldn't because they were being held to the side of her bed with straps.

Chance asked, "Do you want me to see if they can take these straps off?"

"Yes, I want to move my arms."

Chance left to find a nurse to see if they could take Ann's straps off her arms. When he found a nurse she told him he could take the straps off now. They had put them on because when

Ann was semiconscious, she kept trying to take her monitor cable off.

When Chance returned, he and Lee removed the straps from Ann's arms.

After the straps were removed Ann reached to try to take her cables off.

Chance told her, "You can't take them off while you are in recovery."

Ann didn't want to hear that and kept telling them she didn't want them on her and tried to take them off again until Chance grabbed her arm and stopped her.

Then she said, "I've got to have something for pain."

Lee pushed the call button for a nurse and when they answered, Lee asked, "Can Mrs. Clark have something for pain now?"

Lee was told someone would be there in a few minutes to help her.

The few minutes took several minutes before a nurse was able to get there and Ann continued to get more aggravated every second.

Chance and Lee had no idea what they could do. They both kept trying to soothe her, without any success.

A nurse came in with a pain medication injection for Ann and quickly put it in her port. Then the nurse said to Ann, "Give it a few minutes, honey, you'll get some relief from that old pain."

The nurse told them they would be moving Ann to a room as soon as they had a room available.

At one thirty in the afternoon, two nurses came to Ann's cubicle and began removing all of her monitoring cables and everything else hooked up to her except her IV fluid.

Shortly after they finished getting Ann freed from all of their monitoring devices, two men from transportation arrived at the cubicle with a gurney to take Ann back to a room.

Arriving on the floor where Ann had been staying, one of the men asked the nurse at the nurse's station which room was assigned to Ann. The nurse said, "Mrs. Clark will be in Room 1747, in bed number one."

When they took Ann into Room 1747 she found she didn't have a private room, because there was a lady in bed number two.

With the help of a nurse, the transportation men transferred Ann from the gurney onto her bed. Ann was groaning in agony from having been moved around so much.

Chance and Lee arrived in the room just as they finished getting Ann in her new bed. Chance wasn't happy to find Ann had a roommate in her new room because he had been staying with Ann day and night.

He didn't know how he would be able to get any sleep, trying to make his bed on the floor in the small space divided up between bed one and two.

As soon as the nurse left the room, Chance followed her out in the hallway and asked if Ann could be moved to a private room. She told him they didn't have a private room available right now but the lady in bed two was ready to go home as soon as someone came to pick her up and that no one else would be put in with Ann.

Chance thanked her for the information and returned to Ann's room.

Lee had struck up a conversation with the lady in bed two and found out the same thing, that she was waiting very impatiently for her ride home. The lady was on her telephone, screaming at whoever she was talking to about why they hadn't come to get her yet. After the lady ended her telephone conversation, she told Lee, "I'm sorry for yelling, but they were to pick me up three hours ago."

Lee didn't say anything but she smiled and shook her head in a knowing kind of way about why the lady was upset.

Two more hours passed and three more telephone calls made before the lady's husband arrived to pick her up. He tried to tell her he was having car troubles and had to get the car fixed before he could come to get her. The lady wasn't buying any of it. However, her husband did gather up all of her things to take home and an aide came to help the lady out to her car.

Chance and Lee gave a sigh of relief when the lady and her husband finally left the room, not because she was there but because she was always on her telephone yelling at either her husband or one of her kids.

Lee spent a few hours talking to Ann, her older sister, before she had to leave to fly back to Dallas that night. She would have liked to stay longer but she needed to get back home for something she had promised to do with one of her children.

While Lee was trying to make conversation with Ann, Chance went to the van to bring back all the things he had taken down to the van when he had to clear everything out of Ann's previous room before she went to surgery.

Chance was able to get everything back in Ann's new room in three trips and was able to spend some more time with Lee before she had to leave to go home. It was almost eight thirty that evening before Lee said, "I have to go now to make my flight."

Lee kissed Ann good-bye and told her she loved her and to get to feeling better soon.

Chance said, "Call me when you get home, so we know you made it home OK."

Lee promised she would and before she left she kissed Chance and told him to hang in there.

He promised he would.

On June 13, Dr. Garber came to Ann's room late in the afternoon and took off her bandage and checked over the area of her skull where he had done her biopsy. He announced that everything was doing great. This was even though Ann continued to be in great pain.

Before the doctor left, he put a much smaller bandage on Ann's head and told Ann he would check on her again in a couple of days. During the next few days they worked to try to ease the pain Ann was having and started her on treatments of twenty units of Solu-Medrol.

On the morning of June 17, Ann was taken to intervention radiology and they placed a Hickman port on the right side of her chest to use to give her meds and IVs and to draw blood without sticking her with needles all the time.

On June 18, the staples were removed from Ann's head and they put only a small bandage on the site of her brain surgery. They told Chance they would only have to keep a small bandage there a few more days.

On June 19, Ann completed her twenty units of Solu- Medrol and the port put in at the hospital in Big Springs on the left side of her neck was removed. With the port out of her neck, she no longer looked like one of Frankenstein's Monsters, thank God, and the bandage was gone from the top of her head so she looked much better, even if she didn't feel any better.

She continued to hurt all the time in her neck and shoulders and said she hurt all over her body all the time.

The next step of her treatment was to get six doses of Cystoxic with the first one beginning at 6:00 a.m. on June 21. She would get three doses of Cystoxic a day for two days.

The doctor explained he had made arrangements with an oncologist in Big Springs, a Dr. King, to continue doing Ann's treatments in Big Springs. Dr. King would be following the treatments designed for Ann by Barnes doctors. This way Ann would not have to come back to St. Louis every month for the next two years to complete the treatment they had designed for her.

Chance and Ann were both happy to hear about the arrangement for Ann's continuing treatments in Big Springs since it would be costly for them to make a trip to St. Louis every month for the next two years.

It was impossible for Chance to get Ann in and out of her wheelchair in a small space, since she could do nothing to help Chance because she was totally paralyzed from her chest down. The only way to get Ann in and out of her wheelchair was for Chance to pick her up. Besides all that, Ann had a very hard time riding for seven or eight hours.

Ann and Chance were happy to get the opportunity to go home after being at Barnes Jewish Hospital for so long and in the Big Springs Hospital before coming to St. Louis.

Chance counted up the total days Ann had been in the hospital—a total of thirty-five days. Chance thought it seemed much longer to him.

When Dr. Glenn left Ann's room, Chance called Chase and Shane and asked them if they could come to St. Louis to help him bring their mother home. Yes, they would leave early tomorrow morning and drive to St. Louis to help bring Mom home.

The two boys talked after Chance had spoken with them, and Shane told his older brother he would drive over from Fayetteville to The Trout's Inn that night so they could get an early start in the morning.

8

THE TRIP HOME AND MORE TROUBLES

On June 24, 2002, Ann was released by her Barnes doctors to return home.

Ann seemed to be very happy about seeing her two sons, Chase and Shane, but maybe she was even happier to be going home.

Chance had a couple of scripts to fill at the hospital pharmacy before they left. Chase stayed to talk to his mother while Chance and Shane went down to the pharmacy to have Ann's scripts filled. Chance handed the woman working at the pharmacy counter Ann's two scripts and she took them back to a pharmacist. A few minutes later she returned and said, "One of your scripts is pretty expensive and we can't use your insurance at the pharmacy."

Chance replied, "Well, we need both of these scripts filled, so please go ahead and fill it."

The clerk returned again and said, "This script is pretty expensive. Are you sure you want to fill it or do you wait until you return home so you can use your insurance?"

Chance then placed his platinum American Express card down on the counter where the clerk could see it and asked, "OK, just tell me how expensive it is to fill this script?"

"I'll check how much it will cost you to fill the script and I'm sorry we don't take American Express credit cards."

Chance looked at Shane and said, "How much do you think the script is going to cost?"

Shane smiled and said, "It's expensive!"

It took the young lady several minutes before she returned to the counter again and said, "This script is $6,875. Do you want us to go ahead and fill it?"

After Chance recovered a bit from the shock of the cost of the prescription, he said, "No, I believe we will take it home where we can use our insurance."

Chance and Shane left the pharmacy with the one filled script and when they got into an elevator with no one else in the elevator with them they both said, "It's expensive!"

Chance could hardly tell the story of their trip to the pharmacy to Ann and Chase as he and Shane were laughing so much.

Chase enjoyed the story, but Ann seemed only to worry about needing to take such expensive medication.

Ann was right as usual; there was nothing funny about a prescription costing over $6,000.

After loading the van and getting Ann in her wheelchair and loading her into the van they were at long last on their way back home to Big Springs.

Chase would drive the van so Chance could sit in the back to take care of Ann on the long ride home. The decision was made that they wouldn't try to stop except to buy gas, potty, and make a fast food stop.

Shane would follow behind the van in his car and would stop whenever they stopped. They also had cell phones so they could talk with each other during the trip.

Chance knew they could communicate, unlike his experience coming to St. Louis. Chance thought back to his trip from Big Springs to St. Louis and got mad all over again about trying to keep in contact with Ann on their cell phones. Trying to work with an ambulance attendant to operate a cell phone for Ann, when the attendant didn't have a clue about how to use one, was a total disaster.

As the miles passed, it seemed like something happened to Ann and she began talking about a nurse who was following them because she was going to kill Chance, and this nurse had a big knife.

The more Chance tried to tell Ann there was no one following them except Shane following them in his car, the more she insisted yes, there was a nurse with the big knife and she was after Chance and that she wouldn't stop until she killed him.

This went on for hours and nothing Chase or Chance could say eased Ann's mind, and the more they tried, the more agitated she became. Chance knew this was being caused by her medication, but why did Ann have this fixation on a nurse wanting to follow them and kill Chance?

Chance suddenly didn't know what happened to his wife.

He was with someone that wasn't Ann. Her expressions weren't Ann's, this person didn't speak like Ann, and it was all very confusing to Chance.

Ann hadn't been acting like this when she was in the hospital, so what set her off on something like this, thinking some nurse was following them and planned to kill Chance?

Chase didn't know what to think either because his mother certainly hadn't acted this way in the hospital. She seemed just like his mom, not this person riding in the back of the van.

Ann kept telling them all the way to Big Springs, over and over, that this nurse with the big knife was going to kill Chance and nobody could stop her.

They made a stop for fuel once and to get a hamburger to take with them. Ann didn't want anything to eat, and she wouldn't take her medication. She appeared to get angrier with every mile of their trip home.

When Chase pulled the van into their garage, Ann told them to watch out for the nurse with the big knife: she was waiting in their garage to kill Chance.

Chase got out of the van and opened the back doors and put the lift down so he could lower his mother's wheelchair and get her out of the van.

As Chase was doing this, Chance went inside the house and began turning on lights while Shane was busy unloading all their things from the rear of the van.

Chase brought Ann into the house and took her directly into the bedroom as his dad asked him to do. Chance was waiting there to get Ann in her bed.

After Chase delivered his mother to the bedroom he went back in the family room to talk with Shane while his dad was getting Mom into bed.

Chance did all the things he needed to do to get Ann ready for the night, including giving her medications which, thank goodness, this time she took.

When Chance finished taking care of Ann for the night he asked her if he could do anything else for her or if she wanted anything.

The very curt response from Ann was, "No!"

Chance resisted making any smart-aleck response to her curt remark; instead he said, "Good night, sweetheart, I love you and I'll see you in the morning."

Chance went back to the family room to thank their sons for helping bring Mom home and as he was thanking them, Chase said, "Dad, what was that all about where Mom kept saying some nurse with a big knife was going to kill you?"

"Your guess is as good as mine. I don't have any idea where that came from. It must be caused by her medications. It beats the heck out of me. It was weird."

Chase replied, "Dad, it was beyond weird, it was scary. I think if I were you I would be afraid if Mom could get out of bed maybe she would try to kill you or something."

Chance replied, "I have no idea why she kept saying it all the way from St. Louis to Big Springs. She sure made me start watching every car that came up behind us. I sure hope she doesn't keep that up."

Shane said, "Let's hope not. I wasn't in the van to hear what she was saying but Chase told me what she said."

"Thanks again, guys, for coming to St. Louis to help me bring Mom home. I love you and I wish you could stay longer but you better go on home.

"Shane, you're going to stay with Chase over at the resort tonight, aren't you?

"No, Dad, I need to take Chase home and then drive back to Fayetteville. I've got things I have to do there tomorrow."

"OK, but drive carefully, that's a lot of driving and I don't I think I can take having you piled up in a car wreck somewhere on your way home."

"I'll be all right. I'm used to driving at night. I like driving on the road at night because there's not as much traffic."

Chance gave both of his sons a hug before they left and told them he loved them and they both told him they loved him, too.

The next day, Chance called Genell Thomason, the lady he had hired to help take care of Ann to let her know they were home, and he would like for her to start working again if she was still interested in working for them.

Genell told him yes, she was, and if he wanted her to come this afternoon, she would be there. Chance told her to please come on. Chance wasn't sure if he was up to doing things for Ann this morning after the way she was acting yesterday. He hoped she would be back to being Ann again.

When he went in to wake Ann, he did so with plenty of concern that she would be like she was yesterday. If she was, he didn't know how long he would be able to cope with that.

He didn't have long before he found out how she was when he woke her. To say she was hateful and did everything she could do to be uncooperative would have been kind. She was far worse. She didn't want him to do anything to take care of her.

He didn't have any choice except to try to shut out everything she said to him in order for him to do the things he had to do for her. He did get all the things done he had to do to care for Ann that morning.

When he finished all these chores, he fixed Ann's breakfast, which she wouldn't eat, nor would she take medication again.

Chance was totally frustrated and had no idea what he was going to do with Ann if she kept this up for a long period of time. He simply had no answers as to why she became like this after they left the hospital, unless it was caused by her medications. If it was caused by one of her medications, he hoped they could find which one it was and get rid of it.

Chance wanted to get his Annie back and never wanted to hear this woman again.

Chance wondered if there was a possibility that something had happened to her when they did the biopsy of her brain: maybe they hit something that changed who she was.

Chance didn't want to even think about something like that happening and that Ann was always going to be like she was right now. God, what an awful thought.

Genell arrived a few minutes before noon and Chance was really happy to see her. Ann didn't remember who Genell was but she seemed to react better to her than she did with Chance.

Genell got her to eat some lunch and to take her pills; thank goodness, she would do something for someone.

Chance struggled to get Ann to do anything for him, and on so many nights after he got her in bed and finished doing everything he had to do for Ann, he would be lying in his bed, next to Ann's bed, crying softly in frustration and praying for the strength to be able to keep taking care of her.

He didn't know what he was going to do or how he could keep doing it. Ann was so awful to try to work with now.

This pattern continued and went on day after day and week after week.

Dr. Glenn from Barnes had made arrangements with the Big Springs Hospital to have a nurse from their home health care department, beginning on June 28, to check on Ann each week and give her a weekly injection of Solu-Medrol through her Hickman port as part of her treatment plan.

On July 18, Ann had an appointment with Dr. King, the doctor Dr. Glenn had made arrangements with to do Ann's treatments in the Big Springs Hospital.

Dr. King wanted to discuss the treatment plan with Ann, which had been designed by the doctors at Barnes Jewish Hospital for her. Chance had Genell go with them to the appointment with Dr. King, and Chance was pleased to see that Ann behaved decently during the visit.

After Dr. King met with them and gave her a brief exam, he told them he scheduled her to go to the Big Springs Hospital at six o'clock in the morning on July 22 to start her monthly treatments.

Chance thought all along they would be doing these treatments at the doctor's office, but Dr. King told them the treatments lasted too long to do them in his office.

At 6:00 a.m. on July 22, Chance had Ann at the Big Springs Hospital to start the first of her monthly treatments.

Dr. King came in and explained how these treatments would work. First, Ann would receive 1,000 cc of fluid over a three- hour time period, next she would get fifteen minutes of Zofran injections, next came one gram of Solu-Medrol, followed by four hours of Cystoxic, and end with another three hours of fluid. All these medications would be given to her through her Hickman port. Both Ann and Chance were happy to hear they didn't have to have people searching Ann's arms for somewhere to stick her with a needle. At this point in her life she didn't have many veins in her arms left suitable for getting medications in or blood out.

Chance asked Genell to work her regular hours and come to the hospital to be with them any time Ann would be in the hospital. This worked very well because of Genell's long employment with the hospital; she knew many of the people who worked there and how to get things done.

Ann's treatments this day got started about 8:00 a.m. and didn't finish until eight thirty that night before Chance could take Ann home.

After finishing the treatment, Ann didn't have anything to say and was cooperative with Chance getting her into bed.

Ann was truly not doing well for the next three days and was unable to speak so Chance made an appointment for Ann with Dr. Caye to see if anything could be done about her pain and her problem speaking.

On July 25, Dr. Caye examined Ann and said he couldn't make any changes to her meds at this time.

Ann just kept getting worse day by day, so on July 31, Chance took Ann to the ER at Big Springs Hospital. After the ER doctor consulted with Dr. Caye, Ann was admitted to the hospital for observation.

The next morning, August 1, Dr. Caye ordered two units of whole blood for Ann.

The following morning, after she had received the two pints of blood, and Ann woke up, Chance's Ann was back, the person he had been trying to care for was gone and his wife was really back.

Chance believed it was truly a miracle to see Ann back to herself and an unforgettable event in his life. No more was she that strange creature who had entered Ann's body over these past weeks. Thank God!

Chance did exactly that with his prayers. He had really received an answer to his prayers. Praise God!

On August 4, Ann was released from the Big Springs Hospital to go home, but she continued to have multiple problems leading to additional doctors for a variety of new problems.

By August 17, Ann was back in the Big Springs Hospital again with severe pains in her neck, head, and spine.

Dr. Caye contacted a doctor in Springfield who was a pain specialist with Cox Hospital System and asked him for any suggestion he might have to help relieve Ann's pain. He suggested he prescribe Bextra and Neurontin to help with her pain.

From August 29 to November 21, Ann was seen by three additional new doctors for other problems. It seemed like Ann would never get a break from her health problems.

Ann was back in the Big Springs Hospital for another twenty days in September, getting to go home on Chance's birthday, September 20.

It was a very quiet birthday celebration for his sixty-sixth birthday.

Chance was pleased Ann was able to come home from the hospital on his birthday which meant it was a wonderful birthday present. Best of all, Ann was still with him after all she had gone through this year.

Ann's sixty-sixth birthday was on December 4 and she was home and doing fairly well in spite of all her problems.

Both of her sons and their families were able to come on the evening of her birthday which certainly brightened Ann's special day.

She enjoyed her cake and ice cream and the presents she received, but it's pretty hard to think of something to give someone who's confined to a wheelchair and, over the past several years, could buy anything she wanted.

Ann stayed up until after ten o'clock, visiting with her family and enjoying every minute having them with her.

She finally told Chance, "Honey, I have to go to bed. I just can't sit in this wheelchair any longer."

The birthday party broke up with each member of her family giving Ann a careful hug and a kiss as they left the house.

After everyone left, Ann said, "I love you, Chance. You gave me a wonderful birthday party with all of our family. Thank you."

Chance answered, "It was my pleasure doing it. I love you so very much."

As Chance was taking Ann to their bedroom she said, "Chance, I'm sorry you have to do everything for me. I wish you could still work and travel the way you used to. I'm too much work for you."

"You know taking care of you is the hardest job I've ever had, but it's the one I loved the best."

After he finished everything for Ann that evening, he reflected back on their life together and thought about the day they had gotten married.

They were two sixteen-year-old kids who had no idea of the hardships they would face in their life over their soon-to-be fifty years of marriage.

Their fiftieth wedding anniversary would be December 22 of this year, and Chance had to do something special for Ann for their anniversary.

He knew they needed to get their picture made for their anniversary and to plan a dinner somewhere all of their family and best friends could come.

The next day, Chance contacted a photographer who at one time had worked for him at the Superior Parking Meter plant and had left to become an excellent professional photographer.

Chance asked him if would be possible for him to come to their home to take their picture for their fiftieth wedding anniversary. He told Chance it wouldn't be a problem.

Two days later the photographer arrived to take their picture, and with Genell's help dressing Ann and doing her nails, they were ready when he arrived.

Chance had a necklace made for Ann for her anniversary present. The necklace had a large ruby as the centerpiece and the ruby was circled with special high-quality diamonds.

After the proofs of the pictures were brought back to Chance, he knew he had made a mistake. He should have bought Ann a brighter color suit with because the white color made her looked washed out, and because of the amount of weight she had lost, it was too big for her.

It was too bad he hadn't done a better job picking out her pantsuit because these photos would have to do. It had been hard enough for Ann to sit and have pictures taken the first time so there could be no second time.

Chance made reservations for all of their family, called Doc and Susan Schmidt, along with Kathy Jones, the widow of his old boss, Karl Jones, to come to their anniversary dinner at the Station Casino in Kansas City. They agreed to be there for the special occasion.

Chance made plans to drive to Kansas City on December 21 and have their anniversary dinner on their anniversary. He realized their anniversary was only three days before Christmas and everyone was busy, but he wanted to have everyone they loved and who loved them there to help them celebrate.

Chance felt he had everything he could do arranged for their celebration and was just waiting for the day to come. He only could hope Ann was well enough to make the trip.

9

THE LAST FIVE YEARS
OF CHANGE

December 21, 2002, Chance and Ann arrived at the Station Casino and Hotel in Kansas City about four thirty in the afternoon.

It was a cold and windy winter afternoon. They had come to celebrate their fiftieth wedding anniversary tomorrow with their all of their family and a few very close, special friends.

Chance's thoughts went back to their forty-fifth wedding anniversary and how he was too sick that day to go to Branson to celebrate their anniversary and how much their lives had changed over these past five years.

Ann was waiting for him to get out of their van to put the lift down so he could move her wheelchair onto it. Then Chance would lower the ramp so she could get out of the van and inside the hotel as quickly as possible and out of the cold.

Chance keep thinking about just how much Ann's health had changed in those five years; she had become completely paralyzed from her chest down caused by an autoimmune disease called Central Nervous System Vasculitis, the cause of her paralysis.

Chance was very proud of her attitude about her life, considering the pain she had suffered as the parts of her body stopped functioning. She had been on some of the most powerful pain meds made and sometimes they were not enough to give her any relief.

He didn't know how she could stand the pain and smile occasionally. She never complained about the horrible thing that had happened to her. She had to let someone do everything for her. She couldn't urinate or have a bowel movement by herself anymore. For someone who was so private and proper to suffer such indignities had to be so horrible for her.

Chance thanked God every day for the few things that she could still do for herself. She could feed herself. She could brush her teeth, comb her hair, and do her makeup. She could still read and she enjoyed watching TV and could talk with him.

Chance thought the real blessing was that her mind wasn't affected anymore. He wouldn't have wanted to keep taking care of her the way she was when they first returned from her stay at Barnes Jewish Hospital.

He didn't know what had happened to change her personality and have such wild thoughts. He certainly appreciated whoever donated the blood that seemed to bring her back to being herself after she had the blood transfusion.

One thing for sure was her quick mind worked just fine again and her speech wasn't affected anymore as it had been earlier by some of her meds.

A bellman brought a luggage cart to unload their stuff from the van and it completely filled it up. One thing, when they traveled it was like moving a whole household due to all of the equipment needed to take care of Ann: their clothes, meds, and a small fridge to carry applesauce so Ann could take her meds, since without the applesauce she couldn't swallow her meds.

Chance showed Ann around their suite. It had a kitchen, living room, dining room with a bar, two bathrooms, and of course, a bedroom. She thought the suite was very nice and it had plenty of room for their family and friends to sit and visit with them.

Ann said their suite was a lot bigger than their first apartment. However, the cost per night of their suite was higher than four months' rent on their apartment in January of 1953.

Chance thought back to their first apartment and remembered they only had two rooms, a kitchen and combination living and bedroom. They had to share a bath with two other apartments and although their apartment was on the first floor, they had to walk up to the second floor to use the bathroom.

Their life had changed a lot since their first apartment.

After Chance turned on the TV for Ann, he looked through the telephone book and found the telephone number for their best man, Don Smith. They had not seen Don for probably twenty years but Chance wanted to see if he could get in touch with him and have him come to visit with them at the hotel if he could.

Chance was surprised when Don answered the phone because he thought Don would probably be at work. After a few minutes, the two of them were talking like it had only been a week since they saw each other. Yes, Don was retired and could come over to the hotel to visit them tomorrow afternoon.

Chance and Ann were really pleased that Don could come and see them on the occasion of their fiftieth wedding anniversary. After all, he was one of the four people who had attended their wedding: the Baptist preacher, Reverend Thomas, and his wife and Ann's bridesmaid, Betty Shaw.

It would have been nice if Betty could have been there but they hadn't seen her for a really long time and with all their moving around the world they had not kept in touch with her.

As far as Chance and Ann knew, Betty still lived in Webster, Kansas, some two hundred miles from Kansas City.

Chance knew it was going to be a very busy day tomorrow with all of their family and friends coming to be with them. He thought they needed to have dinner early so they had time to relax and get some sleep.

They decided to go down to one of the restaurants and make arrangements for the dinner tomorrow night. They had a simple dinner at one of the restaurants and made a reservation for dinner tomorrow night at the Italian restaurant in the Casino complex. They thought it was the best choice they had for the dinner since everyone coming liked Italian food and it looked like the best of the restaurants in the complex.

Chance couldn't stand not going into the casino for a few minutes, so Ann and he found a slot machine they could play together. One where Ann could reach the play button after Chance put in the money. They were not having any luck with the machine so it didn't take them long to decide to go back to their suite.

After they returned to the room they watched TV for a while and Ann said she thought she needed to go to bed.

Chance took Ann into the bedroom and got her ready for bed and then Chance opened up the small container of applesauce and dipped out a spoonful and placed some of Ann's pills in the applesauce and gave Ann the dose of meds. It took a whole container of applesauce four times a day for Ann to get down all of her daily pills.

Chance knew one thing about that old saying, "an apple a day keeps the doctor away," didn't seem to be working out very well by eating applesauce four times a day. It would be a very rare week if they got by without seeing a doctor or being in a hospital. Rare, indeed!

Last thing needed for Ann to be ready for bed was to get her toothbrush and toothpaste so she could brush her teeth. After Ann finished brushing her teeth and rinsing out her mouth, Ann and Chance kissed each other goodnight.

Chance took the pillows out from behind her, laid her down flat on the bed and then turned her over on her right side, and placed her own pillow they brought from home under her head.

Chance said, "It doesn't seem like tomorrow will be fifty years since we got married, does it to you?"

"No, the time has gone by awfully fast. Maybe I can ask for a rerun.

Chance laughed and replied, "I don't think we can get a rerun."

"No, probably not."

Chance replied, "We should be thankful for all the years we have had together. Several times over the last three years I thought we were not going to make it to our fiftieth anniversary.

"You've been pretty sick and it's taken a lot of prayers and a lot of doctors to keep you with me to make it to this day. I love you so much."

"I love you, too, and I'm sorry you have to do so much work to take care of me."

Chance answered the way he always did, "Hardest job I've ever had, but the one I loved the best."

"I don't know how that's possible, but I glad you feel that way." "OK, Ann, but you better go to sleep or it's going to be the twenty-second and we'll still be talking and I'm not ready for bed yet."

"I love you, so hurry up and come to bed."

By the time Chance was ready for bed, Ann was already asleep so he leaned over and kissed her goodnight again before turning off the bedside light.

Chance woke up early the next morning and made his way to the bathroom while Ann was still sleeping. He managed to go to the bathroom and take his shower before Ann woke up. Before he began shaving, he thought he better check on Ann to see if she was still sleeping.

After finding Ann was still sleeping he shaved, brushed his teeth, and took his morning pills. Thank goodness he had a lot fewer pills and only had to take a couple times a day than one dose of Ann's which she took four times a day.

He found clothes to wear for the day and got dressed. He would change his clothes later in the day for their anniversary dinner tonight.

Ann was awake when he came back into the bedroom. Chance said, "Happy fiftieth anniversary, my love." "Happy anniversary, Chance."

"I bet you're ready to get cleaned up and get dressed for the day. I brought a couple of different outfits for you to look at to wear today before we dress for dinner tonight. You can take your choice of which one you want to wear."

Before Ann had an opportunity to answer him, Chance turned Ann from her right side onto her back and leaned over her and gave her a big good morning kiss.

Then Ann said, "Big deal, you're going to let me have a choice of two different outfits to wear today?"

"OK, you can have more choices if you want, since I brought you four or five different outfits."

"Thanks, you know I don't really care which outfit I wear as long as everything goes with it."

Chance knew that was true after living with her for fifty years. He knew she had to have the right shoes, purse, and jewelry for each of her outfits. He hoped he had packed all the right things to go with her pantsuits.

She had several pantsuits from the same manufacturer in lots of different colors that she loved to wear and he thought she always looked great in them.

Ann picked out the outfit she wanted to wear for the day and with Chance's help she was soon ready for the day.

Chance called room service for their breakfast. He ordered a couple of eggs, over medium, ham, hash browns, and wheat toast. Ann said she wanted oatmeal, bacon, fruit, and decaf coffee. Chance had forgotten to order decaf coffee for himself, so he told room service to please bring a large pot of decaf coffee.

Ann was busy still trying to fix her hair the way she wanted it to look.

Chance knew no woman was ever satisfied with the way her hair looked, even if she had just come from the beauty parlor. There had to be someplace on her head a lock of hair wasn't going to be doing what they wanted it to.

Ann was no different. She kept working on combing the right side of her hair and finally said to Chance, "OK, hand me my hair spray and I'll see if I can hold these hairs in place."

Chance dutifully handed Ann her hair spray.

Ann took the hair spray and squirted some of the spray onto the offending lock of hair and sure enough it finally laid down the way she wanted it to.

Next, Ann asked Chance to give her the bottle of her White Diamond perfume, and she carefully sprayed on just the right amount.

Then he was ready to take Ann out of bed and get her into the wheelchair so she could have her breakfast; about that time the doorbell rang and their breakfast was at the door. That was good because they were certainly ready for breakfast.

After breakfast they spent time talking about their wedding day and how they went back to Ann's house after the ceremony and their mothers had a wedding cake and ice cream waiting for them. To this day they were still surprised their mothers had got together to do that for them, since neither set of parents were happy about them getting married at sixteen.

One thing their parents knew was when Chance and Ann decided to do something, they were going to do it, and they had decided they couldn't wait any longer to get married and they planned to do it even if they had to run away.

Knowing that, both sets of parents reluctantly agreed to let them get married. Their parents would rather have them married and be living near them, than not knowing even where they were.

Their parents loved them that much and wanted to give them every chance of making it. They wanted to keep them living near them so they could still look after them if they needed a little bit of help.

Their parents also realized both Ann and Chance were more mature than their age would indicate. Both of them had jobs and Chance had been working since he was twelve. He started out by shining shoes on the street and then in a barber shop and later got a job working in a supermarket.

Ann worked as a sales clerk in a dress shop and had also worked at taking care of an elderly lady until she died.

Both Ann and Chance were tall and looked and acted much older than their age.

Because they had their breakfast so late they didn't bother to have lunch.

About one thirty their doorbell rang again and when Chance opened the door he found his old friend and their best man, Don Smith, waiting there.

Chance was really happy to see Don because it had been so many years since they had last seen each other, but he was sorry to see his old friend walking with a cane and was having a hard time walking with it.

It seemed Don had been injured at work and hadn't worked for several years. Ann and Chance hadn't known anything about his accident.

Don was pleased to see Ann and gave her a big, but cautious hug. Chance had always known Don thought a lot of Ann. When they got married, Don had told Chance if he didn't take good care of Ann and treat her right he would kick his rear end.

They spent the next three hours talking.

Chance and Ann told Don about all the different places they had lived and all the traveling around the world they had done.

Don told them about his two marriages, about how his first marriage ended in divorce and his second wife had died five years ago.

He had a daughter with his first wife and after they were divorced his daughter wouldn't have anything to do with him until after his first wife died two years ago.

After her mother died, his daughter called him and he flew to California to see her and she was really happy to see him. Now they kept in touch with each other, and Don was really happy about that. His second wife brought two sons with her to their marriage.

His youngest stepson still lived with him and was trying to help look after Don.

Don had been working and living in the Kansas City area since he got out of high school and had continued to work as a butcher in a grocery store—the same work he had done while he was in high school.

Chance thought Don's life had been so much different from his and Ann's.

Chance felt sorry about the way life had worked out for Don as compared to how their life had been. Don's life sounded pretty sad and lonely to Chance.

Then to be injured at work and not be able to do a lot of things, and now Don's health was failing, with heart problem and a diabetic to boot. Chance thought life hadn't been very good for his old friend.

About four thirty their doorbell rang again and this time it was their son Chase and his wife, Marie.

Don had known Chase since the day he was born but hadn't seen him for years. Chase remembered him or at least remembered about him.

They spent a few minutes talking together with Chase telling Don about their trout fishing resort.

Don stayed for a few more minutes and then said he needed to go home before it got much later.

Chase told Don he wished he could meet their son Curt, who should be arriving in a few minutes.

Don told him, "No, my youngest son is expecting me home for dinner."

Chance said, "Don, I'm sorry you can't stay to be with us for our anniversary dinner, but we understand if your son is expecting you, you have to go. Ann and I are really happy you came to see us on our fiftieth wedding anniversary and that you were with us when we got married all those years ago. Thank you, my friend, and please try to stay well."

Before Don left, Chance and Don hugged each other. Chance had a feeling he would never see Don again.

After Don left, their son Shane and his wife, Jan, arrived and a few minutes later. Jan's three kids, Jake, Jerry, and Joanna, arrived. Soon the last of their out-of-town guests made it up to their hotel suite: Chase and Marie's son, Curt, and their best friends, Doc and Susan Schmidt.

They all took a few minutes to visit before they left to go to their rooms to get dressed for dinner wanting to give Chance and Ann enough time to get ready.

Kathy Jones, who lived in Overland Park, Kansas, told them she would be at the hotel about six forty-five.

Kathy was the widow of Chance's old boss and good friend, Karl Jones, and was also Shane's godmother, so she was a very important part of their family, as was Doc and Susan Schmidt, their best friends.

Chance had bought Ann's white pantsuit to wear for their fiftieth wedding anniversary dinner, the same outfit she wore for their anniversary pictures.

He was sorry it didn't fit as well as Ann would have liked it to, but she had lost a lot of weight due to her illness. Chance thought that was certainly not an easy way to lose weight, by getting as sick as Ann was.

He brought the ruby-and-diamond necklace he gave her for their anniversary to wear for their dinner, the same one she wore for their anniversary pictures.

After Chance got Ann dressed, she redid her makeup and recombed her hair as Chance was changing clothes and put on the suit he brought to wear for their dinner.

Ann had finished doing her makeup by the time Chance was dressed.

They were ready to go to the restaurant about forty-five minutes before it was time to leave for their dinner reservation.

Ann and Chance spent the time talking about Don. They both felt he had certainly had a hard time in his life and how lucky they were to have made it together for fifty years.

When it was time to go to the restaurant, Chance opened the door and backed Ann's wheelchair out of their room as Ann held the door open so it didn't close and hit her.

By the time they got to the restaurant, the restaurant staff had everything set up and ready for them. Soon, all of their family and friends arrived at the restaurant for their anniversary dinner.

The dinner was excellent, but it was really hard to have much of a conversation with all the noise from the other diners in the restaurant.

Several pictures were taken by different family members, but when Chance and Ann got the opportunity to see them, none of them came out very well.

They received cards from all of their family and friends wishing them a happy anniversary, which they appreciated very much.

Their son Chase had contacted several important people to get them to offer their congratulations to Chance and Ann on their fiftieth wedding anniversary.

Chase presented the responses to his request to them at the dinner.

They had received best wishes for their fiftieth anniversary from Jimmy and Rosalyn Carter, Bill and Hillary Clinton, Gerald and Betty Ford, Bob and Elizabeth Dole, and from Arkansas' senator, Blanche L. Lincoln and her husband, Steve.

Both Chance and Ann were pleased to get cards and letters from these famous people and appreciated Chase doing that for them.

They didn't have champagne to toast the occasion. Because of Ann's medications, she couldn't have any alcoholic beverages. Except for the symbolic concept of a celebration of a great achievement, such as being married fifty years, Chance would rather have a Coke anyway.

The party ended early since Ann was getting tired and needed to go back to her room to take her nighttime meds and go to bed. Even though the dinner party was over, it took another thirty or forty minutes to say goodnight to everyone.

Chance thought traveling this far away from home was really too much for Ann; although she would never admit it, he could tell she was in a lot of pain and was just plain worn out.

After taking care of the routine tasks required to get Ann ready for bed, Chance had a chance to think back five years and found it hard to believe how much Ann's health and condition had changed since then.

He was so thankful that he still had Ann with him, whatever condition she was in, and thankful she had made it to their anniversary. He thought it was a real milestone for them. Chance had been so afraid over these past two years that Ann wasn't going to live to see it.

He had always thought since they got married at sixteen, they had a real chance of making it to their seventy-fifth anniversary.

Sometimes life didn't work out like one thought it should. Now he was thrilled and grateful they made it for fifty years.

He knew Ann didn't think she was going to make it to their fiftieth anniversary because when she in St. John's Hospital in January and was so bad, she told him she didn't want to be buried in the ground and asked him to buy her a mausoleum.

So he bought them a two-crypt mausoleum, along with enough space in the Big Springs local cemetery for the mausoleum to sit on.

He never realized how much of a construction job it was to install a mausoleum. After it was installed, there was a picture of it in the local newspaper since none of the cemeteries in their small town had ever had a mausoleum before.

Chance thanked God every night and several times during the day Ann was still with him and kept asking God to let her stay with him for a long time.

10

BLIZZARD ON THE WAY HOME

The next morning Chance and Ann had breakfast with Doc and Susan Schmidt before beginning their journey home.

Ann always felt better whenever she was with them. The four of them had a lot of talking to do to catch up with all the things going on with their mutual friends and family.

Ann had to know how Susan's four girls and their families were doing. While Ann and Susan were having their conversation, Doc and Chance were engaged in their own conversation about the people they knew and worked with. Doc and Chance had worked together for several years and knew many of the same people.

When the four of them were together, time always had a way of getting away much too quick.

After several hours Doc said, "We've got to check out of our room before we have to pay for another day. I don't like the latest weather forecast either because they're predicating heavy snow in some areas of Kansas and Missouri."

Chance asked, "Doc, how much snow are they forecasting for Missouri?"

"I don't think they know and they don't know exactly the path the storm is taking, but I'd like to get back to Wichita before it gets too bad."

Ann asked, "Doc, what did they say about southern Missouri and northern Arkansas?"

"I don't think they knew where the storm was tracking the last time I saw it on TV. They only thing they knew then was it was coming out of the Texas panhandle and Oklahoma headed north and east."

Ann sighed and said, "Chance, we better get started home. I don't want to be stuck in a snow drift somewhere on the side of the road."

Susan piped in, "Ann, you sure don't want to take any chances on that."

Chance agreed and said, "We better get packed up and get going while we can."

Doc and Susan gave them hugs and kissed them both goodbye and left to check out of the hotel.

Chance began gathering up all their things and packing suitcases so they could get on the road.

After that was done, Chance called to have a bellman with a cart come up to their suite to take all their things to the van. Next, he called to have their van brought to the front of the hotel.

As soon as the bellman left with their things, Chance and Ann went down to the lobby to check out of the hotel.

Chance took Ann's wheelchair as close to the front door that he could but kept her far enough back away from the doors so she didn't get cold air blowing on her.

He had her scarf, coat, and gloves on her and he had a car blanket to wrap around her when he was ready to load her into the van.

After the valet delivered the van, Chance and the bellman loaded all their things in the van.

Chance left the van's motor running and put the lift down so all he had to do was to get Ann's wheelchair onto the lift and raise the lift up, keeping her out of the cold as much as possible.

It worked very well except it took him more time than normal to climb up into the van, get in the back of the van to pull Ann's wheelchair in, lock it into place in the van, and put on her seat belt. He was too cold and he was trying to hurry too much, which made him fumble more locking the wheelchair in place and putting on her seat belt. His fingers were so cold they didn't want to work. Finally, he got everything put into place, the way it had to be to safely lock the wheelchair and Ann in the van. Then he quickly got out of the van and closed the lift doors.

Chance went around to the driver's side of the van and got into his seat. He had the two heaters working as high and fast as they would operate so it would soon warm up enough for them to leave. It took only a few minutes before the van was at a comfortable temperature. He asked Ann if she was warm enough and ready to start home. She had just thrown off her blanket because she was getting too hot and said, "Let's go home, honey." "You got a deal, love, here we go."

Chance pulled out from under the canopy of the hotel and they immediately had light snow hitting their windshield.

Traffic was fairly light on their way driving south out of Kansas City and the snow had stayed about the same as it was when they left the hotel, just light snow.

Chance thought if this was all it was going to be, it shouldn't be any problem getting home.

After they had been traveling for about an hour, Chance's cell phone rang. It was their son Chase who had left earlier; he told his dad that when they got to Springfield they had encountered heavy snow and Highway 65 south into Arkansas was closed.

He told his dad, "You better find somewhere to stop and spend the night because we had been told to take another highway south to get home to the resort, and even with our four-wheel drive we are having a really rough time even staying on the road."

Chance told Chase as soon as they got to Springfield he would find someplace they could stay the night and see how the weather was the next day before trying to go on home.

From then on, every few miles they traveled south the snow got heavier and the road was harder to stay on. When they were about seven miles north of Springfield the traffic was suddenly stopped and it took them almost an hour to go the next six miles.

Traffic on Missouri Highway 13 which crossed over I-44 was almost completely stopped. It moved inch by inch and Chance swore it had taken them fifteen minutes to move forward only five or six car lengths. The big semitrucks were having a hard time moving on the snow after they stopped, causing the traffic tie-up.

Finally, Chance saw an opportunity to turn onto the westbound ramp onto I-44 and he took it.

He remembered a Marriott Courtyard Hotel near the airport off the next exit west on I-44. When he got to the next exit he turned off and headed directly to the hotel.

Arriving at the hotel he went inside to see if they had a room left because it looked like they had an awful lot of cars there already. When Chance got to the desk, the desk clerk said they didn't have any rooms left but one of the other clerks said, "Well, we do have a handicap room left that they're doing some work on if you could use it."

Chance said, "That's perfect. My wife is in a wheelchair."

Before Chance filled out the registration form, three more people came in wanting rooms for the night and were told they didn't have any rooms available.

They also told the folks they didn't know of any hotels in Springfield that had a vacancy tonight. Chance knew God was looking out for them.

Chance went out to the van and put Ann's blanket on her to try to keep her as warm as possible while getting her from the van into the hotel lobby, because not only was it cold and snowing like mad, but the wind was blowing twenty or thirty miles an hour straight out of the west.

Chance got back out of the van and opened both of the ramp's doors and put the ramp down so he could push Ann's wheelchair onto the ramp.

As soon as the ramp was down in place, he got back in the van and moved Ann's wheelchair onto it. Next he got back out of the van and lowered the ramp down.

As soon as the ramp was on the ground, he unlocked the wheels of the wheelchair and began pushing Ann's wheelchair into the hotel lobby. It was a tough job pushing the wheelchair because of the amount of snow that had fallen and hadn't been cleaned off yet.

As soon as they made it into the lobby, Chance asked the desk clerk where their room was located and was told it was down the hall to the left and it would be the first room on the right past the swimming pool.

Chance got Ann into their room and got her blanket off and then discovered that the room was ice-cold, so he put her blanket back on, found the thermostat, and turned on the heat to the highest temperature he could.

He asked Ann if she would be all right while he went back out to the van and got the things they would need for the night. She said she would be, as long as she had her blanket on.

Chance hurried back to the van, since he had left the wheelchair ramp down on the ground and both of the ramp doors standing wide open and the van's motor running. No one had bothered the van, but Chance didn't really think they would; no decent thief would be working tonight in this kind of weather in Springfield.

He thought to himself that anybody out stealing something tonight would be worse off than if they were working a real job.

Chance tried to think what all he could leave in the van that they wouldn't need tonight and was sorry to realize that he needed almost everything they had in the van to take care of Ann.

Well, he couldn't use a cart in this snow, so he began by carrying in their suitcases and managed to get all of them in his first trip.

Chance was happy the room was on the first floor and he could get back to the van quickly and bring in more of the things they would need for the night, including their travel refrigerator with Ann's applesauce.

He went back the third time to put the van in a parking space and was pleased to find a handicapped parking space where he could still see a sign visible over the snow drifts.

Chance pulled the van into the parking space close to the front door of the hotel which offered some protection for the van from the snow. He shut down the engine and locked up the van and then battled the wind to get his door open so he could get out of the van.

He wasn't too sure who was going to win the battle of the door, him or the wind, but finally he got the door opened enough for him to get out. He didn't have to worry about closing the door because the wind blew the door out of his hand and slammed the door hard against the door frame.

Now, he was battling the wind just to walk back to the door of the hotel. He finally realized how cold it was and how he hadn't paid much attention to how cold he was when he was unloading the van. He was shaking by the time he got into the hotel lobby.

He was still shaking when he got into their room. It took him a few minutes to take off his coat and to begin to feel some of the heat blowing from the furnace.

Ann still had on her coat and gloves and said, "Chance, I am finally getting warm, so whenever you can, could you take my coat and gloves off?"

"It will take me a few minutes to warm up after being outside with that wind blowing on me, but as soon as I do, I'll get your coat off."

"I know, honey. I'm so sorry you have to do everything for me." "You know it's all right. I love being able to take care of you."

A few minutes later, Chance got Ann ready for bed and soon had her safely in bed for the night.

He had just gotten Ann into bed when his cell phone rang. Chance and Ann said at the same time, "I know who that is, it's Chase."

Chance answered the phone and said, "Hello, Chase." Chase replied, "Dad, are you and Mom OK?"

"We're fine. We got a room at the Courtyard Hotel, out by the Springfield Airport, in fact, we got the last room they had.

"How about you and Marie, did you guys get home all right?" "We're fine and finally home after eight hours from the time we left Kansas City. The last hundred miles was awful. I don't know how many times we almost went off the road because of other cars and trucks sliding at us. It was a horrible trip."

"It sounds like it. Was everything at the resort OK?"

"Yeah, we didn't have anything frozen up. I'm glad to say we had drained the water from most of the cabins except the ones we are having guests in right after Christmas."

"Chase, we're not going to try to go home tomorrow until we know the roads have been cleared off."

"Dad, I don't think it will take them too long to clear the snow off the main roads. We don't have all the snow here that they got in Springfield."

"That's good. I'll call you tomorrow after we get home, but I'm sure we won't leave here until sometime around noon."

"OK, I'll talk to you tomorrow."

Chance knew Chase would call tomorrow because he called them every day and sometimes more than one time. They really appreciated him calling every day to check on them.

Their son Shane called maybe once a week, but then he stayed on the phone and talked to them for a long time.

Chance asked Ann if she was getting hungry. She was.

Chance didn't know where they could get anything to eat around here but they certainly couldn't go back out in that storm to find something.

Chance looked through a drawer on the bedside table and found a menu for some small restaurant next door to their hotel.

He had Ann look over the menu to pick out something she thought she could eat. She picked out a corn beef sandwich and some fries. Chance decided to have the same thing along with a couple of diet Cokes.

He called the restaurant and placed their order and the man who answered the phone at the restaurant said that he would bring them their order on his way home.

He told Chance he was closing so he could try to get home before the roads got any worse but he would bring them their order. About forty-five minutes later they heard a knock on their door and there were their sandwiches, fries, and Cokes. Chance paid him and gave him a ten-dollar tip. They really appreciated him bringing their dinner in this snowstorm.

The next morning the sun was shining and the snow had stopped, thank goodness.

After all the things required to take care of Ann were done and Chance was dressed and ready for the day, they got to the breakfast room before the time it closed.

After having a nice breakfast and a few extra cups of decaf coffee, they returned to their room and Chance started packing up their things.

After everything was loaded in the van, Chance backed the van out of its snowy parking space and moved it to the front doors of the hotel. He left the motor running and put down the ramp so he could load Ann into the van as quickly as possible.

The sun was shining brightly to make you think it was much warmer than yesterday, but the truth was it was much colder this morning than when they arrived at the hotel the night before.

Ann was soon loaded in the van and they were on their way home by a few minutes before noon.

The roads were clear as soon as they were out of the hotel parking lot. Getting onto I-44 was no problem today; the interstate was as clear as it could be. The highway department had done a great job overnight clearing the roads.

Turning off I-44 onto US 65 was no problem either and the traffic on it was light.

In fact, the whole trip home the highway and road were all clear and they had very little traffic.

Turning into their subdivision was a lot different. Although Big Springs hadn't gotten nearly the amount of snow as Springfield, their streets and their hills were much harder to drive on.

Turning into their driveway proved even more difficult since their driveway was uphill from the street and the snow had drifted three or four feet deep on it. The van couldn't make it up the drive.

Ann asked, "What are we going to do? We have to get into the garage so I can get out of the van."

"Don't worry, honey, we'll make it somehow."

Chance was able to back the van back out of the driveway and completely back across their street. He pushed the button to open the garage door and it went up without any problem.

After the door was all the way up Chance pushed the gas pedal down and picked up speed as they crossed the street into the driveway and begin climbing the hill but halfway up, the van lost traction and began sliding back down.

Chance took his foot off the gas pedal and applied the brake but the van kept sliding down the drive out into the street and continued sliding across the street until it hit the curb on the other side of the street before he could get the van stopped.

"Chance, do you think you are going to be able to get up the drive and into the garage?"

"I think we can do it. We may have to make a few more runs at it."

"OK."

Chance started the van moving slowly forward and then he pushed the gas pedal down hard but not hard enough to make the wheels spin. The van continued to climb up the drive and made it past where they were on the last try, but again the van lost traction and began sliding back down the drive.

They ended back up against the curb on the other side of the street again.

Chance said, "Ann, this next time we'll make it all the way into the garage."

"Oh, I hope so."

Again, Chance started up the driveway and when the wheels began to spin. Chance pushed the gas pedal down to the floor. This time the tires grabbed on the concrete drive and the van shot forward into the garage. Chance had to hit the brakes hard to keep the van from hitting the garage wall.

Chance yelled, "Wow, that's some way to end our trip!"

Ann was happy to have made it home and into her garage; she didn't care how she got there. Now, she didn't have to worry about getting into her own home.

11

CHRISTMAS 2002

Chance was up early Christmas morning to put the turkey in the oven to give it enough time to cook before the family arrived in the afternoon.

Christmas was a very important day for the Clark family. It was Chance's favorite time of the year and Chance loved buying Christmas presents for everyone. He knew most men didn't like to shop but Chance liked going shopping to search for special presents for each member of the family.

Buying special presents for Ann had always been a particular pleasure for Chance, but now she couldn't really enjoy much of anything that he might give her, which made Chance feel sad, very sad indeed.

However, over these past two years it had to be a lot different. He really couldn't get away from home very long to do much shopping since taking care of Ann was a full-time job. So he made do by ordering most of their presents online or through their J.C. Penney's catalog. He was trying his best to find some things for each member of the family that they might enjoy.

Chance planned to get each member of the family at least three presents and not to spend more than five hundred dollars on each family member.

It wasn't easy to spend that much money with the cost of Ann's meds and the other health-care items not covered by insurance or Medicare. Chance thought to himself this would probably be the last year they could afford to spend that much on Christmas presents for each member of the family.

After putting the turkey in the oven, he went back to the bedroom to see if Ann was awake; if she was he would get her ready for the day.

As soon as he stepped into the bedroom Ann said, "I'm awake.

You woke me up rattling pots and pans in the kitchen." "Merry Christmas to you, too!"

"That's what I thought I was saying, Merry Christmas, Chance!"

"Love, are you ready to get out of bed?"

"I would love to. Wouldn't it be a wonderful Christmas present if I could just get out of this bed all by myself. Wouldn't that be wonderful?"

"Sorry, love, that's one present I can't deliver, so I guess you'll just have to let me help you a little bit. Maybe you can talk to Santa and get that present next year."

"Chance, you don't have to help me a little bit. You have to do everything for me."

"OK, if that's the way you want it, I'll just do everything."

"No, it's not how I want it. I guess God wants it that way, because I sure don't."

Without anything else being said, Chance began doing all the things he normally had to do each morning to get Ann ready for the day. When all of these things were completed it was time to decide what Ann should wear for the day.

To make this decision, he began by asking Ann what she would like to wear on Christmas Day.

She told him she wanted to wear her red pantsuit.

He took it out of Ann's closet and laid it on his bed next to her hospital bed.

Before putting her pants on he put on her knee-high nylon socks. After he had her bra and pantsuit on, he lowered her bed and raised up the head of her bed, moved the hospital bedside table out of the way, placed her wheelchair next to the bed, and then picked her up and placed her in her wheelchair.

Ann said, "I want to wear my silver shoes today, you know, the flat ones."

No, Chance didn't know, but he began looking for her silver flat shoes on the floor of her closet; they were not there. Next, he checked out her closet shoe racks, still no silver shoes.

Ann said, "Look in the guest room closet. Maybe they're in a shoe box up on the closet shelf."

Chance went into the guest bedroom and began taking down boxes of shoes from the closet shelves.

Ann had boxes of her shoes on the closet shelf, six rows wide, and each row stacked four boxes high.

No luck, no silver shoes in those twenty-four boxes.

Chance said, "They're not in any of these boxes. Do you have any more ideas of where they might be?"

"Did you look on the floor in the guest closet? I have a bunch of shoes stacked there, too."

"No, I'll check that out."

Chance moved some long dresses over on the clothes rack and saw more boxes of shoes on the closet floor.

He picked up six boxes of shoes from the floor and began opening the boxes and found the sliver shoes Ann wanted to wear in the third box he opened.

He put all the boxes back in the closet except the one with the silver shoes which he brought back to their bedroom and put in Ann's closet.

He put the silver shoes on Ann's feet and said, "Look, they fit just like the glass slipper fit Cinderella."

Ann just laughed and said nothing.

Chance was in a very happy mood; it was Christmas and Ann had lived to make it to their fiftieth wedding anniversary earlier this month.

He had lots to be thankful for and lots of work left to do to before having dinner ready for the family by five o'clock.

Chance pushed Ann's wheelchair into the family room and asked if she was hungry; she was. So he made her an omelet, with two eggs, pieces of ham, onion, tomatoes, and green pepper and topped it off with a slice of cheese.

He put a couple of slices of bread in the toaster while the omelet was cooking and started the Bunn coffee maker. Everything was ready at about the same time. He took the skillet off the burner, buttered the toast, and got a plate for Ann's omelet and toast.

He poured a cup of decaf coffee and then placed her plate and the cup of coffee on a silver serving tray. He also put silverware, napkin, salt and pepper, and strawberry jam on her tray.

He took the tray into the family room and set it on another hospital bedside table like the one they had in the bedroom.

It made it much easier for Ann to eat without taking her out of the wheelchair and trying to find some way of having her sit up at the kitchen table.

Ann asked him to turn on the TV so she could see what was going on this Christmas Day.

He got the TV controller and turned on the TV for her and put the controller on the hospital bedside table. Then he moved the table over in front of Ann's wheelchair so she could eat her breakfast.

After he had Ann settled with her breakfast and her TV controller, he went back into the kitchen and started peeling potatoes. It took him a while to get enough potatoes peeled for all of the family. He counted ten fairly large peeled potatoes and thought that should be enough for the nine of them.

Chance reviewed the menu in his head that he had planned with Ann's help: turkey, dressing, ham, green beans, corn, mashed potatoes, and sweet potatoes.

Chase and Marie were bringing homemade candy and pies.

Chase made wonderful candy and Marie was making three different kinds of pies.

Shane and Jan were bringing a very large relish tray, salads, and a couple of cakes.

Marie's pies were famous in the family, as were Jan's cakes. Chance thought they should have plenty of food for Christmas with all of this.

Before Ann finished her breakfast, Chance had everything on the stove. The only things left to cook were the ham and sweet potatoes after the turkey was fully cooked.

He would put the dressing into bake at the same time he cooked the ham so he thought he had everything pretty well under control for their Christmas dinner.

He went into the family room to check on how Ann was doing with her breakfast and found she had finished her breakfast and was watching *Christmas Story* on TV.

He asked Ann if she would like to have some more coffee, and she said no, she didn't want anymore.

Chance said, "It's late and you haven't had your morning pills yet."

"No, not yet, I'm waiting for my nurse to bring them to me.

You know he's always pushing pills at me."

"Yeah, I know he is. He must do it because the doctors insist that he give them to you, and I think he loves you."

"You think so?"

Oh, I know he does!

"All right, get me the damn pills."

"Yes, ma'am, the damn pills are coming!"

Chance went back into the kitchen and brought back a glass of water, a spoon, applesauce, and a handful of pills.

He opened the small container of applesauce and took a pill from the stack of pills he had placed on the bedside table and dropped it into the applesauce, took the spoon and dipped it into the applesauce picking up the pill with the spoonful of applesauce, and gave Ann the first of her morning pills.

He repeated the same steps each time until all the pills had been taken by Ann.

After Ann finished taking her pills she said, "Chance, can you bring me my makeup, comb, lipstick, and my perfume?"

"Who did you think was your slave last year?" "You, darling!"

"OK, I'm on my way to get all your things for you and I bet you want your makeup mirror too."

"Right, I do."

Chance went back to their bedroom and gathered up all the items Ann needed to get herself ready for the day and brought them back to Ann.

Ann said, "Thank you, love." "You are very welcome.

Ann went to work getting her makeup on and combing her hair as Chance went back into the kitchen to check on his cooking.

Chase, Marie, and Curt arrived at the house about 2:00 p.m. and came in the house carrying boxes of presents. They began taking them out of the boxes and placing them around the Christmas tree in the front room. After Chase and Curt finished emptying those boxes of presents they went back out to the car to bring additional boxes of presents.

Marie took the box she was carrying into the kitchen and took out three pies and put them on the kitchen table along with two pans of rolls she had baked this morning.

Then she went into the family room and wished Ann "Merry Christmas." She was soon followed by Chase and Chris wishing Ann "Merry Christmas."

Chance had been in the bathroom when they came into the house and was surprised to find Chase, Marie, and Curt talking to Ann when he came back into the family room.

They all wished each other "Merry Christmas" and then began talking about some of their past Christmases, each telling about something special they got one Christmas.

After all of them had told about some special present they received one year for Christmas, they asked Chance what was the most special present he ever got.

Chance said, without any hesitation, "The greatest Christmas present I ever got was given to me a few days before Christmas. I got it on December 22, 1952, and her name was Ann Harris."

After saying that, he had tears in his eyes and got up and went into the kitchen to do something; he didn't want the family to see him crying.

Marie followed him into the kitchen and asked, "Dad, is there something I could do to help with dinner?"

Chance replied, "We do need to set the dining room table. We will have to put the three leaves in the table. Maybe you can get Chase or Curt to help you."

Marie got her son Curt to help her put the leaves in the table and then asked, "Dad, what dishes do you want to use for dinner?

"The ones I brought back from England, there in the hutch next to the table. We need to be sure we put the pads down on the table to protect it from scratches or hot plates. They're in the same place where the leaves were stored."

"Yes, I saw them. Curt will help me get them on the table, won't you, son?"

Chance said, "I'll get a tablecloth and napkins for the table while you are getting the pads."

By the time Chance returned from getting the tablecloth and napkins, Marie and Curt had finished putting the pads on the table. He handed them to Marie and she and Curt began unfolding the bright red tablecloth and putting it on the table as Chance went back into the kitchen to check on the turkey.

He found the turkey was ready to come out of the oven so he took it out to cool and placed the ham and dressing in the oven to cook.

Chance heard the doorbell ring then heard Shane open the front door and yell "Merry Christmas, everybody."

Chase met his brother in the hallway and gave him a hug and wished him "Merry Christmas."

Soon Jan, Jake, Jerry, and Joanna arrived at the door carrying boxes of presents and began putting them under the tree.

By the time Shane and family unloaded their car there wasn't any room left on the floor for even one more present. The presents were now stacked up to the windowsills and spilling over into the dining room.

Jan and Shane carried in three different salads, more rolls, three cakes, and a vegetable tray; now the kitchen table was completely filled.

Chance took one look and said, "Well, I think we will have enough to eat for one meal anyway."

Before they began opening presents, Chase was looking over the mountain of presents they would soon be opening and said, "Wretched excess!"

Ann asked, "What did you say, Chase?

"Mom, I said these presents are simply wretched excess!"

Ann replied, "You're right. There are far too many presents for this family. We need to stop buying so many Christmas presents.

The consensus of the family was this would be the last year of buying so many presents.

Chance wasn't too happy with this idea, because he loved buying presents for everyone. He understood the decision because if there was something any one of the family wanted, they went out and bought it.

It was the Clarks' tradition to open presents one at a time, beginning with the youngest person working the way up to the oldest person, which meant Chance was the last one to get to open his presents. Both Chase and Shane liked this idea because both of their wives were older than they were and sometimes they didn't open their present too quickly, so their wives would have to wait. This wasn't a popular idea with the girls.

The family also had a competition to see who had the most presents to open each year to see who got to open the last present. One by one, each member of the family would be forced to say, "I'm out!" indicating they had no more presents to open.

The competition this year was now down to Chase and Shane, but at the end of the contest, this year's winner was Chase; he had one more present to open than Shane. Shane had won the competition last year.

Finally, the presents were all opened, the gift-wrapping paper picked up and placed into nine thirty-three gallon plastic bags, which Chase would take home to place in the large trash container they used for the resort.

It took more than three-and-a-half hours to open the presents this year, a new record, and Chance was sure it would never be broken with the new Christmas present policy set today.

Dinner was served and when everyone was filled with enough turkey, ham, and all the other fixings that went with such a meal, they all had desserts, some having more than one. The fact was everybody had at least two.

By the time everyone finished their Christmas dinner, the weather was beginning to turn bad and Shane and his family quickly loaded up their things and started home to Fayetteville.

Curt soon left to go home to Fayetteville, too, as the weather continued to deteriorate and since the storm was moving in from the west of Big Springs it made the roads worse between Big Springs and Fayetteville.

Chase and Marie also hit the road because they didn't want to be stuck in Big Springs over the next two or three days. They knew if the snow got much worse they might not be able to go home and their dog was home by herself.

As soon as all of the family left, Chance asked Ann if she was ready to go to bed; she said she certainly was, as soon as Chance could get her meds and get her ready for bed.

It had been a long day with lots of noise and activity going on around her, which was good for Ann, but she got tried very easily and needed her peaceful time.

Chance did all the things necessary to get Ann ready for bed and turned her TV on in the bedroom so she could watch an old Christmas movie on TCM. She didn't see much of the movie because it didn't take long before Ann was fast asleep.

As Chance watched Ann sleeping in her hospital bed, he wondered if Ann would be with him next Christmas and if she was, how many more would she see?

He put the head of her bed down, kissed on her cheek, turned off the TV, got in his bed, said his prayers, and tried to go to sleep, all the time thinking about what a different life they lived now.

12

WASHINGTON UNIVERSITY DOCTORS

*J*anuary 10, 2003, Chance and Ann arrived at Barnes Jewish Hospital in St. Louis to meet Ann's new Washington University doctor who would now become her main contact at Barnes.

Ann's new doctor, Dr. Park, was now Ann's primary physician at Barnes and was taking her case over from Dr. Glenn.

Dr. Park was with Washington University Neuroscience Center, Department of Neurology.

Chance and Ann liked him as soon as they had talked with him for only a few minutes. He had all the details about Ann's condition and her treatment; in fact, he was one of the doctors who designed the treatment she was getting in Big Springs.

Dr. Park made several changes in her meds to help reduce her pain; he increased her Neurontin from 400 mg to 600 mg, four times a day, and prescribed Nortriptyline, beginning with one pill a day and increasing the dosage by one pill per day until she was taking seven pills a day.

Dr. Park told them the pain she continued to have in her neck, shoulders, and under her left breast was all caused by her

Central Nervous System Vasculitis.

Dr. Park also said, "I think Ann has a chance of regaining some of her abilities in the near future.

"However, the longer she's unable to stand or walk, the less likely it will be that she will be able to. She will never be able to walk without a walker or some other type of aid, but maybe if she came to the St. Louis Rehabilitation Institute for a ten-day evaluation, they could decide if she had any chance of walking again.

Dr. Park wanted her to continue on the treatment plan they had designed for her until she completed two years of the treatments.

A week later Chance telephoned Dr. Park who told Chance, Ann's latest blood test looked much better. He felt Ann's treatment for CNS Vasculitis was working and her tests indicated she was improving. The Vasculitis was no longer progressing and her condition was stable.

In February, Ann had a bout of bacteria in her blood and was in Big Springs Hospital for several days before they were able to find the cause.

It turned out to be an infection in her Hickman port. They began treating the bacteria by putting the antibiotics into alternating port openings. The problem cleared up and the Hickman port didn't have to be removed and replaced. That made Ann very happy because she didn't want to go through that again.

Ann was in the hospital for fifteen days with the bacteria in her blood and wasn't able to come home until February 15.

Ann was due for her next monthly treatment at the hospital on February 24, and for the first time after one of her treatments, she couldn't produce any urine which they had to have before she would be able to go home.

Her doctor gave her Lasix through her port but she still couldn't produce enough urine for her test and had to remain in the hospital. She was given more Lasix and after the second dosage, she was able to produce urine. However, they kept her in the hospital for two more days to be sure she didn't have any more problems.

On March 19, Chance took Ann back to St. Louis to see Dr. Park since he was concerned about her problems with her last treatment for her CNS Vasculitis. After he ran several tests, he decided she was doing OK.

Now, he wanted her to do the ten-day evaluation at the St. Louis Rehabilitation Institute, which she agreed to do. On March 21, Ann entered the St. Louis Rehabilitation Institute for her ten- day evaluation.

Ann stayed at the institute until April 5 and returned home to Big Springs the next day after staying the night at the Holiday Inn Express in Cuba, Missouri.

The only positive thing Chance thought was accomplished during Ann's stay at the institute was that she learned to operate an electric wheelchair and the doctor wrote her a prescription for one. Chance contacted the Hoveround Company in Florida, a manufacturer of power wheelchairs, to have someone come to see them about getting a power wheelchair for Ann.

It took about a week for a representative from Hoveround to come from Tulsa, Oklahoma, to see them.

The gentleman was well versed in the type of power wheelchair Ann should have with her condition. He designed the chair with the ability to raise her legs up and to recline the back. The cost of this special power wheelchair was $14,500.

Medicare would get some kind of a discount off the price and their insurance company would pay about another 20 percent of the additional cost, so their cost would be somewhere around $2,000.

Ann wasn't sure they should spend that much money on a wheelchair for her, but Chance thought it would give Ann some freedom to move around the house and it would let her get around outside in their yard. She did love her yard and to see her flowers.

Chance ordered the wheelchair and when it was delivered a couple of months later, even Ann was pleased to get it and was thrilled she could change her position and be able to lay the back of her chair down and raise her legs up all by herself.

She could get around everywhere she wanted to go in the house and the yard and didn't have to ask Chance or someone to take her.

Sometimes, she would even go shopping at Walmart with Chance. She wasn't like the shoppers who used the Walmart power carts because she knew how to drive her wheelchair and didn't run into or over people.

Chance was very happy with Ann's new wheelchair; it did a lot to help him because Ann could drive the chair and he didn't have to push the chair. It was a real help for him and his back.

Ann continued to see Dr. Caye on a regular basis and had to be referred to other doctors for various other problems. She had to keep doing her regular monthly treatments at the hospital until she went to see Dr. Park, and things changed.

On June 13, 2003, Ann and Chance had a long meeting with Dr. Park in St. Louis and he said. "Ann, you are looking better and acting better than I have ever seen you. You're speaking better and your thought process has improved a lot since I saw you earlier in the year. I believe that's because you have been able to reduce your pain medications.

"We feel you don't have to have any more of the monthly treatments with Cystoxic and Solu Medro unless your condition begins to deteriorate. If it does, you will have to restart the treatments.

"The doctors here at Washington University have concluded the reason you're not able to stand and walk is not a problem with your spinal cord. It's caused from small strokes on both sides of your brain and your brain can't fire the message to tell your legs to work anymore. We're sorry to say there is no hope of you ever recovering your ability to stand or walk. There just isn't any cure for your problem.

"I want to see you again in September and check how you're doing and then we can see if there is anything else we can do to help you."

Chance was beginning to have problems with his back due to the constant lifting of Ann in and out of bed. After spending time doing some research on the Internet, he found a system that looked like it could do the lifting for him and save his back.

Chance contacted the manufacturer in Canada to see if he could find a local dealer in Arkansas where he could buy the equipment. They had a dealer in Little Rock who could help him. After about a week, a sales rep came to see Chance and Chance purchased a system from them.

On August 28, the installers arrived to install their Trans Active Lift System in Chance and Ann's bedroom. This system was installed in the ceiling and operated by electric power with a battery backup in case there was a power failure.

The system used a track attached to the ceiling which could move the patient across the bedroom. It could even be designed to move people all around the house if you wanted it too.

In the Clarks' case, the track was just long enough to be able to pick Ann up from her bed and move her over to where her power wheelchair would be parked.

Chance had the track made long enough so they could move Ann as far as his bed was now, in case something happened to Ann's hospital bed.

When the installation of the system was completed, the installer instructed both Chance and Ann on how to operate the system.

The unit was very simple to operate. Chance had to place Ann onto a net type of harness which let her be picked up from the bed and then it was attached to an arm on the lifting device with straps on the harness. The harness was large enough that Ann's body and her head would be totally supported as she was lifted from the bed and over to her wheelchair.

Positioned over the wheelchair Chance just had to lower Ann on to the chair since she was now in a sitting position in the sling or harness. Once she was sitting on the wheelchair, all Chance had to do was to take the straps off the arm of the lift device and place them behind Ann.

When he wanted to put her back on the bed, all he had to do was lower the lift arm and attach the loop straps back on the arm, use the lift to pick her back up, move her back over to her bed, and lower her down on to the bed.

The system worked wonderfully and made Chance's life so much easier. It allowed him the ability to be able to take care of Ann for a much longer time than he might otherwise have been able to without the device. He was already having problems with his back, so the system was a wonderful investment, and he didn't have to worry about dropping Ann during one of her transfers.

Ann was also happier because she felt much more secure in her sling, being lifted in and out of bed, than with someone lifting her up under the arms.

On a meeting on September 19, 2003, Ann and Chance met with Dr. Park at Washington University. He told Ann they had come to the conclusion that she no longer needed to do her treatments of Cystoxic and Solu Medro because they considered she was stable and further treatments would not improve her condition. Dr. Park made arrangements to have the Hickman port removed from her chest. He also made some changes to her medications. Chance thought every time one doctor saw her he was going to change something or other with her meds.

Ann wasn't able to get her port removed by the folks at intervention radiology at Barnes Jewish Hospital until October 2.

Other than some routine doctor appointments to keep checking her general health and tweaking some of her medicines, Ann didn't have any more major health problems or hospital stays.

Christmas was a much happier occasion than it had been for the past few years with Ann's improved health.

She was still paralyzed but she felt much better now and Chance was certainly doing better because Ann was stable and he didn't have as much of a problem with his back after their new lift system had been installed.

13

WHEN ILLNESS COMES FRIENDS FADE

Ann was an avid bridge player so when Chance and Ann moved to Big Springs she joined the Newcomers Club to get acquainted with some other folks who had recently moved there.

She was hoping to have the opportunity to find some ladies who liked to play bridge. She was successful meeting several women who liked to play bridge and she joined several bridge groups. She found Big Springs was a hotbed for bridge players.

Ann became acquainted with a neighbor, Lynn Wilson, who had moved to Big Springs a few weeks after she did and they became good friends. Lynn had two passions in life, golf and bridge. Lynn could play golf in the morning and bridge after lunch. Lynn and Ann became members of several bridge groups together. Both Ann and Lynn were living in a rented house near each other when they first moved to Big Springs. Later, they bought homes in a golf community and their homes were next door to each other.

Neither Ann nor Chance played golf anymore, but they loved the area of their home.

Another woman she met at Newcomers Club was Susan O'Hara. Her husband, Jack, and Chance both worked at Superior Parking Meter Company.

Jack O'Hara had been transferred from Chicago to Big Springs only a few months before Chance rejoined Superior and came to Big Springs.

Chance hadn't known Jack O'Hara before coming to Big Springs; however, he had known Jack's wife, Susan O'Hara, for many years because she was the executive secretary for Ian Stark, who was then vice president of sales for Superior and later its president.

Chance and his old boss, Karl Jones, came to Chicago at least a couple of times a year to meet with Ian Stark when he was the vice president of sales while they were working on bids for parking meters for cities in their sales territories.

Each time Chance and Karl were in Chicago they saw and worked with Susan. She didn't always like it when they were in the office, because she was responsible for typing multiple copies of bids which were submitted to the cities.

This was a time before computers; she was working on an IBM typewriter, therefore, if any small change was made in the proposal, it meant retyping the whole page or several pages. So Chance and Karl were not always some of her favorite people.

Karl and Ian got into long, hard, and sometimes loud negotiations over the price they would be submitting for the parking meters to the cities.

Karl used to say that if they had a penny and a hatchet, depending on which side of the room the bigger piece of the chopped-up penny fell would determine which of them got the biggest piece.

Susan had worked for Ian before he came to Superior and he wanted her to come to work with him at Superior. Susan came to work for Ian at Superior in 1969, so Chance had known Susan several years before they both moved to Big Springs.

Susan retired from Superior just prior to Jack being transferred to Big Springs from Chicago. She knew her husband's health was not very good and she wanted to be available to be home with him if he needed her, so she retired from Superior.

Over time, Ann and Susan became very good friends. After Jack passed away and Chance was traveling internationally, Ann and Susan went to shows in Branson, movies, and lots of other places together. They became very close friends.

Susan was a true people person and she loved to send cards to her friends. She sent cards for everyone's birthday, their wedding anniversary, and every holiday, except Christmas.

Susan didn't send cards for Christmas because everyone else did. She thought the people who received Christmas cards would just look to see who sent the card and then throw it in with all the other Christmas cards they received and never really read them.

She didn't just send a card to people. It was a production; she had inserts of all kinds of things for the different holidays, along with various types of confetti representing each of the holidays and she placed them all into each card she sent.

Ann and Susan had very different personalities. Ann was normally very quiet, but friendly, when she was around a large group of people.

Susan was more outgoing, perhaps because of working for so many years with so many different types of people.

Susan was very smart and accomplished in so many different ways. She had skipped two grades in school graduating from high school at fifteen years old.

Susan thought she wasn't mature enough to go to college at fifteen and didn't start going to college until she was fifty years old, after her kids were grown and her husband died.

She graduated college summa cum laude with the second highest grade point and only a fraction of a point from having the highest one.

Susan was a hard worker and an outstanding executive secretary. She was organized and knew how to get things done in whatever office she worked in.

Ann was an accomplished homemaker and she loved her home; she was someone who would rather be at home than anywhere else in the world. Chance had taken Ann to a lot of places in the world, living in Australia and living a short time in Korea.

Ann had been to almost all the countries in Western Europe, plus traveling to South America and to a few countries in Asia. Ann enjoyed going to these various countries, but given her choice, she would have rather stayed at home in Big Springs, Arkansas.

Susan loved her home but was always ready to go somewhere and liked it better if she was going somewhere she hadn't been to before. Susan had doing quite a bit of international traveling herself but not as extensively as Ann.

They may have had different personalities, but each of them liked and respected the other one, which made a great friendship.

Chance and Ann joined the Big Springs Country Club, a golf club where the second greatest activity was bridge. You could find bridge games going on day and night at the clubhouse.

Ann and her next door neighbor, Lynn Wilson, spent many days playing bridge with different groups at the country club. Playing at the club sometimes meant playing with one table of four women or several tables, depending on which bridge club it was.

Ann was a very good bridge player and normally was either the player with the highest score for the day or the second highest, and being third highest for the day meant she didn't get very many good cards to play.

In addition, Ann had several other ladies whom she met at different places in town. When people found out she liked to play bridge, she was invited either to become a regular member of their bridge club or was asked to become a substitute for their club.

Ann had one group of four women who played every week and they played in the members' home, moving their game each week so every four weeks the game was at your home.

All the ladies in this group, except Ann, were retired teachers, and Ann was also the youngest member of her group. They played together for several years until one of the ladies developed

Alzheimer's disease, and they continued to play with a new member until Ann became paralyzed. Then the two women who were left decided not to continue their group anymore.

Ann had made a large number of friends after she moved to Big Springs. However, after Ann became so sick, the number of her friends who came to see her became fewer and fewer. Even her next- door neighbor, Lynn Wilson, got so she rarely stopped by to see Ann. If Lynn saw Chance outside the house while she was driving by, she would stop and ask how Ann was doing but didn't have time to come in to see Ann. One day Lynn told Chance she just couldn't come to see Ann anymore because she couldn't stand to see her in her condition.

Lynn had a couple of bouts with breast cancer and was now doing OK and kept herself busy all the time. One day after Chance had returned from buying groceries at the supermarket, he said, "Ann, I met Lynn when I first came into the store and I kept running into her in several different aisles as I was filling up my cart. "When I was checking out at the register I saw Lynn at another register and she was just buying a package of gum. I thought it was strange she was going up and down every aisle in the store and only bought a package of gum. Then the other day when I was at Walmart, she was doing the same thing. What's going on with her anyway?"

Ann said, "Lynn hates to be at home by herself so if her husband isn't home, she goes to stores and walks around."

Chance replied, "That's weird!"

Susan O'Hara was the one person who had kept in touch with Ann; she would send get her "get well" and "thinking about you" cards all the time. Plus they received all of her holiday cards and she would drive from Springfield, Missouri, to see Ann and a couple of other friends in Big Springs.

Susan came to see Ann when she was in the hospital in Springfield and a couple of times when Ann was in the Big Springs Hospital. She truly was a very good friend and Ann was always happy when Susan came to see her.

It was very good for Ann to know someone who would take the time to not only think about her but to send her cards all the time and make trips to see her.

Susan had moved to Springfield, Missouri, after Chance had to let her go when she worked as his executive secretary because the folks who were the investors of World Star Parking Systems wanted his office to be in Washington, D.C. so they would always be in the loop as to what was going on with the company.

Chance hated losing Susan; he liked her so much and she did a great job working with him. He hoped she understood he didn't have any choice of ending her job with World Star. He hated not being able to work with her and for changing her life after she didn't have a job in Big Springs any more. She sold her house and moved to Springfield to find a job.

Chance and Ann's closest friends, Doc and Susan Schmidt, would drive to Big Springs from Wichita, Kansas, and stay with them for a week several times a year. The Schmidts had lots of things to do with their family of four girls, who were now grown with several children, so they could only come a few times a year.

Their visits always perked Ann up and it was certainly wonderful for Chance to have their closest friends there to talk to and laugh about all the experiences they had been through together. The best and most reliable person who came to be with them was Ann's sister, Lee. Lee would drive up from Dallas about every five or six weeks to see Ann and stay with them for a week or more, depending on what was going on with her husband and her six adult children and grandchildren.

Lee gave Chance an opportunity to get out of the house for most of the day if he wanted to. Sometimes having Lee with Ann allowed him to go trout fishing at Chase and Marie's resort. He didn't do it very often but he loved the chance to spend time on the river with his son Chase.

Lee was six years younger than Ann and if they hadn't been close before Ann's illness, they sure were now. Ann appreciated her sister so much for all the time she took away from her family to come to be with her.

Chance certainly appreciated it, too. He knew Lee could do whatever it took to look after Ann's needs if he wasn't there; not only did Ann feel comfortable being by herself with Lee but Chance did, also.

Chance didn't have many problems when Genell was staying with Ann but she wasn't physically fit enough to do everything that was required to take care of Ann. Chance knew Genell could look after Ann by herself while he went shopping but he never wanted to be gone from home more than a couple of hours with just Genell at home with Ann.

Lee and Genell became very good friends during Lee's trips to see Ann and if they were both there while he was away from home, he was very sure between the two of them they could handle any of Ann's problems.

As the years went by, all the friends Ann had made over the years living in Big Springs quit calling and coming to see Ann and one by one, they simply all faded away.

As Chance reflected about the women who had been close to Ann for several years and now didn't come to see her anymore, he thought about himself and his failings as a friend.

Chance had always been one those people who thought if people were sick they probably didn't want to have him come to see them. Besides, he felt uncomfortable being with them, being so healthy and strong.

He was certainly sorry now about his attitude about going to see friends who were ill and was ashamed of himself for feeling uncomfortable and not spending time with them. He planned to be a better friend in the future.

14

THE YEARS GO ROLLING BY

Chance and Ann had now settled into a more normal lifestyle, if that's possible with someone who was completely paralyzed from her mid chest down and a stay-at-home husband caregiver.

At least it was normal to them. Ann still had many doctors' appointments in Big Springs and in St. Louis. Overall, Ann's health was much better at the beginning of January 2004 than it had been for the last few years.

2002 hadn't been such a great year with Ann being in hospital for ninety-eight days and in 2003 she had been in a hospital for forty-one days, but her outlook was much better now.

Then on Monday morning, February 23, when Ann woke up she was very sick, running a high fever and having trouble breathing so Chance quickly called for an appointment to take her to see Dr. Caye.

After seeing Dr. Caye, he prescribed some medication to treat bronchitis which she took for several days. She wasn't getting any better so Chance took Ann back to see Dr. Caye on Monday, March 1, and after checking her over, Dr. Caye had

Ann admitted to the Big Springs Hospital and kept her there until Friday, March 5, when he released her to return home to continue recovering from her bronchitis.

This would be Ann's only stay in the hospital in 2004, just a total of six days—what an improvement from the last several years!

In June, Chance and Ann took a trip to Wichita, Kansas, to be at the fiftieth wedding anniversary celebration of their friends Doc and Susan Schmidt, which they had been invited to by the Schmidts' four girls.

Chance and Ann wanted it to be a surprise visit so they didn't tell Doc or Susan they would be there. Chance and Ann wanted so much to be with them as Doc and Susan had come to their fiftieth anniversary party in Kansas City in December 2002.

The Schmidt girls had planned to hold their parents' party at one of the city parks in Wichita on Saturday, June 23, so Chance and Ann drove to Wichita on Friday to be able to be there.

Saturday morning it took some extra time to get Ann dressed and to do all the necessary tasks required for taking care of Ann each morning. It was much harder working at the Comfort Inn Suites than doing these things for Ann at home.

Finally, they were both ready to go and they didn't have too much trouble finding the park; however, it turned into more of a problem finding which one of the buildings the Schmidt party was in.

Once Chance thought he found the right building but after seeing the people who were going in and out of the building was no one they recognized, they thought that was probably the wrong building. So Chance continued to drive around the park and when Chance spotted Doc's car, he knew he had found the correct building. Chance got Ann out of the van as quickly as he could and they made their way to the entrance. Chance opened the door and Ann drove her wheelchair inside the building and everyone circled around Ann in her wheelchair the moment she arrived.

Everyone was thrilled to see them and was so happy Ann was well enough to make the trip for the anniversary party. Chance and Ann had a wonderful time with all of Doc and Susan's family.

After the party ended, Chance and Ann returned to their room at the Comfort Inn Suites and spent the rest of the day in their room.

On Sunday, Chance and Ann spent the entire afternoon and evening at Doc and Susan's home visiting just like they used to do so many times over so many years. They all loved each other very much. Monday, the Clarks drove back home to Big Springs and were pleased they had been able to make the trip and to see all of their best friend's family. Chance felt so good about Ann being able to make that long trip and was healthy enough to do it. Thanks, God.

The Clarks' trip to Wichita was the happy point of their year.

In 2005, Ann had an even better year for hospital stays; she didn't stay one day in the hospital during the whole year. *Wow*!

In April 2006, Ann had a couple of spots on her face and a small growth in her hair on the left side of her head and Chance was concerned about a spot on her right ear as well.

Since Big Springs didn't have a dermatologist, Chance called their son Shane, in Fayetteville and asked him if he knew a good dermatologist in Fayetteville.

Shane told him they used a dermatologist in Springdale and gave his dad the number for Dr. Worth. As soon as Chance finished his conversation with Shane, he called Dr. Worth's office for an appointment for Ann. They made an appointment for Ann on April 27.

During the visit with Dr. Worth the doctor froze the two spots on her face and the one of the left side of her head. Dr. Worth took a scraping of the spot the spot on her ear and had it sent it to a lab for testing because he was concerned it wasn't something he could just freeze off.

On May 13, a nurse from Dr. Worth's office called and told Chance the spot on Ann's ear was melanoma and the doctor needed to remove it from her ear.

This was the only major medical problem for Ann in year 2006, which was bad enough that she had to have surgery on her right ear for the melanoma, but was lucky enough she didn't have to follow the surgery with chemotherapy.

Dr. Worth managed to get all the melanoma from her ear and the sample of the tissue removed indicated the tissue was cancer- free. The doctor did have to cut off a part of her ear, but he was able to do a great job of reshaping Ann's ear so you never knew he had to cut away part of her ear.

Ann continued to have various health problems throughout 2006 but still managed to be in the hospital for only three days in 2006.

In July they heard their friend and next door neighbor Lynn Wilson's cancer had returned and she was in the hospital, and then they got word she passed away on July 23, 2006.

Chance thought maybe that's why she didn't want to spend any time with Ann when Ann was so ill because she was afraid she would be in the same way one day.

Chance was very sorry for her husband and her two sons; it was going to be a lonesome life for them without Lynn.

Chance and Ann didn't plan to go to Lynn's funeral because Ann thought there would be too many people and it would be hard for her to drive her wheelchair in the church where her funeral was to be held. Chance and Ann did go to the funeral home to pay their last respects to Lynn during visitation and Chance signed the guest register for them.

Lynn would have been pleased with the way she looked. She was dressed just like they had seen her a hundred times before. She was in her golfing outfit, ready to play a round of golf, complete with the cap she always wore. Maybe she would have also liked to play a few hands of bridge after lunch.

Ann's seventieth birthday would be on December 4, 2006, and Chance planned to have as big a celebration as possible with their family at home.

Chance was working hard to have all their Christmas decorations up before Ann's birthday and had finished decorating the Christmas tree in their front room when Ann's sister Lee and her daughter Lynn arrived on the night of December 3.

Lee, Lynn, and Chance were talking in the kitchen as they were bringing in their suitcase and the food Lee had made to bring for the birthday party when they heard the noise of something crashing in the living room.

Chance ran into the living room and saw his just-completed, decorated Christmas tree had crumbled to the floor with ornaments everywhere. One of them was inside the kitchen and several were under the dining room table. What a mess! Chance found the Christmas tree stand was broken and had come apart, letting the tree crash to the floor.

Chance knew he had to get the Christmas tree mess cleaned up and all the broken ornaments picked up before Ann's birthday party the next night. Since Lee was there with Ann, Chance asked Lynn if she wanted to go with him to Walmart to find a replacement tree stand. She did.

Chance and Lynn drove to Walmart and began looking for a new tree stand; they found several different ones and Chance finally chose one that looked a lot better than the one that had just broken. They purchased the stand and went back home. With Lynn's help, Chance was able to hold up the Christmas tree while Lynn put the tree stand on the trunk of the tree.

After Lynn had securely fastened the tree stand, Chance sat the tree back upright and the two of them began picking up the ornaments and putting the ones that were OK back on the tree and throwing away the broken ones.

The whole episode took them almost three hours from the time the tree came crashing down until they bought the new tree stand, put the new stand on the tree, got the tree standing upright, put over half of the ornaments back on, which had been on the tree already, and to clean up the broken ornaments.

All the time Chance and Lynn had been working on the tree problem, Ann and Lee had been in conversation. By the time Chance and Lynn returned to the family room, Ann announced she had to go to bed because she was worn out from doing all the talking.

Lynn came and gave her aunt a hug and a kiss and told her she was glad to see her looking so good. Lee told her goodnight and Ann drove her wheelchair into their bedroom where Chance was waiting to take care of all of Ann's bedtime chores.

The next afternoon Chase and Marie arrived to have the opportunity to visit with Ann, Lee, and Lynn.

Chase and Marie's son Curt was coming over after he got off from work and they knew Shane and Jan would be along sometime. Chance and Lee fixed Ann's birthday dinner using some of the food Lee had brought from Dallas. They didn't know how many of the family would be there or when they would arrive so they fixed dishes the guests could have when they got there.

The kitchen table was filled with things to eat so Chance was certain no one would go away hungry.

The idea was that as the guests arrived they could just graze on all the different dishes they had prepared.

Chance had a large birthday cake made for Ann with numerals seven and zero in the center of the cake. It was a white cake with white frosting and trimmed with pink and yellow flowers. They had done a great job at Walmart decorating the cake. It looked terrific! A little after seven o'clock all their guests arrived. Chase and Marie's son Curt got there first. Then Shane's stepchildren arrived, Jake and his wife, Ireland, from Springdale,

Arkansas, and Jerry and his sister Joanna came from Fayetteville.

Everyone had their fill with all the food Chance and Lee had prepared and everyone was having a very good time, especially Ann. It was her night. She blew out the two candles on her cake and enjoyed all her birthday presents. Chance was pretty sure Ann never expected to live to see her seventieth birthday.

Chance was sure with all the health problems she had had these past eight years she would never make it, but Ann was a fighter, and here she was on her seventieth birthday.

After everyone had gone home, except Lee and Lynn, who were staying with them for one more day before going back to Dallas, Chance waited in their bedroom for Ann so he could help her get ready for bed.

Chance heard Ann tell Lee and Lynn goodnight and could now hear her wheelchair coming down the hallway to come to bed so he knew she would soon be there.

After Chance had Ann ready for the night he asked her if she had had a good time and enjoyed having all her family there with her.

Ann assured him she certainly did and thanked him for making her birthday such a wonderful event and told him she loved him.

Chance kissed her goodnight and went over to his bed to get some sleep; it had been a long day for him.

15

BIG CHANGES IN CHANCE'S LIFE

*I*n 2007, everything was going very well at the Clarks' house.

Ann had only been in the hospital for three days in 2006.

They didn't have to make trips to Washington University in St. Louis to consult with Ann's doctors anymore. Nor did Ann need additional treatments of Cystoxic and Solu Medro to control her CNS Vasculitis, a real blessing for Ann when they were able to stop these treatments.

Their friend Susan O'Hara and her daughter Christy had driven down from Springfield to visit them a couple of times already this year and both of them really appreciated seeing them.

Ann loved the fact that even though she had been ill for so many years, her loyal friend Susan continued to send her cards all the time.

In April, their best friends, Doc and Susan Schmidt, came from Wichita and spent ten days visiting with them. The four of them had a ball for ten whole days laughing, talking, and eating.

Ann sister Lee was with them for a week in March and was back for another week in May and had plans to come back to see them in August.

Ann's pain was under control and she didn't have to keep going from doctor to doctor to see about getting new meds.

Ann's health was as good as it had been for years.

Their sons Chase and Shane and their families came to see them as often as they could.

Ann was in good spirits almost all the time and enjoyed having Genell come and stay with her while Chance went shopping or was there with her while Chance was working at home. Ann liked having another woman around to talk to when Genell was helping Chance take care of her.

Genell would do Ann's fingernails every Friday. Ann really liked Genell doing her nails and she did such a great job. Ann's nails always looked great.

Chance and Ann spent many hours watching movies and sports on TV. They loved to watch the old movies on TCM. They made sure they watched it on Saturday nights; there always seemed to be a good picture on that night.

They also had hundreds of movies on VHS and DVDs to watch; many of their favorite films they watched over and over. Both Ann and Chance loved the movies.

So even though Ann was still completely paralyzed and had no feeling in her lower body, the Clarks had settled into a very normal life.

Chance loved the fact he was able to care for Ann and she loved the fact he would do whatever had to be done to take care of her. Ann felt bad Chance wasn't working anymore and that he was tied down staying at home with her after he had spent so much of his life traveling.

The last several years before she became sick he had traveled the world and he had loved it.

When Ann first became paralyzed, Chance confessed to her one day that staying at home all the time was like being in jail. He had never been in jail, but he thought the people in jail must be feeling like he did staying at home.

One night around July 2, the Clarks finished watching a movie on TCM and after Chance did all the necessary things to take care of Ann, he gave her a kiss goodnight and started around the end of Ann's bed to go over to his bed.

Ann said, "Chance, if sometime happened to me would you go with Susan?"

Chance stopped dead in his tracks at the end of Ann's bed and tried to think about what Ann just asked him.

A second after he heard and understood what Ann asked him, Chance blurted out, "Susan! Susan! We're way too much alike!"

Neither Chance nor Ann said anything else. Chance went on over to his bed and wondered whatever brought something like that up in Ann's mind.

Chance had known Susan O'Hara for almost forty years and they had been friends and coworkers but he never thought about Susan in any way but a professional way. It wasn't like Ann to bring up a subject and just drop it but she never said anything more about it.

Chance and Ann spent a lot of time talking every night when Chance was getting her ready for bed and after he finished taking care of all her nightly needs.

Sometimes they talked about their children and their own lives and the places they lived and traveled to and about their friends.

Shane's stepson Jake Johnson was the oldest of Jan's three children and he had a hard time with several problems in his life until his stepfather Shane stepped in and got him help in getting his life straightened out.

As a result of Shane's help, Jake legally had his last name changed from Johnson to Clark to have the same last name as his mother and stepfather's.

Jake had met his wife, Ireland, while working together, and fell in love and they were married, and then both got their college degrees. They waited a couple of years after they finished college before starting a family.

Now they had a son, Robbie, born June 9, 2007, and they had brought him over to see his great-grandparents.

Chance and Ann were pleased his grandmother and mother brought Robbie over to Big Springs to see them.

On Monday night, July 16, after Chance had Ann ready for the night, Ann said, "Chance, I'm afraid to die."

Hearing what Ann said, Chance replied, "Ann, everybody is afraid to die because even when we think we know what happens to us, there is always a place in our mind that questions it.

"I'm sorry, honey, I don't know what else I can say. We do know Jesus said he promised the ones who believed in Him would have eternal life.

"Ann, I wish I could say something that would help you more but I don't know anything else to say."

Chance went over to Ann, hugged her, and gave her another goodnight kiss, then went to his bed and laid down.

He lay there for a while and said, "Goodnight, Annie, I love you and I'll see you in the morning."

Ann answered, "Goodnight, Chance. I love you."

Ann was having problems with a toothache the next morning so Chance made an appointment with their dentist for Ann on July 19.

When the nineteenth arrived, Chance took Ann for her appointment with their dentist.

After the dentist checked over Ann's teeth, he said, "Ann, I'm sorry to tell you this but with all of those high-powered drug treatments you had, it has really done a number on your teeth. You're going to have to have seven of your teeth pulled."

Ann said, "You can't save any of them?"

"I wish I could, Ann, but they're too bad to save." "When can you do it?"

"You know I don't pull teeth. We'll make you an appointment with Dr. Jenkins who's a specialist in tooth extraction."

"Sorry, I remember you don't pull teeth because you sent me to Dr. Jenkins to pull one out for me before."

Chance asked, "Doctor, what can you do to replace Ann's teeth after she has them removed?"

"I can make Ann some replacements for most of her old ones after she gets these out."

The doctor asked his assistant to call to see how soon Dr. Jenkins could get Ann an appointment. The doctor's assistant returned a few minutes later and told them she had an appointment on Monday, July 23.

Ann thought that was good because she didn't want to wait very long thinking about having seven teeth pulled.

One thing that made it nice going to Ann's dentist was the doctor and his assistant always lifted Ann in and out of her wheelchair and in and out of the dental chair, which meant Chance didn't have to do it all by himself.

Ann wasn't happy thinking about needing to have so many teeth pulled and then getting replacement teeth made. She knew this was going to cost a lot of money.

Friday night, July 20, after Ann was ready for the night and Chance was getting into his bed, Ann said, "Chance, I don't know why I ever said I was ever afraid to die, I never have been."

Chance didn't know how to answer her. Finally he said, "That's good, sweetheart, I'm glad. Goodnight, I'll see you in the morning."

Chance said that to Ann every night.

Saturday night Chance asked Ann, "What would you like me to fix you for dinner tonight?"

Ann thought for a moment and replied, "I want one of my favorite meals, a loaded baked potato from Wendy's."

"OK, you've got a deal and I'll get chili, Wendy's chili is almost as good as what I make. Do you want anything else?"

"Yes, I want a chocolate frosty, too."

"I'll go get our dinner right now and we can have it while we watch one of our DVDs."

Chance didn't ever like leaving Ann alone even for a few minutes. He knew she had a phone on the family room bedside table, but he didn't want to think about if something happened to her while he was gone.

What if something happened to him while he was gone, how would Ann get help? Who would look after her if he was gone?

Wendy's was the closest restaurant to their home and by using the drive-through at Wendy's, Chance was back home in fifteen minutes.

Chance selected a movie from their collection of DVDs and as they had their dinner in the family room they watched their movie.

When they had finished watching their film, Ann said, "Let's go to bed before it's time for the late movie to come on TCM. I read what the movie was, but I can't think about the name of it right now. I know it was one I wanted to see."

"OK, I'll get your pills while you go to the bedroom."

Chance moved Ann's bedside table away from her wheelchair and Ann started driving her wheelchair back to their bedroom. By the time he got her nighttime pills from the kitchen, Ann was already in their bedroom.

As soon as Chance got to their bedroom he hooked up the harness from her sling to the arm of their ceiling-mounted lift system. He used the lift to pick her up from her wheelchair and then he used the lift to move her over to her hospital bed.

Then, using the lift he gently lowered Ann down onto her bed. What a wonderful system their lift was; he was so glad they made the investment to buy the lift system. He knew it had saved his back and was one of the things that had allowed him to be able to take care of Ann at home by himself.

After she was on her bed, Chance rolled Ann over on her left side and pushed the sling under her right side. Next, he turned Ann over on her right side which let him pull the sling out from under Ann's body. Then he turned her onto her back.

Chance put the sling on the wheelchair and he drove the wheelchair into his office next door to their bedroom. He plugged the wheelchair's power cord into the wall outlet so Ann's wheelchair's battery would be fully charged up in the morning.

Chance went back to their bedroom and began taking off Ann's clothes and got her ready for the night. After Chance finished doing all the things he had to do for Ann, she raised the head of her bed up as Chance was moving her bedside table over to the right side of her bed, positioning it so Ann could sit up and wash off her makeup and brush her teeth.

When all this had been completed, Chance gave Ann her bedtime pills. Ann continued to get her pills one pill at a time with a spoon of applesauce with each pill. Then she had a glass of water to drink after she had taken all of her pills. This was the only way Ann could swallow her pills without choking.

Chance turned on the TV in their bedroom and turned it to TCM to watch the film Ann wanted to see. It was a comedy and they were both laughing a lot at the picture and enjoying it very much; around twelve thirty their telephone rang and it was, of course, Shane.

Shane knew his folks were always up late on Saturday night and he wanted to see how they were doing and spent some time talking with his folks about all the things he was up to.

Chance talked with Shane for several minutes before Shane asked to talk with his mother before she went to sleep. Chance gave the phone to Ann and she talked with Shane for even a longer time than Chance had.

Chance didn't know what the two of them were talking about but Ann was laughing so hard it must have been very funny. Ann finally told Shane, "I need to go to sleep. I've got to hang up the phone now."

The telephone conversation with Shane ended around one o'clock Sunday morning.

Chance got out of bed to kiss Ann goodnight and as he got back into his bed he said, "Goodnight, Annie, I love you. I'll see you in the morning."

Ann didn't answer; she was already asleep.

Sunday morning Chance woke up about nine thirty and went into the kitchen and made coffee for them. He went back into their bedroom and Ann was still sleeping so he decided to go ahead and take his shower and clean up and let Ann sleep.

After he made himself ready for the day he checked on Ann and she was still sleeping. So he went back into the kitchen and fixed himself a bowl of cereal.

After he ate his cereal Chance again returned to their bedroom and tried to wake Ann up and found he couldn't.

He checked her all over and even though he was moving her around in the bed she didn't wake up.

Ann still seemed to be sleeping although she appeared to be breathing harder than normal.

Chance kept talking to Ann all the time but she wasn't responding or waking up.

Chance went to the phone next to his bed and called 911 and gave them his name and address and told the 911 operator he couldn't wake his wife up.

He told the 911 operator he wanted an ambulance to take his wife to the hospital as soon as possible.

Living in a small town had a lot of advantage; one of them was it didn't take long for an ambulance to arrive at their front door.

Chance met the ambulance attendant at the door and told him it would be easier to take his wife out of the house through the patio sliding glass doors and told him to bring the ambulance around to the back of the house and they could pull the ambulance up on the grass.

While the ambulance driver moved the ambulance around to the back of the house the attendant Chance had been talking to came into the bedroom to try and see if he could get any response from Ann. He couldn't rouse Ann either.

The ambulance driver came into the bedroom bringing a gurney to put Ann on to take her to the hospital.

As the ambulance crew was getting the gurney into the bedroom a police officer came to the bedroom to check on what was going on since Chance said he couldn't wake his wife up in his 911 call.

The ambulance driver told the officer it was all right, he knew this lady and she had been ill for a long time. Hearing that, the police officer turned around and left as the ambulance attendants were moving Ann off her bed and onto the gurney.

When they started trying to move Ann out of the bedroom, Chance told them they would have to sit Ann up on the gurney in order to make the turn out of their bedroom into the hall.

Chance was right, since Ann had been moved by ambulance crews in and out of their bedroom many times before. He knew it was the only way they could get the gurney and Ann out of the bedroom.

After Ann had been loaded into the ambulance, Chase grabbed his hospital suitcase which was filled with all the things he needed to take care of Ann in the hospital.

He locked the house up, got into Ann's van and drove to the hospital as quickly as he could.

Arriving at the hospital Chance went directly to the ER where he knew Ann would have been taken. As soon as Chance told them at the desk he was Chance Clark and his wife had just been brought in by ambulance he was taken to the Ann's ER room. She still looked the same way she did at home when he began trying to wake her up a few hours ago.

Dr. Caye's associate, Dr. Chelsea, was making the rounds in the hospital this Sunday morning, seeing all of his and Dr. Caye's patients. Dr. Chelsea was in the room with Ann when Chance arrived there. Dr. Chelsea said, "Chance, I've ordered some tests for Ann to see what's happened to her."

"Thank you, Dr. Chelsea, I appreciate it."

"After I have an opportunity to look at the results of the tests, I'll get back with you."

"Thanks again, Doctor."

It took a couple of hours for them to do a CT scan and several X-rays for Ann. While they were doing these tests Chance telephoned Chase and Shane and told them what was going on with their mother. Both said they would be at the hospital as soon as they could.

Chase told his dad he would call Ann's sister Lee and Chance's brother Will and tell them what had happened to his mother.

Chance telephoned Genell to let her know that Ann was in the hospital and she told him she would be at the hospital as soon as she could get dressed.

Genell came to the hospital in less than an hour and after she saw Ann, she told Chance, "I don't think they're going to be able to do anything to help Ann."

Working with Ann for almost five years, Genell thought of Ann like she was her daughter. She loved her and Chance could see Genell was ready to break down with grief.

Some three hours later, Chase, Marie, Shane, and Jan came into Ann's ER room. Chance was relieved to see them and they all hugged each other and said hello.

Dr. Chelsea found Chance sitting by Ann's bedside, while the rest of the family was standing beside Ann's bed just staring at her. Dr. Chelsea said, "Chance, I've had a chance to look over the

X-rays and her CT scans and had two other doctors look her test over and none of us have ever seen the amount of blood pooled at the base of Ann's brain. There isn't any hope she can survive this, she only has a short amount of time left. I'm sorry, there isn't anything we can do to help her.

"We will be moving her to the fourth floor in a few minutes and you can all go up to her room with her. The best we can do is to keep her as comfortable as possible."

Chance said, "Thank you again, Dr. Chelsea."

"Chance, I didn't know if you would want us to take Ann to another hospital to see if they could do anything for Ann or not, but I wanted to ask you if you did."

"Do you think if she was at some other hospital they could do anything to help her?"

"No, I don't."

"Then no, we don't want to move her."

Two attendants came into Ann's ER room and said, "We're here to take Mrs. Clark up to Room 442. Is that OK, Doctor?"

"Yes, it's OK. You can take her to her room."

The attendants transferred Ann onto a gurney to take her to her room.

All of Ann's family followed Ann's gurney up to her room.

A nurse on the floor led them into Room 442 and told them she would get them more chairs so everyone could sit down.

The attendants transferred Ann onto her bed.

A few minutes later the nurse returned with a couple of additional chairs and promised to find them some more.

After several more hours passed, Chance asked his family if they had had anything to eat for the day: no, they hadn't.

Chance suggested they should go get something to eat and suggested they go to Colton's Steak House, which was OK with everyone. They didn't have a lot of choices of restaurants in Big Springs anyway.

Genell told them she was tired and felt like she had to go home and would see Chance sometime tomorrow.

The family had dinner with little or no conversation since each of them were lost in their own thoughts.

They returned to the hospital and Chase, Jan, Shane, and Jan stayed until around 9:00 p.m.

Chance said "You guys might as well go home since Mom's not going to wake up from the coma she's in and none of us can do anything to help her. Besides, I don't want to have to worry about all of you driving home."

Each one of them gave Mom a kiss and told her they loved her and left to drive back home.

Around eleven o'clock that evening an aide came in to see if she could do anything for him or if he wanted anything: no, he didn't. Ann continued breathing very hard and when the aide came into Ann's room again around four thirty on Monday morning, July 23, Chance asked her if she would help him turn Ann over on her right side for a while and get her off her back.

She agreed to help him, and as Chance was using the bed pad to turn Ann onto her right side, Ann gasped and stopped breathing.

Chance said to the aide, "She's gone."

The aide ran out of the room to get a nurse.

Chance stood over Ann and put his arms out over her and like some ancient priest raised his palms up to the ceiling and said out loud, "Father, I can do no more. She's in your hands now."

Chance would never know where the words came from; all he knew was he said it.

He sat back down on his chair next to Ann's bed, put his hands down, and placed his right hand on Ann's shoulder.

The aide and a nurse came into Ann's room and the nurse confirmed something Chance already knew, that his love was gone.

His everything was gone.

The nurse left the room and came back in a few minutes and said she spoke with Dr. Chelsea and asked him if he wanted one of the ER doctors to come up and pronounce Ann.

She said, "Dr. Chelsea told her no, he would do it himself when he got to the hospital."

For the next two hours Chance sat by Ann talking to her and telling her she needed some more blankets because she was getting so cold.

Dr. Chelsea arrived a little before seven o'clock and checked her and told Chance that he and Dr. Caye were so sorry they couldn't do anything to help her.

Dr. Chelsea left Chance sitting in Ann's room.

A few minutes later a nurse and an aide came in and the nurse, who knew him from the many times Ann had been in the Big Springs Hospital and knew he did everything for Ann when she was in the hospital including giving her baths, asked, "Chance, do you want to help give Ann her last bath?"

Chance was so struck with the words "her last bath" his tears started flowing and all he could do as he ran out the door was mutter, "I can't."

Chance found his car and had to work hard to be able to drive Ann's van home with the tears in his eyes and the emotions he was feeling with the loss of his love.

When he got home he struggled with the thought his Ann would never return to this house she loved so much.

When he got into his house he went straight to his office and first called Chase and told him his mother was gone.

Next, Chance called Shane and told him his mother died about four thirty this morning.

The next call he made was to Ann's sister Lee to let her know Ann was gone. She told Chance, "I'll be there this afternoon to help you."

The last call Chance made was to his brother Will who had been only seven years old when Chance and Ann were married, so Ann had been part of his life since he could remember.

Will and his wife, Betty, lived in Webster, Kansas, the town where Chance and Ann had met in junior high school and were married.

When he told Will, Ann had passed away this morning, both of them started crying and neither of them could talk anymore. Chance mumbled something like, "I'll talk to you later."

After these calls were made, Chance sat down in his blue chair and began alternating between crying and yelling at God for taking Ann away from him.

This went on for the next two hours or more except the yelling at God taking Ann lasted only a few minutes, before Chance was just crying and asking his God to take care of his Annie.

16

CELEBRATIONS OF ANN'S LIFE

Chance stopped crying and screaming from the pain in his heart at the loss of Ann sometime after eleven o'clock that morning, and he had to start thinking about all the things he needed to do.

Chance remembered Ann had written some information about what she wanted done for her funeral and he thought she had put it in the family bible.

He got up from his blue recliner chair and went into the living room and found the family bible on the shelf of one of the end tables next to the couch.

Chance searched through all of the funeral home cards of their dead family members, which had been saved in their Bible, and found the note Ann had written about things she wanted for her funeral.

She had a poem and a list of songs she wanted sung at her funeral and Chance knew all the songs except one: "You've Got a Friend." Chance didn't have a clue about this song.

He remembered Ann had an appointment to have several teeth pulled today so he called to let the dentist know that she had died earlier that morning. Chance knew Ann didn't want to have her teeth pulled, but this was an awful way of getting out of it.

Ann had also noted she wanted their friend John Charles to sing at her funeral.

John had been a music teacher and was involved in all kinds of music productions in Big Springs. He had quit teaching and bought a travel agency which Chance and Ann used all the time.

Chance figured he was John's biggest client when he had been doing all his world traveling.

Chance telephoned to let him know Ann had passed away that morning and she wanted to have him sing at her funeral. John told him he would be honored to sing at her funeral.

Chance hung up the phone and less than thirty minutes later his doorbell rang. When Chance opened the door it was John.

Chance asked John in and after he was in the house John put his arms around Chance and said, "I'm so sorry about Ann. I know how much you loved her."

Chance asked John to come and sit down in the living room; he wanted to tell him about the songs Ann wanted him to sing at her funeral.

The songs Ann asked for were: "Amazing Grace," "The Lord's Prayer," and "You've got a Friend."

In Ann's note she asked for two poems be read at her funeral, one called "A Most Unusual Gift of Love" and second one "To Those Who Love Me."

John told Chance he wouldn't have any problem singing two of the songs Ann wanted but he didn't have any idea about the last one, the one called, "You've Got a Friend."

John told Chance, "Don't worry, I'll find the song."

Chance was so pleased John had come over to be with him. It meant a lot to him that his friend had taken time to be with him.

After John left, Chance sat down and read the poem Ann had written her note on about what she wanted at her funeral.

Chance read this poem by an unknown author: "To Those I love and Those who Love Me."

After Chance looked some more through the Bible, he found the other poem Ann wanted read, by Robert Saxton, titled: "A Most Unusual Gift of Love."

After reading the poems Ann chose for her funeral, his eyes began to flow tears again.

Chance tried to think about all the things he must do with Ann no longer here with him.

In the first place, Ann had died too young.

Husbands were always supposed to go first. He tried over the years to help make Ann independent and to prepare her for when he died, trying to get as many things arranged for her so she would be able to take care of herself.

It was all wrong: she was the one who should be left, not him! At two o'clock in the afternoon his doorbell rang and when Chance opened the door there stood Lee; she had already made it from Dallas. Chance reached for Lee and they held each other and Chance said, "Honey, you sure got here quick.

"I didn't make but one potty stop and I filled my gas tank on the same stop."

"I really glad you're here. You don't know how much I appreciate it."

"I wanted to be here to help you take care of things for Ann's funeral and do whatever else I can do to help."

"Lee, you have been so faithful coming to be with Ann so often. She loved having you here. Let me get your things out of the car and into the guest room."

Lee handed Chance her car keys and said, "You can start getting things out of the trunk while I make another potty stop."

Chance took her car keys as Lee made her way to the bathroom. Chance walked to the car, opened the trunk, and saw Lee had brought a lot of things with her. He brought in her suitcase and a garment bag and put them in the guest room.

Chance met Lee in the hallway as he was going back to her car to get more of the things she brought with her.

He said, "It looks like you brought a bunch of pop and food with you."

"You know I can buy pop in Dallas so much cheaper. I figured you would have a lot of people here this week that drink pop and eat snacks."

"Well, it's certainly true of the Clark family."

Chance opened the garage door and began unloading the pop and the snacks into the garage as Lee was loading up the extra refrigerator in the garage with cans of pop she brought with her from Dallas.

After Chance and Lee had her car unloaded they closed the garage door and went into the family room.

Chance said, "It doesn't feel right to walk into the family room and not have Ann in her wheelchair sitting here watching TV. No, it's not right she's not here."

"No, Chance, it's not going to feel right for you for a long time." "I guess I better call the funeral home and set up an appointment to make the arrangements for Ann's funeral."

"You need to do that soon so we can contact our family and let them know when Ann's funeral will be."

"OK, I'll call them. I guess we have to do it."

"The sooner we get it taken care of, the better it will be for everybody." Chance took out a telephone directory from a drawer in the kitchen and found the number for the funeral home he had Ann's body taken to and called their number.

Kate Olsen, the lady who owned the funeral home, answered the phone and Chance told her it was Chance Clark and he needed to make an appointment for Ann's services.

Ms. Olsen set up an appointment for him the next day at two in the afternoon.

The rest of the day Chance and Lee spent talking about Ann and all of her illness and all the suffering she had gone through.

Lee was particularly pleased to hear about Ann's last day and how she was laughing at the movie they had watched and during her conversation with Shane at twelve thirty on Sunday morning.

Lee told Chance it sounded like Ann's last day was certainly better than most folks' and she even had one of her favorite meals, Wendy's loaded baked potato and a chocolate frosty.

Chance said, "With all the problems with Ann's CNS Vasculitis and her awful treatments, she died from a cerebral hemorrhage, the same thing your dad died from, the aneurysm in her carotid artery. It was the one thing wrong with Ann that none of her doctors ever wanted to try to do anything with."

"Well, she made it eight years without having any problem with it. Maybe that's eight years more then she would have had if they had tried to do surgery on the aneurysm. Who knows?"

Chance hadn't eaten all day and Lee had had only a bowl of cereal for breakfast before she left Dallas, so they needed something. Chance knew Lee and Ann always liked to go to the Catfish Wharf in town, so they went to dinner there.

When they returned to the house both of their bodies needed rest so they went to bed.

Lee hadn't gotten a lot of sleep after Chance had called her about Ann, then she had gotten up early and had driven all the way from Dallas. It didn't take her long to get ready for bed or to fall asleep.

Chance, who had a hard time most nights getting to sleep, took a couple of Tylenol PM to help him sleep. He sure didn't get any sleep anytime on Sunday. Chance wasn't used to taking any type of sleep aids so it worked very well for him.

Chance didn't wake up until eight thirty the next morning and he could smell coffee brewing. He had a little problem remembering Lee was here and would be the one fixing coffee. He got out of his bed and walked past Ann's hospital bed to the bathroom.

Chance got into the shower and while standing under the showerhead with the warm, refreshing water cascading over his head and body, he wished the water could wash away the pain in his heart as well as it was doing washing away the shampoo and soap.

After he finished his shower, Chance toweled his hair and body, then blow-dried his hair, shaved, brushed his teeth, and took his morning pills. He hadn't taken any of his meds yesterday so he thought he better do it this morning.

He dressed and went into the family room and found Lee sitting there reading the morning newspaper.

Lee looked up from her newspaper and said, "Morning, Chance, can I fix you some breakfast?"

"Morning to you, Lee, we can go out and have something. You don't have to fix breakfast."

Lee replied, "It's not a problem. I saw you have eggs, bacon, and bread to fix some toast. Besides, I'm not cleaned up yet. I'm still in my gown and robe."

"OK, Lee, let's have breakfast here and I'll help you fix it." "Good, you can make the toast."

After breakfast was made, eaten, and the kitchen cleaned up, Lee went in to take her shower and get dressed for the day.

At 1:30 p.m., Chance and Lee got into her car and Lee drove them to the funeral home. It took them only about ten minutes to get there and they sat in the car for a while without talking, each of them lost in their own thoughts.

A few minutes before 2 p.m. Chance said, "I guess we better go in and meet with Kate Olsen."

Chance knew Kate Olsen from seeing her at the country club, and Ann had been in bridge clubs with her.

When Chance and Lee went inside the funeral home, Kate was walking past the front door and saw them come in. Kate greeted them and Chance introduced Lee to Kate. Kate asked them to come into her office and the three of them began discussing plans for Ann's funeral.

The decision was made to hold Ann's funeral on Friday, July 27, at eleven o'clock in the morning. This would give their family members time enough to travel to Big Springs for Ann's service.

They talked about the pallbearers for Ann and who would conduct the service for her.

Chance said he would contact the people he wanted to act as Ann's pallbearers and would bring Kate a list of them as soon as he talked with each one of them to see if they were willing to act as pallbearers.

Chance said he would like to have a Methodist minister do Ann's service but he had to confess he didn't know one. All the time they had lived in Big Springs they had never attended church here; they still had their membership in the First United Methodist Church in Webster, Kansas.

Kate told him Don Dalton was the minister at the First United Methodist Church and she had worked with him a lot. Kate assured them Don was a very good man and she could call him for them. Chance told her he would appreciate her doing that.

Chance said, "I have a list of songs Ann wanted sung at her funeral and I've already spoken with my friend John Charles and asked him to sing the songs for us."

Kate asked, "Do you want us to write Ann's obituary or do you want to write it yourself? Either way, we will submit it to the newspaper for you."

Chance said, "I'll have my son Chase write Ann's obituary for the newspapers. He's a very good writer. We will want to run it the local paper and in the *Webster Daily News* in Webster, Kansas."

She said, "That's not a problem. We can do that for you."

Kate asked, "Would you like to have us make a video for you to show during Ann's visitation Thursday night?"

Chance asked, "What do you need from us to be able to make the video?"

Katie replied, "We would need pictures of Ann at various ages during her lifetime and for any special occasion you would like to include, things like that."

Chance asked, "What type of device would the video be shown on? Is it a special piece of equipment?"

"No, it's a regular DVD player the video will just operate on a loop. It will play the DVD over and over."

Chance said, "Since we would have to find the pictures for you, I think I'll have my son Shane make it for his mother. He's made a full-length motion picture, I'm sure he can make a DVD for us." Kate said, "OK, I guess the only other thing we need to do is to have you pick out a casket for Ann and tell me if you are going to furnish the clothing you want Ann to wear, or do you want to pick out something from our stock?"

Lee answered, "We'll bring all the clothes we want her to wear."

Kate said, "Then let's go into our casket display room and I'll let you select Ann's casket."

The three of them went into the casket showroom and after some time, Chance and Lee chose a blue Tuscany-model casket. It had a white interior with beautiful embroidered pansy flowers on the side of the interior of the casket.

Kate said, "You have the mausoleum that's in Maplewood Cemetery, don't you? In fact, I remember you actually bought and installed the first mausoleum we ever had in Big Springs some time ago. I read it in the newspaper since they had a picture of it right after it was installed."

"Yes, we did."

Kate said, "Then you don't need anything else from us. You certainly don't need a vault for the casket."

"No, we don't."

"Ann's funeral will be the first one we have ever done with entombment in a mausoleum."

Kate continued, "I'm sure Don Dalton will phone you and want to meet with you to know how you want Ann's funeral done."

When Chance and Lee returned to the house, Chance began contacting the family he wanted to act as pallbearers.

He asked Randy Roberts, Lee's husband; Will Clark, Chance's brother; Doc Schmidt, Chance's best friend; and grandsons: Curt Clark, Chase's son; Jake Clark, Shane's stepson, and Jerry Johnson, another of Shane's stepsons. Of course, all of them agreed to be pallbearers for Ann.

Chance added two honorary pallbearers to his list: Ann's local doctors Dr. Charles Caye and Dr. Bob Chelsea.

Wednesday was a very busy day. Chance got a call from Don Dalton, minister of the First United Methodist Church and he set up an appointment with Chance and Lee to discuss Ann's funeral at one thirty that afternoon.

Next, Chance received a call from John Charles telling him that with the help of his son, a music teacher in Texas, he had found out the song "You've got a Friend" wasn't a gospel song, but a popular song written and performed by Carole King.

John said, "I think you should use her recording of the song for Ann's funeral. I've looked at it and I don't think I can do it justice."

Chance asked, "John, do you think you could find the song on a CD we could use?"

"I have it, and I can drop it off at the funeral home." "Thanks, John, I appreciate it."

Chance had talked on the phone the night before with both Chase and Shane about what he wanted them to do and both agreed to do their jobs.

Chase e-mailed a copy of Ann's obituary to Chance early that morning and Shane was coming over that night to look for pictures to make the video and would have it back to the funeral home by tomorrow right after noon.

Chance and Lee checked over the obituary and thought Chase had done a good job on it so Chance called Kate Olsen and told her he was e-mailing it to her.

After Kate received the copy of the obituary, she said she would get it in the newspaper this afternoon and send it on to the newspaper in Webster.

At one thirty, Chance and Lee went to the Big Springs First United Methodist Church office to meet with Reverend Don Dalton but when they arrived, they found he was still in a meeting with someone else.

The woman working in the church office told them Brother Dalton was expecting them and would be with them in a few minutes.

Chance had been involved with a Methodist church his entire life until they moved to Big Springs, and he and Ann decided they would wait awhile before transferring their membership from Webster to Big Springs but he had never heard of a Methodist minister being referred to as Brother.

Time had slipped away without them ever attending church in Big Springs.

Chance knew going to church required it to become a habit but after they got out of the habit of going, they never got back into the habit. Chance knew going to church was a good habit to have and it was too bad they never went to church in Big Springs.

Chance had begun traveling all over the world and then when he was home, there always seemed to be something they had to do on the weekends.

A young man left the minister's office and following directly behind him was another man. When the man saw Chance and Lee waiting outside his office, he introduced himself to them and asked them to come into his office.

Reverend Dalton invited them to sit down at his conference table. It looked to Chance that the conference table was being very well used, with stacks of papers at one end of the table and just enough empty space for the three of them to sit down around on the other end of table.

Chance introduced himself and Lee to Reverend Dalton.

Reverend Dalton immediately expressed his sympathy for their loss of Ann and said, "I understand from Kate Olsen that you would like for me to do the service for Ann. I'd be pleased to do Ann's service for her. I would like to know how you would like her services done."

Chance replied, "I want to thank you for agreeing to do the service for Ann and would like the service to be 'A Celebration of a Life Well Lived.' I don't want her service to be a sermon."

Reverend Dalton said, "That's no problem. I would like for you to tell me all you can about her, if you would, things she liked, what she didn't like, and what kind of things she liked to do. I need to have information about her family and where she was born, lived, and something about her personality."

Lee said, "We can certainly do that for you."

For the next hour and half, Chance and Lee talked about Ann, her family, the place she was born and lived, things she liked and things she didn't like, how long Chance and Ann had been married, her illness, and the things she liked to do.

All the time the two of them were talking, Reverend Dalton was writing on a yellow legal pad, making notes and asking them to explain this or that and when Chance and Lee finished talking, the legal pad was filled with information about Ann.

Chance told Reverend Dalton Ann had chosen the songs she wanted sung at her funeral and the two poems she wanted read, and Chance gave Reverend Dalton copies of each of the poems for him to read at Ann's services.

Reverend Dalton said, "Although I never had the opportunity to meet Ann, I know a lot about her and would have enjoyed knowing her. I think I can do a nice service for her."

Chance thanked him for his time and told him on behalf of Ann's family they appreciated him being willing to do Ann's service for her.

As soon as Chance and Lee finished their meeting with Reverend Dalton, they drove directly to Springfield to Dillard's department store to look for an outfit for Ann to be buried in. After searching Dillard's for some time neither could see anything they liked.

Lee suggested they try Kohl's department store. She told Chance she bought a lot of things there and was pleased with her purchases. Chance had never shopped there but was willing to try it, so they went there.

Just when they were ready to give up shopping at Kohl's, they found a beautiful pale green pantsuit that they both liked, so they bought it, along with a green pin and a scarf to go around her neck and a pair of knee-high stockings and a pair of panties.

After making their purchases they first stopped at home and picked up one of Ann's bras and then went directly to the funeral home and delivered the clothes.

That evening Shane and Jan came over to get pictures so he could make the video for Ann's viewing, scheduled for tomorrow.

After Shane searched through several albums and selected several pictures from them, he took a DVD which contained all the slide pictures they had taken over the years to make Ann's video.

Shane and Jan left around ten that night and Shane promised he would have the video at the funeral home late the next afternoon before it was time for the viewing.

Thursday morning Kate Olsen called Chance and asked him and Lee to come to the funeral home to see Ann and make sure they thought she looked OK.

Chance and Lee drove to the funeral home to see how Ann looked in her new outfit and took all her rings and the diamond bracelet she normally wore every day, along with her glasses.

On their arrival at the funeral home Kate was waiting at the door for them to take them to see how Ann looked, and both Chance and Lee agreed she looked fine but thought she should have her glasses on, since everyone was used to seeing her wear glasses.

Chance gave Kate, Ann's glasses and she put them on her, and then he asked Kate if she would put Ann's rings and diamond bracelet on her.

Kate took the jewelry and put them on Ann.

Now, both Chance and Lee felt Ann looked more like what she normally looked like.

They were both happy with the way Ann looked now.

Kate told Chance she would take Ann's jewelry off at the beginning of Ann's service when they closed her casket as Ann had requested and return them to Chance.

Several members of Lee's family arrived in Big Springs on Thursday afternoon and checked into the Comfort Inn motel, including Lee's husband, Randy Roberts.

Lee packed her things and moved over to the Comfort Inn to be with her husband and family, for the first time since Ann died leaving Chance alone.

Sure enough, Shane arrived with a completed video of Ann at four o'clock Thursday, after staying up all night to get it finished, and as soon as he got to the house, Chance and Shane took the video to the funeral home.

One of the funeral home employees put the DVD into their player and pushed the button to start the video but it didn't play; both he and Shane tried to play it but nothing happened. Shane couldn't understand it, as it was playing at home. Finally the man from the funeral home decided to change DVD players.

He put the DVD into a different machine. He pushed the play button while Chance and Shane were each saying a little prayer that the DVD would play. Sure enough, the video flashed a picture of Ann on the screen with words and music playing in the background.

By the time the visitation was set to begin, all of Ann's family was there and the chapel was filled with flowers and still more flowers were being delivered.

Dr. Caye and his wife and many of the nurses from the hospital and the doctor's office came to Ann's visitation, along with many people who had worked with Chance at Superior.

Several of Ann's bridge club members came to extend Chance and the family their sympathy.

Their dentist and his assistant came to see Ann and expressed their sympathy to Chance for his loss.

Genell and Judy, the lady who cleaned their house for them every couple of weeks, made plans to come to the house to serve food for everyone after Ann's funeral.

Genell told Chance losing Ann was losing the daughter she never had after being with her for five-and-half years. Genell was having a very hard time with the loss of Ann.

It would be the first night Chance would be in the house all by himself. He didn't know until late Thursday night how much comfort it was having Lee come to be with him right after Ann died. Now, he was completely by himself and thinking about living through Ann's funeral tomorrow. He didn't get much rest and was up early, took his shower, dressed, and drove to the funeral home to have time to be by himself with Ann before her funeral service at eleven.

Chance went from standing next to her casket to sitting down staring at her or sometimes staring off into space; he didn't know what he was going to do without Ann.

As Chance was sitting with Ann, more flowers were delivered to the chapel. They were running out of space in the chapel to put them; finally they decided to start putting the flowers in the back of the chapel until that, too, was filled.

Later, when more flowers came, they placed them in the entrance foyer. Ann would have loved all her flowers.

Kate Olsen told Chance this was the most flowers they had ever had for a service in the chapel; there were even two different arrangements from his old friend Jimmy Kim from Korea.

Their best friends, Doc and Susan Schmidt, came to the chapel well before it was time for Ann's service was to begin, and Chance took them up to see Ann.

The three of them stood by Ann's casket for a long time just remembering all the times the four of them had been together and all the fun they always had had.

Chance went out in the foyer of the chapel and greeted people as they came in; several of his cousins came from Kansas, Illinois, and Indiana, as well as Ann's cousins who lived in Kansas City and a couple of small Missouri towns.

Chance was surprised that so many came from far away to be at Ann's funeral, but just moments before Ann's funeral started, Chance got the biggest surprise when his old boss from World Star Parking, David Metzler and his son Marc came into the chapel.

They told Chance they had chartered a jet and flew in this morning and had a car and driver waiting for their arrival at the Big Springs Airport to bring them to the funeral home.

Chance was so moved that they would do that for him. He had really admired and liked them before; now he loved them.

Chase and Shane and their families held up very well through all of Ann's funeral service although Chance knew they were hurting the same as he was, with the loss of their mother.

Moments prior to the service was to begin, Chance went to Ann's casket, took one more loving look at his love, leaned down, and kissed her good-bye for the last time. He took his seat and then Ann's service began.

Kate and one of her assistants went to Ann's casket and Kate removed all of Ann's jewelry except the new green pin they had bought to go with her pantsuit.

Then they closed and locked the lid on Ann's casket. Chance felt like they were closing the lid on the best part of his life.

Everything went perfectly for Ann's service; everyone did what they were to supposed to do, and each of them did their part well.

After the service was over and Ann's casket had been placed inside the mausoleum and the last prayer had been said, Reverend

Dalton invited everyone to the Clarks' house for lunch as Chance had asked him to do.

All the family and most of their friends came to the house, along with David and Marc who arrived at his house before he did. Chance was pleased so many people came to the house and had something to eat and several folks stayed a long time visiting with him and his sons and their families.

David and Marc were some of the last ones to leave the house to fly back to Washington.

Before David left, he asked Chance to renew his passport so he could go with him to Korea soon. Chance promised David he would do it and thanked them again for coming to be with him.

After they left, Chase and Shane told their dad they couldn't believe David and Marc chartered a jet and flew into Big Springs for Mom's funeral.

After Chance's daughters-in-law, Jan and Marie, helped Genell and Judy clean up the kitchen, Chance's family all left to go home. After Doc and Susan said good-bye, the only one left with Chance was Lee; her husband, Randy, had gone back to their motel with one of their kids earlier.

Lee said, "Chance, I guess you still have a mess to clean up after we're gone but there is still lots of food left for you to eat, so you won't have to do much cooking for a while."

Chance replied, "Lee, thank you. I don't know how I would have been able to do everything without you."

"We're going to leave early in the morning to drive back to Dallas. Randy has an appointment some place in West Texas on

Monday so we won't see you tomorrow."

"Lee, thank you again. I really have appreciated you being here with me, I love you."

Lee gave Chance a hug and a kiss on the cheek and said, "I love you, and it's going to be all right."

Then Lee left, and Chance was alone.

17

CHANCE'S LOST WORLD

After everyone had left the house, Chance drove to the cemetery to see if the people had replaced the front of the mausoleum and to have a chance to talk to Ann alone.

Chance was pleased the front of the mausoleum was back in its place and all secured. Now the only thing they needed to do was to engrave the date of Ann's death of it.

Chance stayed about twenty minutes thinking and talking out loud to Ann; he knew she couldn't hear him, but it made him feel better talking to her anyway.

He told her he didn't know what he was going to do without her: you know you have been my life.

Chance knew the one thing he should never, ever say was to say he wasn't going to do something. Because he always wound up doing it or having to do it, but he said it and meant it, *"The one thing I know is that I'm not going to make any decisions about changing anything in my life for a year."*

Chance returned home and tried to think of all the things he needed to do the next day and decided he couldn't do it tonight.

Saturday morning he went back out to the cemetery to see if everything was OK with Ann's mausoleum and found it was the same as it was when he was there the night before.

He spent about thirty minutes talking to Ann, telling her he missed her and now everybody had gone back home and he was by himself.

Returning home, Chance fixed something to eat and worked at straightening and cleaning up the house from all the folks being there yesterday.

Chance went to the cemetery twice more to check on Ann this day.

Sunday morning he dressed and went to church at the First United Methodist Church for the first time since living in Big Springs and found being there was comforting to him.

Chance felt at home being in this church; it was a much smaller church than what they had been used to in their church in Webster.

When the church service ended, Chance stopped and shook hands with the minister and thanked him again for doing Ann's funeral service.

Reverend Dalton was very gracious and told Chance he was pleased to have him attend church today and hoped he would come back. Chance assured him he would be coming.

After church, Chance went by the cemetery to tell Ann he had gone to church and liked it very much and wished they had started going years ago when they had talked about it.

Chance was back at the cemetery one more time to see Ann that Sunday.

Monday, Chance made a trip to the local Social Security office to let them know Ann had passed away. He didn't want to become involved in paying back any money to Social Security.

Chance had read about people whose Social Security monthly checks kept coming for years before Social Security discovered they had passed away and the people who had gotten the money had to repay the money, plus interest.

Chance knew these people were crooks, but he didn't want to take any chances with Social Security.

Next, he stopped by the funeral home and met with Kate Olsen, paid her for Ann's funeral, and thanked her for the good job they did with Ann's services.

After that Chance drove to the cemetery to let Ann know what he had done this morning.

Chance returned home and began trying to decide what he was going to do with all the equipment they had accumulated over the years that had been required for taking care of Ann.

First, he thought about what he was going to do with his bedroom. He certainly didn't want to keep walking around Ann's hospital bed to go to the bathroom.

He thought about moving the king-size bed he had in the guest room into his bedroom.

Chance and Ann had a king-size bed before Ann needed a hospital bed. They had moved it over to a storage building and then after several years he gave it to his brother.

He decided not to move the king-size bed into his bedroom but to move the hospital bed out and instead of buying another single bed for his room, he would get his old rocking chair out of their storage building and put it in his bedroom.

After getting the hospital bed moved out of the bedroom, Chance brought his rocking chair back from the storage building, bought a cushion set, and put it on the chair. He thought it looked pretty good in his bedroom.

Chance talked to his sons every day and with his son Chase sometimes twice a day. He thought they both seemed to be doing pretty well after losing their mother but knew, too, that people don't always let you know how much they are hurting, including himself.

One day he saw his next-door neighbor, Bill Wilson, and stopped to talk with him and Bill said, "I guess you didn't remember it, but Lynn died on July 23, 2006, exactly one year to the day before Ann did. I figured Lynn needed a good bridge partner and she asked for Ann."

"Bill, I didn't remember that Lynn died on the twenty-third." Bill said, "I'm sorry you lost Ann. She was a wonderful woman." "Thank you, Ann was a wonderful person. She and Lynn sure had a good time when they were together." "Yes, Lynn told me that all the time."

Bill told Chance he had to go; he had an appointment and would see him later.

Chance didn't remember Lynn had died a year ago and certainly didn't remember she died on July 23.

The next project he had was a yard and garage sale he scheduled to try to sell as much of the equipment he bought to take care of Ann as he could, plus to sell a lot of Ann's clothes she had in two clothes closets, as well as other odds and ends around the house.

Chance had asked Genell to come to help him with the sale. She came over a couple of days before the sale date to help him get things ready for the sale. While she was there, Chance gave her one of Ann's diamond bracelets and she really appreciated it.

The day of the sale, Genell had asked her daughter-in-law to come along and help them with the sale. So they had three working the day of the sale and before the day was over they could have used a couple more people helping them.

At the end of the day they had sold all the equipment used to take care of Ann and lots of her clothes and other items. Chance ended up with just over two thousand dollars for all the items sold that day.

All the rest of Ann's clothes Chance loaded up in his van. Chance knew his friend Susan O'Hara had been one of the people who had started a thrift store for the Big Springs Hospital, so he took all the clothes left from the sale there.

Chance's van was totally filled up with all the clothes left over from the sale, so he knew the thrift shop was going to have a nice selection of good clothes to sell.

Chance had been trying to keep himself as busy as he could so he didn't have so much time to think about missing Ann. Sometimes it worked but most of the day and night he thought about things she said and things they did together.

He missed her and was sure he always would.

His son Shane called him one day and said he had a good idea for a business and told his dad about his idea of starting a magazine as a restaurant guide, which listed all the information about when they were open, telephone number, address, type of payments they accepted, and their menus, for four cities in Northwest Arkansas.

Shane said, "One day when we had all the family at our house, we decided to order dinner and couldn't make up our mind about what kind of food we wanted to order. I thought if I just had a restaurant guide with the different restaurants and their menus in it we could have decided what we might want to order.

"I thought since nobody has a guide like that we should make one ourselves and want you to help sell the listing to the restaurants."

"What cities are you talking about, Shane?" "Fayetteville, Springdale, Rogers, and Bentonville."

"How would you distribute them and where would you distribute them?"

"We would send them out to every house and business in the four cities."

"How many books would it take to cover all four cities?"

"I don't know, probably about two hundred and fifty thousand."

"I don't think so, Shane. Besides I live too far away from those cities to work trying to sell the listings."

"Dad, I think it's a good idea anyway."

"I tell you what I'll do. I'll think about it."

Chance didn't understand that Shane was trying to get something for his dad to do so he didn't just give up living after his mother died.

Chance thought about the idea and a few days later called Shane back and told him he would consider trying the magazine idea, but instead of doing it in Northwest Arkansas he would want to do it in Branson, Missouri, and instead of trying to send the magazine to homes and businesses, they would take them to hotels, motels, and resorts.

Shane agreed they should try it in Branson since it wouldn't be such a long drive for his dad to go to work there. Chance wasn't sure about how much he wanted to work trying to sell something again, but he would try it.

18

THE ONLY SURE THING
IN LIFE IS CHANGE

Thursday, August 16, Chance answered his telephone and was pleased to hear an old friend's voice on the other end of the line. It was Susan O'Hara who told him she was in Big Springs to visit some friends and wondered if she could stop and visit him. Chance quickly agreed to her visit and told Susan he would put on a pot of coffee for her.

Susan told him she would be at his house in about an hour, as she was finishing up her visit with her friend Nancy and then she would come to see him.

Chance made sure everything was picked up in the living room and the family room. He was sure that it was, since he was the only one living there but he checked the rooms anyway. He turned on the lamp in the living room and the lights in the two curio cabinets in the combination living and dining room.

Chance went to the kitchen and made a pot of decaf coffee. Then he took a couple of cups out of the kitchen cabinet and sat down waiting for Susan to arrive.

True to her word, Chance saw Susan's car pull into his driveway just an hour later.

Chance opened the door and was waiting at the front door for Susan to come into the house. As was normal for Chance and Susan to do when they met or parted, Chance gave Susan a big hug and told her he was glad to see her.

He invited Susan to sit down in the living room and asked, "Do you still use Sweet'N Low in your coffee?"

"Yes, I do."

"Good, I'll get you some coffee and be right back."

Chance put Sweet'N Low in her cup and poured both of them a cup of coffee.

Chance brought the coffee back into the living room and pulled out a Formica-covered shelf from the end table next to Susan's chair and sat her coffee on the shelf.

Chance sat down on the couch across from Susan and asked how she was doing.

She said, "I'm doing OK. I'm so sorry you lost Ann. I thought the last time I saw her she was doing pretty well."

"She had been. Then that Sunday morning I just couldn't wake her up and she died the next day."

"Chance, I don't go to funerals and I can't make myself send flowers to funerals but I stopped by to see you and see if I could contribute to some cause Ann would like or if you can think of something I could do for you."

"Susan, I am getting ready to order a couple of bronze flower vases for our mausoleum. If you would like to do one of those, it would be great."

"OK, do you know how much they cost?"

"No, I can't but I could let you know after I get them ordered."

"That's fine. Just let me know and I'll send you a check."

They took a sip of their coffee and Susan said, "Chance, you know you're fresh meat now with Ann gone. The widows will start bringing you so many casseroles your refrigerator won't be able to hold them."

Chance kind of smiled and said, "Well, so far I'm still cooking my own food."

Then they spent the next hour talking about Ann.

Susan knew from her own experience after losing her husband, Jack, that people always tried to avoid talking about a lost loved one, when the one who has lost someone wanted nothing more than to talk about them.

After they had a couple of more cups of coffee, Susan said, "I think I'd better get on the road home. I don't want to drive home in the dark, but after three cups of coffee, I think I better use your bathroom before I start home."

Susan went into the bathroom and when she returned to say good-bye to Chance, she found he was in the kitchen putting their coffee cups into the dishwasher.

When Chance came back to the living room Susan was studying the grandfather clock which was not running, and then she saw an anniversary clock in the living room which also wasn't running.

Susan said, "Chance, did you know you have two clocks in here that aren't running?"

Chance looked at the two clocks and replied, "We weren't in this living room very often and I don't know what's wrong with the grandfather clock. I've been able to keep it running for a long time and now I can't.

"I think the anniversary clock just needs a new battery. I haven't spent a lot of time looking after things other than Ann these past few years."

Chance gave Susan another hug and they said good-bye.

Chance walked Susan out to her car and said, "I see you've got a pretty new car. I like red cars."

"Yeah, red cars are my favorite."

Susan got into her car and backed out of the drive as Chance watched until her car turned the corner and he couldn't see her car any longer.

The next day Chance thought about what Susan said about his clocks not running.

He had done everything he could to fix the grandfather clock. He found the name and telephone number for someone who claimed to fix grandfather clocks.

Chance called the clockmaker, who came over that afternoon, and after the clockmaker looked over the clock mechanism, he told Chance he would have to take the works out of the clock and take them back to his shop to fix.

Chance agreed the clockmaker could take the clock mechanism with him.

The following week the clockmaker returned with the clock mechanism and reinstalled it back into the clock. Chance was surprised the cost of fixing his clock was four hundred dollars.

Chance thought back to when his brother Will and he had bought the clock for their parents' thirty-fifth wedding anniversary for about three hundred and seventy-five dollars.

Susan's birthday was August 31 and Chance made an effort to send her a birthday card every year. He thought it would be funny to write in her card "Thank you for costing me four hundred dollars to get my clock fixed."

So he did, because he knew Susan had a great sense of humor and thought she would get a kick out of it.

About a week or so after Susan's birthday, Chance called her to say he was coming to Springfield on Saturday to buy some shoes and wanted to know if she would like to help him pick them out and then he would take her out for coffee.

Susan said, "OK, I can go with you while you buy your shoes. Then maybe you can buy me some coffee, but I can't stay too late, because I'm going to a performance of the Springfield Symphony."

Chance replied, "I've never been to a symphony."

Susan said, "Would you like to go with me if I can get a ticket for you?"

"That sounds great. What time does the performance start?" "Eight o'clock."

"OK, how about I come to Springfield about two o'clock? Then I should have time to buy my shoes, and we can get something to eat before we go to the symphony."

"Chance, I call you back to let you know if I can get you a ticket to go with me."

Susan called Chance back and told him she had a ticket for the symphony for him and would see him Saturday afternoon.

Chance knew Susan was a very good friend to both Ann and him for a lot of years and he liked being with her, so they should have a good time.

Since Chance didn't want to wear a suit to go shopping, he brought a suit and tie with him to wear for the symphony.

He was sure he could change out of his casual clothes at Susan's before they went to dinner and to the symphony. He wasn't used to wearing a suit anymore, as he had done every day for over forty years when he was working.

Arriving at Susan's, he asked her if it would be all right if he brought in his suit and things to change into before they went to dinner and the symphony.

She said, "Sure, it is no problem. You can put your things in my office and change in there after we finish shopping for your new shoes."

They drove to Dillard's department store in the shopping center and made their way to the men's shoe department. Chance knew exactly the shoes he wanted; it was a wing-tip dress shoe made by ECCO.

When Chance told the sales clerk what shoes he wanted and his size, he was surprised when the clerk told him ECCO didn't make the wing-tip shoe anymore.

Well, Chance didn't know what he wanted then, so he asked the clerk to show him dress shoes that ECCO was making. The clerk went to the back store room to locate dress shoes in Chance's size which were made by ECCO.

While the clerk was gone, Chance told Susan his experience about having heel spurs after working in Sao Paulo, Brazil, to lay out parking spaces and walking on their cobblestoned sidewalks there.

Chance said, "When I came back from there, I could hardly put one foot in front of another and went to a podiatrist who told me I had heel spurs and injected cortisone in both my heels. The shots hurt worse than my heel spurs. Anyway after all the pain the shots caused me, they didn't seem to help me much.

"Ann and I went to a shopping center in Overland Park, Kansas, for something she wanted to buy. As I was walking by the men's shoe department in Dillard's, a clerk saw me and said, 'Bet you've got heel spurs and I'll bet you I've got something that can help you.'

"I said to the clerk, 'I doubt that.'

"The clerk then said, 'I've got several clients who were suffering with heel spurs and when I got them to try an ECCO shoe, they started walking a lot better and with a lot less pain.'

"Anyway, Susan, I sat down and the clerk measured my feet and came back with a pair of ECCO wing-tip shoes, put them on my feet, and told me, 'OK, walk around a little and see if the shoes help you.'

"I didn't believe how much better my feet felt walking around in the shoe department, so I bought the shoes and told the clerk I would wear them. My heel spurs went away a short time later and I don't wear any other shoe now."

The clerk returned with a very plain pair of black ECCO dress shoes and Chance told him he didn't like them very much but he bought them anyway since they didn't have the wing-tip shoe he wanted.

After Chance finished his shoe purchase he asked Susan, "Would you like to go have coffee somewhere?"

Susan said, "Yes, I'm always ready for a cup of coffee. In fact, I have a coupon for two dollars off Starbucks Coffee."

Chance looked at Susan a second before answering her and then replied, "I'll tell you what I'll do, I'll pay you two dollars for the coupon and let's go anywhere else for our coffee except Starbucks. Their coffee is too strong for me."

"I agree their coffee is really strong, so we can find somewhere else to have coffee or why don't we go back to my house and I'll make the coffee?"

"Sounds like a deal to me."

They drove back to Susan's house and she made the coffee and they sat and talked until it was time to get dressed and go to dinner and then on to the symphony.

The Springfield Symphony performs at Hammon's Hall and Chance was impressed with the theater and the symphony orchestra was the largest live orchestra he had ever seen.

The music was stirring and Susan was into every movement and seemed to be well versed in classical music.

Chance was strictly into country and western music but was surprised that he enjoyed the music very much. He was pleased Susan had gone to the trouble of getting him a ticket to go with her.

As they left the theater Susan was in a joyful mood as the last piece of music played was one of her favorites.

She was swinging her arms and hands and as they walked along on a beautiful moonlit night, she took Chance's hand in hers and when she tried to take it away, Chance continued to hold on to her hand.

Susan thought to herself, What have I done?

Chance continued to hold her hand until they got to the parking garage, and there he took out his keys and opened the car door for Susan and then went around and got into the car.

Nothing was said on the way back to Susan's house and when they arrived, Susan almost flew out of Chance's car but by the time she got to the front of his car Chance was standing there to thank her for going shopping with him and for taking him to the symphony.

"Susan, thank you so much, I really enjoyed the day."

Chance reached to hug Susan as they had done for years. He gave her a kiss that maybe was a little longer than they ever shared before when they had said good-bye to each other.

Susan almost ran to the door, but she stopped, turned, and said, "Goodnight, Chance, be careful going home."

Susan had vowed never to date anyone after her husband died and hadn't in all the years she had been a widow. She told herself she wasn't really on a date; she was only with an old friend.

Susan had been through the years of pain caring for a sick husband and then to have him die was more pain than she ever wanted to go through again.

Sunday after Chance came home from church, he sent Susan an e-mail thanking her again for spending the day with him and for taking him to the symphony.

They continued to e-mail each other every week and Chance told her in an e-mail he had been invited to a birthday party for him on September 20 at his son's resort.

Susan decided she would call him to wish him happy birthday so she called him on his cell phone just as he was about to cut his birthday cake at Chase's.

They talked only for a couple of minutes, just long enough for her to wish Chance happy birthday. Susan hated talking on the phone after needing to talk on the phone so much when she worked as an executive secretary and she didn't like spending money on long-distance calls either.

Susan asked him to e-mail her a picture with his birthday cake and Chance promised he would do it.

Chase told his dad that it was very nice of Susan to call him on his birthday.

After Chance returned home, he sent an e-mail to Susan thanking her for the call and sent her a copy of his picture with his birthday cake on his seventy-first birthday.

A couple of days later, Susan sent Chance an e-mail telling him she had always wanted to take the train ride at Branson, which made a trip down into Northern Arkansas and then returned to Branson. In her e-mail, she told him she never wanted to just go by herself and wanted to know if Chance would like to go with her. She said she would take him there as a birthday present. She also told him Saturday nights would be the best night for her to go and that they served dinner on the train on that night.

After Chance read Susan's e-mail, he answered it trying hard to be funny and sent Susan an e-mail which said, "You pony up the dough and I'll go."

As soon as he sent that e-mail he thought, Susan is going to think I'm awful. Reading it over the fifth time it sounded to Chance like he was some kind of cad. He was horrified at what he had sent her. Chance quickly sent Susan another e-mail apologizing for the e-mail he had sent her, and then for good measure he called Susan to tell her he was sorry for the flippant way he had responded to her gracious invitation.

Susan couldn't believe Chance was so upset with his answer to her e-mail. She had known Chance for almost forty years and took his response to her invitation the way he had meant it to be, funny. Susan made arrangements for tickets for the following Saturday night and sent Chance an e-mail telling him she planned to come to Branson Saturday and would be staying at the Palace Hotel.

Chance sent her back an e-mail and told Susan he would pick her up at the hotel around five o'clock Saturday afternoon to go on the train ride.

Saturday afternoon, Chance drove to Branson and made his way to the Grand Palace Hotel. He arrived there about fifteen minutes before five o'clock. He found a parking place for his car and waited until it was almost five before going in to get Susan.

Chance picked up a house phone and asked to be connected to Susan O'Hara's room. As soon as the phone rang, Susan answered the phone.

Chance told Susan he was in the lobby and would wait for her there.

A few minutes later Susan came down to lobby and Chance gave her a hug and a light kiss.

He thought she looked very nice and was looking forward to being with her and on their train ride this evening.

Today Chance had bought along his 2002 Thunderbird, which Susan hadn't seen before.

He had the top down and when Chance opened the door for Susan he said, "I can put the top up if you like so it doesn't blow your hair."

Susan said, "No, leave it down. It should be fun driving through Branson with the top down."

As they drove along Highway 76, or the Strip as it was known locally, a lot of people stared at the T-Bird as they drove by.

Susan asked, "Chance, when did you get the T-Bird?"

"In September 2002. I wanted a T-Bird when they first came out in the nineteen fifties but I couldn't afford a hubcap for one of them back then, so when they brought them back in 2002, I bought one. I love it, but it's not a very good road car for a long trip. It rides too rough and doesn't have any room for luggage."

They found a parking place and walked to the train station in old downtown Branson to wait for the time the train was to leave. They realized they were there way too early. There wasn't any place to sit down and the air was really humid.

Susan was trying her best to cool off by using a brochure and fanning herself with it. However, between the heat and maybe the thought of being here with Chance, she thought she was going to pass out.

Chance was worried about her and managed to get her some cool water to drink. It helped some, but she was still having a problem standing in the heat.

At last the train pulled into the station, and an announcement was made they would soon be boarding the train and would everyone please have their tickets ready and to check which train car their tickets were for.

Susan took the tickets out of her purse and handed them to Chance. She didn't like women always being the ones who paid for meals at restaurants and presenting tickets at shows, so she wanted Chance to be the one who took care of their tickets.

They were thankful when they were seated at a table in the train. It was cool, the train left the station right on time, and the meal service was not only good but the food also was terrific.

When Chance found out the meal was provided by the Golden Corral Restaurant he was both surprised and pleased they did such a great job.

The train trip was fun and the scenery in Northern Arkansas was beautiful; they even went through a fairly long tunnel on the trip.

Chance took Susan back to her hotel and asked what Susan planned to do the next day. She told him she planned to stay in Branson for most of the day and do some shopping and look around in different places.

Chance asked if she would mind having company, and she told him she would be delighted if he wanted to come back to Branson the next day and spend some of his day with her. He assured her he did.

When he opened the door of the T-Bird, he gave Susan a hug and a kiss and said, "I think I'm falling in love with you."

Susan didn't have anything to say. She was confused and scared: what had she gotten herself into with her friend? Finally, after she was almost in the hotel she turned and said, "I'll see you tomorrow.

19

WHAT DO WE DO
NOW, COACH?

Chance left the hotel parking lot to drive back to Big Springs thinking, as he drove, about Susan: What was happening with him? Why the change of feeling about his longtime friend?

Maybe he had loved Susan for a long time but certainly not like he was feeling about her now.

He'd only lost Ann a little over two months ago: How could he start feeling about Susan like he did about Ann?

He had loved Ann since they were fifteen years old and had been married to her for more than fifty-four years.

Ann was the only girl Chance had ever even had a date with.

It was craziness to think he could be falling in love with someone else so soon after losing Ann.

Chance discovered young people were not the only ones who could fall in love with someone so quickly.

He was seventy years old and had fallen in love with Susan that quick; maybe it helped that she had been his friend for forty years.

Whatever it was, all he could do was think about seeing Susan again tomorrow.

When Susan left Chance in the parking lot she almost ran to get away from him and when she got into her room she kept thinking, What have I done?

All she was trying to do was to be a good friend and spend time with Chance so he wasn't feeling so alone. She knew too well about how it felt losing your spouse.

How could he tell me that he thought he was falling in love with me?

Susan had been a widow for over seventeen years and wouldn't ever consider dating anyone. She had been through losing her husband of thirty-three years and the heartbreak she suffered after he was gone was more than she ever wanted to go through again; no fleeting bit of happiness would be worth the pain of losing a husband again.

Plenty of men had asked Susan to go out with them but she always said "No" and meant it, because she thought she might fall in love with someone, get married, and lose another husband. No, sir, she never wanted to go through that again; it wasn't worth it!

She told her daughter Christy, "If God wants me to get married again he will have to 'plop' the man right down in front of me."

Susan went to bed trying to sleep but kept thinking, this whole thing is craziness. Susan had her life just the way she wanted it: she had a house she loved and she had her cats and worked for her dad three days a week and looked after him seven days a week.

She had cared for her mother until she passed away a few years earlier and now she was taking care of her ninety-year-old father.

Susan's husband, Jack, had been a diabetic and had a very long history of fighting the disease, with Susan helping him through every painful step. He lost an eye, a leg, and finally both legs.

Then he suffered heart problems and had open-heart surgery. It seemed to her she had been a caregiver for almost all her life. So she didn't need or want another husband to look after and then have him die.

Why would she want another husband?

Both of her kids and her two grandchildren lived in Springfield, so she could see them any time she wanted to. She had loads of friends, she had enough money to buy and do whatever she wanted to do, and she certainly didn't need a husband, no way.

How did she feel about Chance? Well, she liked him for a friend but she wasn't looking for anything more. She didn't get much sleep thinking about Chance and what she was going to do about him?

Morning came both in Big Springs and Branson to two people who didn't have a whole lot of sleep. Since each of them had been thinking about last night what was going to happen today.

Chance made his breakfast and ate it, got ready for the day, ventured outside to pick up the Sunday newspaper, returned to the house, and sat back down at the kitchen table and read his paper. He finished reading the paper about the same time as he drank his last drop of coffee.

It was ten thirty in the morning when Chance backed the T-Bird out of the garage and the T-Bird still had its top down from yesterday. He thought about the drive home last night from Branson with the top of the T-Bird down. It was such a beautiful night with a full moon. It was a magical night. What a glorious ride home in his beloved T-Bird.

The T-Bird was the only expensive possession Chance had ever bought in his life. When he bought it, they already owned a Chrysler Town& Country van, Ann's Chevrolet custom-made handicap van, and a two-year-old Lexus.

Chance had never bought a toy for himself before as so many men did, who bought boats, motorcycles, three-wheelers, four- wheelers, campers, and motor homes.

The T-Bird was strictly his toy.

Chance traded in Ann's Lexus on the Bird, since she was never going to be able to drive it again. He sold the Chrysler Town& Country Van and finally sold Ann's handicap van after she died.

Then he bought an old Lincoln Town Car since he found traveling any distance in the T-Bird hurt his back. It was really only a car to drive around town; it certainly wasn't meant for the road.

The drive to Branson was still very nice this September morning and he found the traffic on 76 was very light compared to last night's traffic when Susan and he were going downtown to the railway station.

By 11:15 a.m. Chance was pulling up in front of the Palace Hotel and was soon talking to Susan on the house phone.

Susan told him she had to check out of her hotel by noon, so she would finish packing her things and be down in the lobby in a few minutes.

Chance found a chair near the elevators to wait for Susan and before too many minutes passed, one of the elevator doors opened and Susan was there.

Chance thought she looked very nice this morning and offered to take her bag out to the car for her. Her lack of sleep didn't show to Chance at all.

Susan gave Chance her bag while she turned her keycard into the front desk. She had prepaid her room for the night, so dropping her keycard off was all she needed to do at the desk.

Susan led the way to her car, which was parked on the west side of the hotel. Chance didn't know there was additional parking for the hotel on the side and also there was more parking at the back of the hotel. Chance placed her bag in the trunk of her car and they went to the front of the hotel where the T-Bird was parked.

Chance opened the door for Susan and handed her the seat belt and Susan said, "You know how bad I hate seat belts?"

"No, I didn't know you hated them. They might save your life someday."

"I still hate them."

They made a right turn out of the hotel parking lot and began driving toward old downtown Branson. Before they had driven three blocks, it started to rain.

Chance pulled into the first parking lot he could get into, stopped, got out of the car, took off the tonneau cover, put it into the trunk, pushed the "raise top" button, locked the top down, and put up the windows.

Then they continued driving in the direction of downtown Branson and it quit raining before they had traveled another five blocks.

Chance said, "Susan, I don't think the weather can make up its mind whether it's going to rain or let us have sunshine."

Susan smiled and replied, "Right now it looks like we are going to have sunshine and I love riding with the top down."

"Me, too. I love convertibles."

When they reached the parking lot at Branson Landing, Chance parked the T-Bird, unlatched the top, pushed the "lower top" button, lowered the windows, popped open the trunk, got out of the car, put the tonneau cover back on, and got back in the car.

Chance asked, "Where would you like to go shopping?"

Susan said, "I would like to go to the Red Roof Factory Outlet Mall, if that's OK with you. There are a couple of stores I would like to go to there."

"Sound good to me. I want to look for a couple of shirts and that should be a good place to do it."

Chance turned the car around and started back down 76 toward the Red Roof Factory Mall and after they were about halfway there, the sky opened up and the rain was just pouring down on them.

As soon as Chance could find a place to get off 76, he pulled into a parking lot and went through the same drill as he did before to get the top put back up.

After the top was up and he was back inside the car Chance said, "You know, Susan, I don't think we want to put the top back down again today. Maybe we will have better luck next time."

Susan had been busy trying to dry herself off and she appeared to agree with him.

They spent the rest of the day together, shopping, having lunch, and talking about everything, without saying anything about how they felt about each other.

It was almost 6:00 p.m. when Chance took Susan back to pick up her car at the hotel to drive back to Springfield. When they arrived at the hotel, Chance was very sorry she was leaving; he enjoyed being with her so much.

Chance walked Susan to her car and after she pushed the button to unlock her doors, Chance opened the driver's door for her, but before she got inside the car she told Chance she enjoyed the day.

Chance said, "Thank you for the train ride and for spending the day with me." He reached over, put his arms around her, and gave her a good-bye kiss.

Then he told her he would call her later to be sure she got home all right.

Susan drove away on her way back to Springfield and Chance followed her down 76 until he turned south on Highway 65 south and she turned north on 65.

Beginning from this weekend on, Chance and Susan talked on the phone if Chance called her, and they communicated by e-mail every day. Susan hated talking on the phone and didn't like to make long-distance telephone calls.

Either Chance went to Springfield to see her or she came to Big Springs.

One weekend, Susan came to Big Springs and planned to stay overnight at the Holiday Inn Express. The two of them planned to have a movie weekend.

Chance, like Susan, had an extensive library of DVDs and videos of movies and they were only going to watch movies and take time out to have something to eat. Chance was a big fan of the John Wayne films so they watched lots of them that weekend.

Chance and Susan sat together on the family room couch to watch the movies. A few times it would have been hard to tell which love scene was better, the one on the screen, or the kisses on the couch.

Chance told Susan she didn't have to stay in the Holiday Inn; she could have used his guest room, but Susan said, "No, I can't. I'm too much of a dinosaur. I can't stay in your house overnight."

Chance understood exactly what she meant and he was just fine with it.

Chance and Susan had a great time watching the movies and kissing on the couch that weekend and it was really hard for Chance to watch Susan leave him to go back home to Springfield.

After Susan left, Chance felt very conflicted about his feelings for Susan after losing Ann such a short time ago. He decided he needed someone to talk to about it and on Monday he made an appointment to meet with his new pastor later in the week.

Chance went to meet with Reverend Dalton and had a frank discussion with him about being in love with Susan and wanting to marry her, but was concerned about getting married so soon after Ann's death and what people would think.

Reverend Dalton was a good listener and said, "Chance, I think the best thing for you to do is to pray about it and then to follow your heart."

Chance replied, "I've been praying about it and my heart is telling me I should marry Susan."

Reverend Dalton said, "Then I think you should follow where your heart is leading you."

After Chance finished thanking Reverend Dalton for his help, Chance made up his mind to ask Susan to marry him.

The following weekend Chance was coming to Springfield and made plans to stay at the La Quinta Hotel in Springfield and planned to talk to Susan about getting married.

Chance spent a lot of time at Susan's house and over coffee he said, "Susan, I think we should get married."

Susan replied, "What would we do if we got married? In the first place, my first commitment in life right now is to my dad."

"I understand that, but I'm sure we can work around being married and you can still take care of your dad."

"I love my cats and I know you're allergic to cats. Your eyes tear up and you start sneezing being in my house for just an hour. What would you do if you're with them all the time?"

"Susan, I don't have all the answers. I just know I love you and want to marry you."

"I think you're just lonesome."

"Susan, I love you and want to be with you all the time. I can't think about anything else."

"OK, I think you're just lonesome, but I'll think about it."

Nothing more was said about the subject of marriage for the rest of the weekend.

As Chance was leaving to go home to Big Springs, Susan walked him to his car. Chance reached for her and held her body as close to his body as possible with his arms around her; he kissed her long and hard and said, "Think about it."

20

TELLING THEIR FAMILY

After several days and daily telephone calls and e-mails three times a day from Chance to Susan, he decided to send Susan an e-mail asking her two direct questions.

He composed the e-mail which ended with these questions: "Do you love me and will you marry me?"

An hour later Chance's telephone rang as he was sitting at his desk; when he answered the phone he heard Susan say, "I do and I will."

Then she hung up the phone.

Chance sat there looking at his phone for a few seconds and then called Susan back. When Susan answered the phone she said, "I knew you would call me back."

Chance replied, "You win. That was the shortest telephone call I've ever gotten in my life and the best one.

"I love you, you know, so let's get married on Valentine's Day.

Where do you want to get married?"

"In my church in Springfield, if that's OK with you."

"Sounds good to me. Tomorrow is Tuesday. Since you're not working for your dad tomorrow, I'll come to Springfield.

"We should see if we can get your church for our wedding on Valentine's Day. Since Valentine's Day is a special day for people to get married, we might not be able to get the church then."

"OK, Chance, I'll see you tomorrow."

Susan hung up the phone again and thought, What did I just do? I said I'd marry Chance, that's what I did.

After Chance finished his phone call, he remembered the statement he made not long after Ann's death: " The one thing I know is that I'm not going to make any big changes in my life for at least a year."

Chance remembered thinking to himself at the time he made that statement to several people. I know better than to make a statement like that because every time I say something like that, it's exactly what I did or had to do.

Early Tuesday morning Chance drove to Susan's house, arriving there a little before nine o'clock.

First, he wanted to be sure she hadn't changed her mind about getting married after talking with him last night.

Second, he needed to see and hold her in his arms; he really loved Susan.

Susan was surprised to see Chance arriving at her front door before nine in the morning but she was glad to see him. As soon as she opened the door she was in his arms and after a long kiss she said, "You really got here early."

"You know, Susan, what they say. 'It's the early bird that gets the worm.'"

"You calling me a worm?"

Susan had a way of twisting statements around to cause Chance and others folks a little bit of squirming and embarrassment. Her quick wit was one of the things Chance loved about her.

However, sometimes he didn't have a smart answer to come back at her with; this was one of those times.

The one defense he had in this kind of situation was to take her in his arms and tell her he loved her, so he did.

Then Chance said, "You like to give me a bad time, don't you?"
"Well, it's pretty easy."

"Yes, I know, but you love me anyway." "Yes, I do."

Susan poured Chance a cup of coffee and they talked for a while and then left to go to Susan's church.

Arriving at the church they first met with the church secretary and booked the church for their wedding on February 14, 2008.

Susan asked if the minster was available and was told he was. Susan introduced Chance to her minister and then Susan told him she and Chance planned to get married and wanted him to do their wedding ceremony for them.

The minister told them he would be glad to marry them and said he normally liked to counsel the couple planning to get married a few times before the wedding.

However, since Susan and Chance had eighty-eight years of marriage between them, he didn't think he was qualified to counsel them.

Susan and Chance now had the church and the minster for their wedding date.

After their meeting, Chance told Susan he would see her Saturday and that he planned to tell his son Chase and his wife, Marie, the next day that they were getting married and he would ask Chase to be his best man.

Susan planned to ask her daughter Christy to be her maid of honor.

The next morning Chance drove to the Trout's Inn Resort to talk with Chase and Marie about Susan and him getting married. The closer he got to their home, the more nervous he became. He didn't know what they were going to think about him talking about getting married so soon after Mom died.

By the time he arrived at the resort, he was literally shaking and when he was getting out of the car he saw Marie coming out of the office door.

When she saw him she said, "Dad, what's wrong with you? You look sick."

Chance answered, "I've got something to talk to you and Chase about."

"Come in, Dad. Are you sick?"

"I have something to tell you and Chase and I just want to tell it one time. Can you get Chase?"

"Sure, Dad, come and sit down at the table in the office and I'll get Chase."

Marie came back into the office with Chase following close behind her.

Chase asked, "What's wrong, Dad?"

"Nothing, I just have to tell both of you something and I don't know what you're going to think about what I'm going to tell you."

"OK, Dad, tell us."

"Susan and I are going to get married next Valentine's day, and I want you to be my best man."

Chase said, "Wow, we thought you were going to tell us you had something wrong with you and you didn't have long to live or something.

"I've been pretty sure you were going to marry Susan for a while. She's all you ever talk about when we're talking on the phone.

"Sure, Dad, I'll be your best man. I'd be honored to."

Hearing Chase's reaction, Chance felt like someone had just lifted two tons off his chest.

Marie said, "Dad, you scared me. I thought when you got out of your car and the way you looked you were going to tell us you were really ill. I'm glad for you and Susan. I think it will be good for both of you."

Chance, Chase, and Marie continued talking about the upcoming wedding and where they were going to live.

Chance said, "Since Susan is still taking care of her father, we'll have to live in Springfield."

A few minutes more passed before Chance said, "I need to go home and write some checks and get them in the mail to pay a couple of bills."

Riding home, Chance thought it went pretty well with Chase and Marie, telling them Susan and he were going to get married.

Now, he only had to tell Shane and Jan he was getting married. He'd asked Chase and Marie not to say anything to Shane and Jan about getting married until he had time to go to Fayetteville to meet with them.

Chance could only hope it would go as well with them as it had with Chase and Marie.

When Chance returned to Big Springs he went directly to the Big Springs diamond store and met with the owner of the store, Charles Stone, and told him he wanted to buy a two-carat diamond engagement ring with matching diamond wedding bands.

Charles checked over his stock and told Chance he didn't have a good two-carat diamond engagement ring, but he showed him one that was one-and-three-fourth carats. Charles told Chance, "It's the best diamond we have in stock. You can just look at the fire and sparkle in that diamond."

Chance agreed the diamond had plenty of sparkle and he liked the matching diamond wedding bands so much he agreed to buy all of them.

The following Saturday, Chance went to Susan's house and after they hugged and kissed hello, he asked Susan to sit down for a minute.

He got down on one knee and said, "Susan, would you marry me?"

Susan answered, "Yes, I will."

Then Chance handed her a ring box with the engagement ring he had chosen for her.

She opened the box and was very surprised he had bought her an engagement ring but decided she loved it. Susan had thought that someday soon they would go together and pick out rings.

Chance gave Susan one more box and Susan couldn't imagine what Chance could be giving her now. When she opened the box she found it contained car keys for Chance's beloved Thunderbird and note saying, "This is your engagement present.

Chance had given her his T-Bird! If she ever had any doubt about him loving her before, this had to prove how much he loved her. She knew he loved that car.

Chance said, "Now all I have to do is to find a way to get up off the floor after being down here on one knee."

They both laughed even knowing it wasn't a very good joke since Chance had problems with his knees. Using the arm of the couch to help pull himself up, Chance managed to get up off the floor.

Later, he took out a third box which held their wedding bands and showed them to Susan.

Susan thought they looked beautiful but hesitated a few minutes before saying, "Chance, I don't know how to say this, but I don't want my wedding band to have diamonds in it. When you put a wedding band on my hand at our wedding ceremony, I never intend to take it off.

"It's all right if you want to have your ring with the diamonds in it, but I only want a plain gold band for me."

"Sweetheart, that's not a problem. In fact they have a plain gold wedding band that matches your engagement ring. We can just exchange this one for the plain one, OK?"

"Great, I love my engagement ring. One more thing, I want to pay for your ring. It's just a Susan thing."

"OK, it's not a big deal to me about who pays for the ring." "It is to me. I want to buy your ring myself."

"OK, sweetheart, while I'm here in town, there's one more thing I want to do today."

"What do you want to do, Chance?"

"I want to go see your father and ask his permission to marry you.

"You know, I think he might like you doing that."

They both got into Chance's car and went to Susan's father's assisted living apartment at Creekside at Elfindale.

Arriving at the apartment complex, Chance and Susan went hand in hand into Susan's dad's apartment.

Her father was surprised to see Susan coming into his apartment and said, "Susan, what are you doing here? It's Saturday." Susan replied, "Well, Dad, I can come over to see you on Saturday. Besides, Chance wants to ask you something."

Mr. Christenson turned his power wheelchair away from his computer and around to face Chance and said, "How are you, Chance?" Chance was speaking louder than normal because of Mr. Christenson's poor hearing and he was a little bit nervous.

Chance replied, "I'm fine. I asked to see you because I wanted to ask you for your permission to marry Susan."

Mr. Christenson was surprised by Chance's question and responded, "I guess that's up to Susan if she will say yes to you, but you have my permission to marry her."

"Thank you, Mr. Christenson. Susan has already said yes but I wanted to have your permission to marry her."

"You've got it."

The three of them visited for a short while more and Susan told her dad, "We have to go, Dad. We have a late lunch date with my son William and his family.

Before they left Chance said, "Mr. Christenson, I want you to know I will do my best to make Susan happy."

This would be the first time Chance would meet Susan's son William and his wife, Wanda, and their two children, Scarlett and Skip.

Chance liked Susan's grandchildren's names, Scarlett and Skip O'Hara.

They met at the Lone Star Steak House and Susan said, "I would like for you to pay for dinner for them, but I want to pay you back since I'm the one who invited them for dinner to meet you.

"That's not necessary. I'll buy their dinner."

"Yes, it's necessary, because I want to pay for their dinner." "OK, love."

When Chance pulled the T-Bird into the parking lot he pulled into a parking space just next to where William's van was parked.

Scarlett and Skip got out of their van and came over to give their grandmother a hug and kiss.

After they greeted Susan, she introduced them to Chance.

Scarlett was twelve and Skip was eleven; both acted older and were very polite when introduced to Chance. Chance liked them immediately, as well as their parents when he met them. He felt William made an effort to be extra nice to him when they were introduced to him by Susan.

The dinner went well and they had an opportunity to get to know Chance a little bit and he got to know Susan's son and his family. Since he already knew Susan's daughter Christy, Chance felt he had received a warm welcome from all of Susan's family and was pleased about that.

The next Saturday, Chance was going to a Clark family reunion and asked Shane to go with him to Miami, Oklahoma.

Chance told Shane that he and Susan were planning to get married on Valentine's Day.

Chance was a little shocked at Shane's reaction to his news. Shane told his dad it was too soon and he wanted him to date Susan for more than a year. He told his dad it was fun dating and getting to know someone before they thought about getting married.

Chance said he was sure that was true for eighteen- to twenty- year-olds but it was a lot different if you were seventy years old and had known the person you were going to marry for over forty years. Shane didn't understand how his dad felt about getting older and how his dad felt about having his wife with him one day and the next day she was gone forever.

Shane didn't realize when his dad made up his mind to do something, whether it was right or wrong, he was going to do it and he was marrying Susan. Who knew how much time Susan or he had to live and be together? They wanted to be together and have as much happiness as they could with the time they had.

Shane and his family weren't happy at all about his dad getting married so soon after Ann died.

Chance returned home after the reunion and after dropping Shane off in Fayetteville.

He called Susan to let her know he was home safely and to tell her about Shane being very upset about them getting married.

Susan was sorry Shane was upset, and she told Chance she was getting concerned about their wedding next year. She had heard from her nieces and many of her friends and other relatives who told Susan they were coming for her wedding and the number was growing daily. There were people coming from several Midwestern states to be there for her wedding.

Susan was afraid her wedding was getting way out of hand with so many people planning on coming, especially since she and Chance were leaving right after the wedding and going to Kansas City for their short honeymoon.

They would only be gone over the weekend, since Susan had to be back at work for her dad the following Monday afternoon.

Susan said, "I was telling my daughter Christy and her husband, Steve, that I was getting stressed out thinking about the wedding with all the people coming and us leaving right after the ceremony.

"I told them I didn't know what to do about it.

"Steve said, 'Mom, why don't you go to Vegas and have Elvis marry you?'"

Chance said, "I don't think I'd want to get married by Elvis, but I kind of like the idea of going to Vegas to get married. I'll look into some of the wedding chapels they have there."

21

It's a Wonderful
Day in Vegas

Chance opened up his computer, got on the Internet, and started searching for Las Vegas wedding chapels and found several of them.

One by one he eliminated chapels until he thought he found the right one; it was called Little Chapel of the Flowers. Chance thought it sounded perfect for Susan and him.

Next, he called Susan and asked her to get on the Internet and check out the web site for a chapel called Little Chapel of the Flowers and see what she thought about it for their wedding.

Susan called him back and told him she thought it looked perfect for their wedding and liked the idea that their kids could watch the ceremony live on the Internet.

Then Chance asked Susan what date in November she wanted to get married, and Susan suggested the twenty-fourth. Susan told Chance that was the date Jack and she were married and it would be exactly fifty years on that day from when she first married and it had been a good marriage.

Chance asked her if it would be OK if they got married a week earlier so they had their own date. Susan agreed but thought it would have been nice to get married on the same date fifty years later than her first marriage.

Susan booked the chapel for their wedding but they had only a few choices about the time of day available to be married on that day. After talking about it with Chance, they took the 9:00 a.m. time slot. They hadn't realized the chapel would be so busy with people getting married all day and into the evening.

Chance made reservations for them on Allegiant airlines leaving Springfield on Friday, November 16, at seven thirty in the evening, arriving in Las Vegas at 9:00 p.m.

He also booked a room at the Luxor Hotel and Casino for them, beginning on Friday night and checking out Monday.

They would be flying back on the same airline, leaving at 2:00 p.m. on Monday and arriving back in Springfield at 7:00 p.m. Susan made arrangements with the lady, who normally worked Tuesday afternoons taking care of her dad, to switch to Monday and Susan would work on Tuesday.

When Susan told her kids Chance and she had decided to go to Las Vegas to get married and asked her kids not to come to her wedding, they were not happy about it at all.

Susan was afraid if her kids came to the wedding, several of her nieces and their families would decide to come and then she would be right back to trying to entertain people while she was getting married.

Chance's kids were happy enough not to be going to their wedding.

Chase and Marie had a hard time getting away from the resort and Shane and Jan didn't want dad to get married so soon.

The following Tuesday Susan called Chance and told him she and her daughter Christy were driving around some neighborhoods in Springfield and she said she thought she might have found a house for them.

Chance told Susan he would come to Springfield on Thursday and asked if she would call and make an appointment for them to see the house. She did, and they had an appointment for 1:30 p.m. on Thursday to look at the house.

Chance drove to Springfield Thursday morning and after they had lunch at Perkins Restaurant, they drove to the house to meet the salesman who had the house listed.

When they arrived and spoke with the salesman he told them the house had been on the market for a while and thought they could make a good buy on the house if they liked it.

They liked the location of the house, which was just off one of the major streets in the city, and still close to Susan's dad.

When they went into the house they found it had three bedrooms, two baths, living room, and a small kitchen with eating space on the first floor of the house, as well as a three-car garage. Downstairs, there were two more bedrooms, a full bath, and a very large family room with a walk out into the backyard.

From the front of the house it didn't look like a house with almost four thousand square feet of living space.

The two of them really needed a house this size, right? This house was bigger than any house either of them had ever lived in even when they had families.

They liked the house and decided to buy it without looking at another house. They made an offer on the house for a few thousand dollars less than the asking price and the owner accepted it.

Now, between them they had three houses!

Chance had a twin bed in his bedroom and Susan had a regular full-size bed in her bedroom. They needed a bedroom suite with a bigger bed for the master bedroom. No problem, they drove to Furniture Row and bought a large bedroom suite with a king-size bed.

They were closing on their new house on November 14, and their new bedroom suite would be delivered on November 15.

They were flying to Las Vegas on November 16, and when they went to the airport to check in for their flight, they had accomplished everything they had planned to do.

They had bought and closed on their new house, listed both of their houses for sale, had their new bedroom suite delivered and set up, and they were plenty early for their flight to Las Vegas to get married.

Their plane was scheduled to leave at 7:30 p.m. However, their plane was delayed coming in from Orlando and they didn't board their plane until almost nine o'clock Springfield time.

Chance had checked online on the office hours of the license bureau and found the office now closed at midnight due to cutbacks in the county's budget. In the past, the license bureau office had been open twenty-four hours a day, but not anymore.

Chance figured with the two-hour time difference between Springfield and Las Vegas they would still be able to make it to the license bureau without any problem. Once they were in the air the flight went smoothly enough and they landed not too much after nine Las Vegas time.

It seemed like it took them forever to make their way to the baggage claim area and then they couldn't find the right carousel for their flight to reclaim their luggage. Chance kept going from one carousel to another each time the luggage started coming out onto a carousel.

Susan went to a carousel she thought was going to be the one that the luggage was coming on for an Allegiant Air flight. Chance had given up finding their luggage when he saw Susan dragging both of their bags from the carousel she had been waiting by.

Chance went to her as quickly as he could because it was now 10:40 p.m. and they still needed a taxi to take them to the license bureau to get their marriage licenses. They exited the terminal to the taxi stand and Chance saw the largest number of people waiting to get a taxi he had ever seen at an airport anywhere in the world.

They dutifully got into line and after being in the line for a taxi for five minutes and not moving a foot, Chance could see they were never going to be able to get to the license bureau in time to buy their marriage license before it closed at midnight if they didn't do something besides standing in this taxi line.

Chance told Susan, "Let's go find a limo so we can get to the license bureau before they close." It took them less than five minutes to get a limo and they were on their way.

The driver knew what he had to do to get them to downtown Las Vegas without going on the Vegas Strip and he pulled the limo up in front of the license bureau at eleven forty-five: they were going to make it on time.

Chance and Ann rushed into the office of the license bureau and were able to get someone to help them right away and they were back in the limo before twelve midnight and on their way to the Luxor Casino and Hotel.

Arriving at the hotel Chance gave the driver a hundred-dollar bill and thanked him for getting them to the license bureau in time to pick up their marriage license.

New York was known as the city that never sleeps but Chance decided Las Vegas was no different; at twelve forty-five in the morning the city was jumping.

When Chance and Susan got inside the hotel to check in for their room they had to wait in another line before getting their room keycard. Chance told Susan, "I see it doesn't pay to come to Vegas late Friday night. All the times I've been to Vegas I've never had to wait so long to get a taxi or get my room."

When they got to their room, Chance had to call the chapel and leave their room number for the limo driver who was to pick them up later this morning and take them to the Little Chapel of the Flowers for their wedding ceremony.

As they were getting ready to go to bed Chance said, "Three weeks before Ann died, as I was walking around the foot of her bed after finishing all the things I needed to do to get her ready for the night, she asked me, 'If something happens to me would you go with Susan?'

"Her question really took me by surprise and I thought a second and said, 'Susan! Susan! We're way too much alike.' Ann never brought it up again."

Susan wasn't too happy with Chance saying *Susan! Susan!* like it was a bad thing.

Then she told Chance that a long time ago, she and Ann had been somewhere while he was working in Australia, China, or someplace far away, and this was years before Ann became paralyzed, and she had said to Susan, "If something ever happens to me I want you to marry Chance and take care of him."

Susan laughed and told Chance she said to Ann, "No way, we're too much alike."

"Well, Susan, I guess Ann is getting her wish."

A few short hours later, Chance was up and dressed, and since they didn't have a coffeemaker in their room, he went down to the lobby level to get some coffee for Susan because he knew she loved her coffee.

Arriving at the lobby area Chance found the only place he could easily get coffee for Susan was at Starbucks. It was against everything he felt in his heart to buy Starbucks coffee but he knew Susan would need her coffee this morning, so he ordered the mildest coffee he could get.

Chance got several packets of Sweet'N Low which he hoped might cover up the flavor of Starbucks coffee enough for Susan.

By the time he got back to their room, Susan was up and had had her shower and was getting dressed.

He came over to her, put her coffee down on the bedside table, took her in his arms, and kissed her good morning.

After their embrace and kisses Susan said, "Thank you for my coffee. I needed it."

"You're very welcome, my love. I'm sorry it's Starbucks, but it was the only coffee I could find this morning, but I brought you a lot of Sweet'N Low so maybe you can drink it with extra sweetener."

"I'll manage, it's coffee."

Chance took a quick shower, shaved, and got dressed in his best suit which was too big after he had lost thirty-five pounds over these past six years.

He and Susan had found a tie and pocket square in silver, which matched Susan's dress.

Susan loved giving cards for every occasion and their wedding day was certainly a very special occasion so she gave Chance a card and inside the card was a poem she had written, which read:

My dear, dear cowboy

As we say the words today that begin our life together,
I pray we' ll be happy and safe, no matter the weather
Bright sunny skies or dark gloomy rain
This is our chance to begin to love again.
Whatever the future holds and for however long
You've made me feel that I truly belong
In the world of couples who have paid their dues
In a world that has always marched in twos.
We affirm our chance to begin anew
No matter the tears, the problems, the sorrows
That will surely, somehow, march into our tomorrows
We have family and friends to share our joy
In a love that life's knocks cannot destroy
So hang tight, sweetheart, it may be a wild ride
But we' ll be all right if we stay side by side.

Susan handwrote at the bottom of her typed letter: *I love you with all my heart now and always! Hugs, Susan*

After Chance read Susan's wonderful card he gave her a kiss and thanked her, and also being a Virgo like her, Chance handed her a wrapped package. When Susan took hold of the package it felt as if it had a picture frame in it and when she opened it she found it was a gold picture frame. However, it didn't have a picture in it but a letter Chance had written for her; it read:

Susan My Wife

November 17, 2007, we begin a new life together. We've each had wonderful loving spouses in the past, but now it is our turn as husband and wife to find our own way together as mates, lovers, and partners for the rest of our lives.

We both thought we could never find a love like we had before, but God was kind and merciful to us and in his own way brought us to be together. We didn't believe it at first that it could be love, just friendship from days and years gone by. Then, wow, we found we were so deeply in love it couldn't be denied even if we tried.

Now you are my wife, my love, and my life. From this day forward you come first in my life until we leave this earth. No one or nothing will come before you. The past will only be the past. Though it's filled with loving tender memories it can't be above you, my love, for here you are and here you'll stay, first in my heart and deed.

No one knows how much time we have to be together so it's important to be together, laughing and loving every day. We must be patient with one another because we're new together we won't always agree, but together we'll work it out so neither seems a fool. Life is far too short to spend it in woe and worry. It's better to spend it laughing and loving and sometimes even forgiving.

Just one thing for you, my dear wife and friend, to know, I'll always be there for you no matter what life throws at us. Together we'll find a way to make the day bright and cheery. Live one day at a time is all we have to do. Then we can cherish the day when it is through. We'll laugh and love a lot. You'll see then you will always be proud to say my name is Susan, I'm the wife of Chance, who loves me dearly.

Susan, my dear wife, you are so precious to me. Even on this day that we wed you' ll always be the girl I love, want, and need to eternity. To the world you may be called Mrs. Clark, which will be right enough, but to me you will always be, my Susan, my love, my wife, and now my life. This little poem is all I can say to tell you how proud I can say now, this is my wife Susan Serene Clark. I' ll love you forever.

November 17, 2007
Luxor Hotel and Casino
Las Vegas, Nevada

My Love Always
Chance Clark

Susan wasn't surprised Chance had written something for her on their wedding day but was pleased he had his poem framed for her. She knew exactly where she was going to hang it, right next to her side of their new bed.

The two of them hadn't been dressed and finished with reading their poems for very long when their room telephone rang.

It was their limo driver and he was waiting for them in the lobby. The limo ride didn't take long and soon they were pulling into the driveway of the Little Chapel of the Flowers.

Susan and Chance thought the chapel looked nice; in fact, it looked just like the picture they had posted on their web site. This certainly wasn't true of some places they had seen on web sites that didn't look nearly as good when they saw them for real as they did on their web sites.

Inside the building they were met by a lady who showed them to an office and told them their minister would be with them in a few minutes. She was right because a few minutes later the minister who would be performing their wedding ceremony came into the office.

He introduced himself to Chance and Susan and when he heard they were from Springfield, Missouri, he told them he attended seminary in Springfield and was ordained as a minister there.

The minster asked if they had their marriage license and Susan gave it to him. The minister filled out all the information to have the State of Nevada send them copies of their certificate of marriage.

The minister talked to them a while, wanting to know if they had written their own wedding vows or if they wanted him to do a traditional wedding ceremony. They wanted the traditional wedding ceremony.

The minister said they would be ready to begin the ceremony in a few minutes; he just had to check if their photographer was ready for them. He was back a couple of minutes later and said everything was ready.

They approached the actual chapel where they were to be married and the photographer met them at the chapel door and told them to wait until the minister was in his position at the altar and then the wedding march would begin.

Then they should go directly down the aisle, arm in arm or holding hands, to where the minister would be waiting for them.

The minister was now in his place and the wedding march began.

Chance and Susan went down the aisle arm and arm with huge smiles on their faces.

As they arrived at the altar in front of the minister he began the service and their photographer was taking photos of them all during the ceremony.

The ceremony was going perfectly until the minister asked Chance, "Chance, do you take Susan to be your lawfully wedded wife, to have and to hold from this day forward, in sickness and in health, in poverty or wealth till death you do part?"

Chance broke up laughing and he was trying very hard not to, but two things made him laugh: first he'd never heard the words "in poverty or wealth" in a wedding ceremony; the words he had always heard before were "for richer or poorer" and he was always teasing Susan by saying "you poor girl" and her response was always "I'm not poor."

Chance regained his composure and finally was able to answer, "I will."

The rest of their wedding went fine, and of course, Susan had no problem responding to the minister when she was asked in the same way.

They kissed at the end of the wedding ceremony. Then they almost flew down the aisle and out of the chapel with even bigger smiles than they had going down the aisle to get married.

After their wedding, the photographer took several more pictures of them outside, using different settings as backdrops for their pictures around the grounds of the chapel.

When the photographer finished taking their pictures, she took them into her studio and after only a few minutes she was able to show them all the pictures she had taken during and after their wedding.

They chose to buy a lot of the pictures she took, and the finished pictures would be sent to them.

The limo driver took them back to the Luxor and they had a small lunch. When they returned to their room, they found they had received a box made of solid chocolate with pieces of chocolate candy inside from Chase and Marie wishing them all the best on their wedding day.

They spent the rest of the afternoon talking and walking around the Las Vegas Strip going to one casino after another. They weren't having much luck playing the slot machines but they thought they had very good luck finding and marrying each other.

During lunch Chance made a reservation for their wedding night dinner at the steak house in the Luxor Casino.

They arrived at the steak house that evening and when the staff found they had just been married that morning, they couldn't have been more attentive if we had been the king and queen of England. And the dinner was spectacular, the champagne was exquisite, the salad was fresh and delicious, the steak with a slab of blue cheese on the top of it was heavenly, and a scoop of ice cream topped it all off.

Then their coffee at the end of the meal was great and it sure wasn't Starbucks.

When they made their way to their room Chance said, "This was one of the best days of my life."

22

LIFE AFTER MARRIAGE

Chance and Susan returned to Springfield and had lots to do since the only furniture they had in their new house was the bedroom suite moved in the day before they left for Las Vegas and they had two houses chock-full of furniture and their collections.

Tuesday and Wednesday Susan went to work at her dad's as she had planned to do, and on Thursday they had been invited to Chase and Marie's for Thanksgiving dinner at the resort.

They drove to the resort on Thanksgiving morning and had a very nice time visiting with Chase and Marie. The dinner was excellent and everyone had more than enough to eat. Marie had fixed Chance's favorite pie, chocolate, of course, along with pumpkin and apple pies.

On the way back to Springfield they stopped by Chance's old home and loaded up the car with lots of Chance's clothes.

Chance and Susan surveyed the furniture in each room and tried to decide how much of it would work in their new home.

Chance had collections of different types of Santa Claus, David Winter's English Cottages, and items he had collected from all the countries he had visited while traveling the world. In addition, he had a lot of tools and a huge collection of paintings and pictures.

When Susan opened up some cabinets in a room adjacent to the kitchen where Chance had dishes and glasses stored, which Ann and he had bought or inherited, Susan almost gasped at the number of glasses.

They decided Chance had a lot of furniture and things they couldn't use in their new home and they hadn't looked over the furniture and things Susan had in her house yet either.

Between the two of them, they had one heck of a lot of things to get rid of and with both of them being collectors they were going to have to work out where they were going to put them.

Susan had a collection of nativities, cups and saucers, plus all kinds of items she had bought on her international travels.

The following morning when Susan woke up she told Chance, "I had a horrible dream last night that all of your dishes came out of the cabinets like the scene in the Disney movie *Beauty and the Beast,* where the dishes and glasses came out of the cupboards and flew all around. Your dishes were chasing me."

Chance talked with Shane and asked him if he thought Shane's stepdaughter Joanna could use any of the furniture. Shane was sure she could. Shane called back a few minutes later and told Chance that Joanna wanted the furniture. Shane would rent a truck and come over to the house and take the furniture and other household items to Fayetteville. That would take care of most of the furniture Chance and Susan didn't want to move into the new house.

Chance made arrangements with the moving company Two Men and a Truck to move the items from his home they had decided to move from his house in Big Springs to Springfield. This took up one whole day.

Chance made sure not to have all of his dishes and glasses moved to Springfield so Susan wouldn't have to worry about them chasing her around the house.

Next, they had Two Men and a Truck move the things from Susan's home over to their new home. Since Susan had a much smaller house and they only had to drive a few blocks from her old house to the new home, it only took about three hours to complete this move.

The following week Shane and Jan came to Big Springs and met Chance there. They loaded out everything left in the house to go to Fayetteville. Now both houses were cleaned up and empty.

Less than a month later they had sales contracts on both of their houses and sold them very close to their asking prices. So they did well selling their old homes.

Susan continued to work for her father and Chance was going to Branson the three days a week Susan was working, trying to get the magazine started that he and Shane called *The Eateries Restaurant and Show Guide.*

Chance had been lucky to find a couple of good people to do most of the selling of ads for the magazine and he worked at getting the hotels, motels, and resorts to put them into their rooms.

Shane managed to get the magazine laid out and to the printers in time for him and his dad to deliver them to the hotels just a week or so after the Memorial Day weekend.

They didn't sell nearly enough ads to pay for the commissions for selling the ads or to pay the printer so Chance and Susan lost money on the business that year.

In the fall of 2008 Chance and Susan took a trip called the *Grand Tour of France.* It was the first tour Chance had ever been on even though he had been to France many times before, always working, never as a tourist.

They began the tour by flying into Paris and their hotel was only a few steps away from the Eiffel Tower. It was a nice hotel and they loved spending time visiting the Eiffel Tower.

The tour took them all around the famous sights of Paris, including a night boat ride on the Seine River. Although it was a rainy night, Paris by boat was very romantic and they loved all the bridges they passed under.

Seeing the Eiffel Tower lit up with blue lights was spectacular; it was lit that way because France at that time was the lead nation of the European Nations.

They visited the Louvre, of course, and during their visit someone stole something in the area they were visiting. Suddenly, alarms rang, doors and gates swung shut, and they were trapped in the area they were in for about thirty minutes. They never found out what was stolen or if they caught the guilty person.

Before they left their Paris hotel they traveled by bus to Versailles Palace. They loved the gardens there but were so disappointed when they went into the famous Hall of Mirrors because they had on display a huge, hot-pink, plastic-looking dog. They couldn't understand why it was allowed because no matter how much the artist paid to have it on display, it ruined the whole effect of this magnificent room.

From Paris they went by one of the French fast trains to the southeast of France. It took two-and-a-half hours to arrive there and it took two days for their tour bus to come from Paris to meet them. The ride on the train didn't seem to be going so fast until Chance and Susan started looking at the telephone poles along the rail line: the telephone poles were just a blur.

When Susan tried to take a picture from the train the picture turned out to be nothing but a blur. Even her fast camera couldn't capture a decent picture.

The tour took them to several chateaux and quaint towns, like St. Michel built out into the sea, but the highlight outside of Paris for Chance and Susan was visiting Normandy Beach and seeing how hard it had been for American troops to make the landing to free Europe.

Chance's Uncle Tommy was one of the men who had made the landing and lived to come home. His Uncle Tommy had five Bronze Stars for the major battles he lived through in Europe.

They truly loved the trip and Chance thoroughly enjoyed his first visit to France as a tourist.

Before Susan and Chance were married, Susan told Chance her favorite thing to make in the kitchen was reservations for dinner.

This wasn't a problem for Chance, who had spent most of his life traveling for his work and living in hotels and eating in restaurants. Even when he got home, Ann would say, "Let's go out to eat," and that was always fine with him.

Susan did always want to make two big meals every year and those were Thanksgiving and Christmas dinners. Both Susan and Ann were fine cooks but they had their fill doing it for their family over a lot of years and were just tired of cooking. Who could blame them?

23

LIFE AND LOVE TOGETHER IS FUN

Chance and Susan discovered being too much alike actually worked out very well for them.

They both loved traveling and going to new places and would have liked to take more than one major trip a year, but as long as Susan was looking after her father they didn't want to be away from him more than three weeks a year.

Chance and Susan both loved baseball. However, Susan, in general, was *not* a sports fan nor was either of her children or her grandchildren.

Chance loved to watch football games and college football and basketball games on TV. Susan bought Chance a sign to go over the TV that read "*Life is a game FOOTBALL IS SERIOUS.*"

Chance watched his games on TV and Susan read books.

Chance liked writing books much better than reading them.

Susan loved to give Chance things and one thing she gave him was a sign he hung in his upstairs office which read *LOVE YOU MORE!* which was what she was always telling Chance.

They found both of them liked the St. Louis Cardinals and although Chance had been a fan of theirs since he had listened to their games on the radio with his mother when he was only six years old, he had never been to a game to see them play.

Susan had been to several of their games, going on bus tours sponsored by the local Springfield radio station *KTXR* which carried all of the Cardinals' games.

So Chance and Susan made a trip to St. Louis in order for Chance to see his first Cardinals' game in 2011. It turned out to be a great time to see his first Cardinals' game, since they went on to win their eleventh World Series later that year. Eleven in '11. Great! Chance loved playing slot machines. He wasn't often a big winner but he loved to play them anyway. Susan had gone several times to Las Vegas where she enjoyed playing the slot machine herself but was much more cautious about how much money she would play.

Then Chance introduced her to the Oklahoma Indian casinos around Miami, Oklahoma, and she soon loved playing there because she could go for a day and be home in her own bed later the same night, not like going to Vegas.

Chance continued working with Shane doing *The Eateries Restaurant and Show Guide* for Branson, Missouri, and Susan continued to work three days a week for her father. She began spending much more time each week helping to care for him even though he had full-time help twenty-four hours a day, seven days a week.

The two of them loved their house and decided in 2009 to remodel. They were lucky to find a great contractor to oversee the work. They expanded the size of their house by another one thousand square feet, on two levels.

The addition gave them a nice size dining room, a larger living room, and larger kitchen with an eating space for the two of them, and they remodeled the two upstairs bathrooms, added an elevator for Chance so he didn't have to walk up and down the stairs to their lower level with his bad knees, plus they added a second, larger office downstairs for him, a spa room for Susan, and a very large patio.

It was amazing to them that when the project was completed, from the front of their house it didn't appear to have changed. It took nine months to complete the project so it took away their normal vacation time in 2009.

Susan loved to send cards and when her family and friends had a decade birthday, she would send them a card to arrive every day for a full week before their big day.

Chance knew Susan's seventieth birthday was coming up on August 31, 2009, so he thought he should try to do something special with cards for her on her decade birthday. He was pretty sure no one had ever done something like this for one of Susan's decade birthdays.

Chance thought if she could send a week's worth of cards for her friends' decade birthdays, he would buy her thirty-one cards to give to her for her seventieth birthday.

Each day for the month of August 2009, Chance had a birthday card sitting alongside the morning coffee he made for her. Chance had made her coffee every morning since they had been married.

She loved the thoughtfulness of the daily cards delivered next to her morning coffee for a whole month, and he duplicated her cards only one time during the thirty-one days.

Susan did have a great birthday in 2009!

Chance enjoyed making and bringing Susan her morning coffee; it seemed to Chance such a small gesture for all the things Susan did for him.

❦

In 2010, their travel plan was to rent a newer car to take a road trip to see a lot of the western part of the USA. The trip was planned to take them from Springfield, Missouri, to Sioux City, Iowa, on the first day.

One thing they did when they took a driving trip was to play a kid's game Chance called *Horse.* It was a simple game where each one of them counted the number of horses they saw on their side of the road, scoring one point for each horse they saw on their side of the road, ten points for a white horse and five points for a horse with a rider or for a Clydesdale.

Susan loved the Budweiser Clydesdales and they had visited the Budweiser Clydesdales' breeding farm, Warm Springs Ranch, near Boonville, Missouri, to see them. It was a great place to be able to see them and stand next to them. They were magnificent animals, so they earned extra points.

If you had a cemetery on your side of the road, you lost all of your horses and had to start over at zero; the game ended when you reached the destination city for that day. Because it was easy to lose track of the number of your horses, Susan kept a scratchpad in the car to keep score.

So it was only a kid's game, but it gave both of them something to do to pass the miles away and they saw a lot more of the countryside while looking for horses.

Besides, it was better not to try to be too old; just maybe you might live a little bit longer if you were playing like kids.

On day two, they drove across South Dakota from Sioux City to Rapid City and spent a couple of days there. They made the obligatory stop at Wall Drug Store before arriving at Rapid City. Chance hadn't been there in a long time and was surprised how much larger and better it was now.

They enjoyed seeing the full-size bronze statues of US presidents in the downtown area of Rapid City. They were really very well done and Susan had a ball taking pictures of every one of them.

From Rapid City, they traveled to Custer State Park to see the large herd of buffalos, well, Chance had bragged about how large a herd of buffalos they had there, and at the very entrance to the park, a nice large buffalo was standing just inside the cattle guard, used to keep the buffalos inside the park.

After driving every road through the park, they never saw another buffalo.

Chance had been there several times in the past and sometimes you could hardly drive through the park because of all the buffalos. Susan was *never* going to forget to give Chance a bad time about the "largest herd of buffalos in America," yeah, what buffalos?

The next stop was in Deadwood, South Dakota, in the Black Hills. From there they visited Mount Rushmore, which had changed so much since the last time Chance and Susan had been there, they didn't recognize anything about except the carvings of the presidents. The facilities were so much bigger and nicer then when Chance was last there.

The next day they went to see the Crazy Horse Monument; it too had changed so much since Chance and Susan had been there with their families. All the facilities had been improved greatly and the only problem was it was so foggy they couldn't see the monument at all.

The next stop was in Hot Springs, South Dakota, to visit the Mammoth Museum. It was a wonderful opportunity to see the bones of these huge creatures who once roamed the area of what is now South Dakota. They were so much larger than the present-day elephants in Africa, unbelievable.

Chance and Susan's next stop was to be in Cody, Wyoming, to visit Buffalo Bill's Museum. Before they could get that far though, they had to stay all night in Greybull, Wyoming. The trip from Sheridan to Cody proved to be just too far to make it all the way because of crossing the mountains coming through the Bighorn National Forest on Highway 14.

The following day they made the drive into Cody and visited Buffalo Bill's Museum and stayed in Cody overnight.

The next morning they left Cody and entered Yellowstone National Park at the East Entrance and drove north through the park. They couldn't believe how much the park had been damaged from the fire back in 1988.

They drove on to West Yellowstone, Idaho, and stayed the night. When they awoke the next morning, their car had four inches of snow on it. This is June. What the heck is it doing snowing this time of year?

They found out later in the day that the East Entrance to Yellowstone National Park was closed and all the roads in the north part of Yellowstone National Park they drove on yesterday were all closed due to the heavy snow.

After Chance cleaned the snow off the car, they left to drive back into the park and found a large number of buffalos along the roadway.

Susan said, "I guess the buffalos moved from Custer State Park to Yellowstone National Park."

As they were both laughing, Chance replied, "Yeah, smartypants, it looks like they did." Which made both of them laugh even harder.

They drove to Yellowstone Lodge and had lunch there.

Then went outside to watch Old Faithful and sat down on benches to wait for it to erupt. They sat there and sat there and sat there, waiting in the cold, windy weather until it went far past the time it was expected to erupt. Chance said, "Honey, I think it's froze up and if it hasn't, certainly every part of me has."

"Chance, we can't come to Yellowstone and not see Old Faithful erupt."

Although his heart wasn't in it, he agreed to stay and wait. They waited another ten or fifteen minutes and finally a little spurt of water spewed out of the ground and then another little spurt and finally it began erupting, sending water high up into the sky and blowing spray over on to the people who were watching it, including Chance and Susan.

Slowly the eruption ceased and they made their way to the car and turned the heater on as hot as it would go.

They soon headed out of the park headed to Jackson, Wyoming, driving past the Grand Tetons, but they were very disappointed since rain was blocking any kind of view of the Tetons.

They stayed overnight in Jackson and walked around town so Susan could take pictures of the park which was located in the center of town. There, a nice lady offered to take both of their pictures at the entrance to the park. The park had a beautiful arch formed out of deer or elk antlers over the sidewalk leading into the park.

Leaving Jackson they drove south to Kemmerer, Wyoming, the town where J. C. Penney opened his first store, and their next stop was in Vernal, Utah. The following day they left Vernal, Utah, and drove into Western Colorado to get to Moab, Utah. It was the shortest route Chance could find to go there.

Staying in Moab they discovered the town and surrounding area was used in a lot of motion pictures and many of the town's people had been extras in these movies.

The stayed for two nights in Moab, visiting Arches National Park the day after their arrival in Moab, and the next morning they continued their Utah National Park tour.

They visited Canyon Lands National Park, Capitol Reef National Park, Grand Staircase-Escalante National Monument, and lastly, Zion National Park.

All the national parks were interesting and each had its own different features and personality, but Chance thought Arches and Zion were the most interesting. Susan was a big fan of Bryce Canyon.

Leaving Utah, they headed to Las Vegas where they spent the next two days and nights before leaving for Arizona.

When they passed through Boulder City they thought they would have a chance to stop at Hoover Dam but due to construction of the new bridge across the dam and the traffic, the best they could do was to just get over the dam on the way to the new Skywalk overlooking the Grand Canyon.

Getting to the new Skywalk proved to be a horrible experience. Driving over more of a trail than a road, some of the holes in the road were half the size of their car and due to the amount of dirt on their car when they arrived at the Skywalk, you couldn't tell what color their black car was.

The Skywalk was made of special steel and glass made in Germany and Chance wasn't too wild about going out on it in the first place. Chance didn't like taking risks any time and standing on a piece of glass over the Grand Canyon sounded like a risk to him.

Susan was determined to get her opportunity to walk around on the Skywalk but didn't like the idea she couldn't take pictures on it since the folks who ran the Skywalk would be taking your picture. This way they could get a lot more of your money.

When they got ready to go onto the Skywalk, they found you were not allowed to take anything on it with you.

You had to leave your bags, purses, cameras, and cell phones in a locker and put some cloth booties over your shoes to walk out onto the Skywalk. Also, you could only stay on it for a short amount of time.

Chance thought looking down through the Skywalk glass, even if the Germans made it, didn't make him feel any better about being up this high over an arm of the Grand Canyon and walking around on glass. Chance did feel that the Skywalk was an engineering wonder and to be able to suspend something as big and heavy as the Skywalk out over an arm of the Grand Canyon was quite a feat.

Susan, on the other hand, loved it and would have spent a lot more time on the Skywalk if they had let her.

When they finished their time on the Skywalk, they visited the gift shop and looked at the pictures that were taken by the Skywalk personnel and, of course, they bought the picture. It cost $30 for one picture and it didn't even show the glass walk!

Susan couldn't take pictures of the Skywalk when she was on it, so she took several pictures of the Grand Canyon and of the Skywalk from the ground.

When they left the Skywalk, they had to drive back down the same horrible road; no, it was a trail they came on, it certainly wasn't a real road.

By the time they got to Kingman, Arizona, and before they checked into their hotel for the night, Chance stopped and washed the dirt off their car.

Leaving Kingman, they drove to Flagstaff, then took Highway 89 traveling to Highway 160, then going on to Four Corners.

The only site where the corners of four states come together in the United States, thus named Four Corners, is the borders of the states of Utah, Colorado, Arizona, and New Mexico.

After hours of driving, they arrived at Four Corners and found it was all fenced off due to construction to build a gift shop and snack bar, so Chance didn't get the opportunity to stand on four states at the same time. Susan had been there several times before, so she had had that experience.

So they did the only thing they could do; they pushed on to Durango, Colorado, where they spent the night and had the opportunity to purchase tickets for the next day on the Durango to Silverton Narrow Gauge Railroad and return.

The next morning they made their way to the train station to ride the Durango to Silverton Railroad train, which Chance had wanted to do for several years. He bought tickets in a car with open sides, so Susan could take her pictures. It was great for taking pictures but Chance was freezing; however, they did have blankets for the passengers on this car.

Chance really enjoyed the trip and both he and Susan loved the history and story of the building of the railroad by a Chinese crew. Both of them were history buffs.

One thing they were learning on this trip was just how much they loved being together all the time and doing things together. It was wonderful!

From Durango they drove to Taos, New Mexico, and spend the night and most of the next day looking around the city.

After Taos they drove to Albuquerque and had a wonderful time taking a ski lift to the top of Sandia Mountain and having dinner. It was a great evening and on the way down the mountain, seeing the lights of the city spread out below them was like looking at a wonderful fairyland.

The rest of the way back to Springfield was just driving and trying to get home as soon as they could. But all in all, it was a marvelous trip and they always loved the time they were together and the fun they always had.

Chance thought that Susan won far too many times playing *Horse* on the trip. In the future, he knew he was going to have to get a lot more horses on his side of the road to stay up with Susan.

24

DIDN'T WE TRAVEL AND DIDN'T WE HAVE FUN?

Their vacation in 2011 was The Great Train Adventure. Susan and Chance had always wanted to take a long train rides across the USA, so they decided this was the year.

Because they didn't have Amtrak service in the third largest city in Missouri, Chance and Susan drove to Kansas City to begin their *Great Train Adventure,* since Kansas City is on one of the Midwest's Amtrak main lines.

It had always struck Chance as being rather strange that in Europe every little village has some kind of a train service and in the USA with one of the largest rail networks in the world, you had to drive two hundred miles to board a train. Figures!

They drove to Kansas City and spent the night at the Westin Crown Center Hotel, directly across the street from Kansas City's Union Station to have easy access to their early morning departure time.

Chance hated to have to get up in the middle of the night to catch planes, trains, or any other form of transportation after having done it for so many years when he was working.

Early the next morning they checked out of the hotel and drove across the street to Union Station. Chance parked the car in front of the station and unloaded their luggage so they didn't have to carry it on the long walk from the long-term parking garage to baggage check-in.

Susan stayed with the luggage while Chance parked the car. After the car was securely parked, he made his way to the station after a very long walk to meet Susan.

Then they took their luggage to the ticket and luggage check-in area of the station and found it wasn't opened yet. A sign on the door said the offices would open at seven o'clock, so they sat down to wait or try to find some coffee or breakfast but they found there was nothing open in the entire huge building, not even the coffee shop.

Around seven fifteen in the morning, someone finally opened the doors to the Amtrak ticket office and baggage check area of the terminal.

However, after they made their way to the luggage check-in point they found it didn't open until seven thirty. They decided to stand in line and wait until it opened. The waiting area to check the baggage wasn't very large and it was soon packed with people and luggage. When it opened they were the second ones to get their luggage checked in.

OK, so they made it to the train station on the date and time they were scheduled to leave and they had checked in their luggage, then the announcement was made their train was running late.

Chance and Susan had done the things they were suppose to do: how about Amtrak doing what they were supposed to do and run the train on time?

Since they couldn't do anything about their train arriving on time for their departure, they decided to find coffee and something for breakfast.

One of the restaurants was just opening and the lady opening the restaurant told them they could have a seat. She told them she had just started the coffeemaker and when they asked if she had decaf coffee, she said she would start a pot of decaf for them.

Chance and Susan went to a table and sat down. A few minutes later the woman came back and gave them menus. After a few more minutes passed, she came back with their decaf coffee and they placed their order for breakfast.

When they were finishing the last bites of their breakfast, an announcement was made that their train was arriving and would be boarding a short time later.

Chance paid the check and he and Susan returned to the boarding area to get on the train.

They found they had to climb down a very long staircase to get to the platform to board the train, and Chance with his bad knees and Susan with her replacement knees were not happy about climbing stairs. They did it, but the pain each of them endured wasn't something they enjoyed.

After they made the painful descent down the stairs, they saw an elevator was available for people who had problems like they had. Great timing! Chance was certain he would remember the elevator when they returned to Kansas City.

The plans for the trip specified they would first travel to Chicago on the train called the Southwest Limited and spend two nights at the Hilton Garden Inn Downtown/Magnificent Mile in Chicago and visit with Susan's best friend, Julia, and Susan's niece Jeannie and her family.

They had a nice visit and dinner with Julia and a lively breakfast with Jeannie, her husband, and their two little ones. Chance and Susan remembered what it was like to have young children out for breakfast and now they knew why you had children when you were young. Now they could laugh about parents trying to keep little ones entertained when you were out for breakfast since their kids were old now.

Chance and Susan left Chicago on Amtrak's train the Empire Builder leaving at 2:15 in the afternoon on October 1 and would arrive in Seattle on Monday, October 3 at 10:25 a.m. Well, that's what the schedule said anyway.

They found out once they were on the train just how small their bedroom was; it was a really tight fit.

In the bathroom, Chance's shoulders rubbed against both sides of the bathroom walls if he stood up straight.

After you took a shower you had to take your towel and wipe up the toilet and the bathroom floor, since the shower drain was in the middle of the bathroom floor.

The walls of the bedroom must have been made of a heavy, well maybe not so heavy cardboard, because you could hear every sound in the next compartment, from every word to every bathroom sound. If you could hear your neighbor's every sound, you could be sure they heard yours too.

The trip on the *Empire Builder* was going fine, until they got into North Dakota and then the train came to a stop out in the middle of nowhere.

Then came an announcement, a freight train traveling in front of them had hit a car and killed two people and they would be sitting in the middle of nowhere for the next three hours.

They were told the train would make up the time they lost and they would arrive in Seattle on time. Chance found that hard to believe that they could make up three hours.

Chance planned to step off the train when they stopped at one of the stations in North Dakota, because North Dakota was the only state in the Union he had never set foot in.

However, since they had had so much flooding in North Dakota earlier in the year, they couldn't stop at the station where he planned to get off, so he stayed on the train through all of North Dakota.

They found out later that due to the flooding in North Dakota the *Empire Builder* hadn't been able to make the trip from Chicago to Seattle for several weeks. So they found out they were very lucky it was back running when they planned their trip.

The train arrived in Seattle on time, as they had been told it would. They retrieved their luggage and took a taxi to the Best Western Pioneer Square Hotel to stay for two nights, then they would take the *Victoria Clipper* at 8:00 a.m., traveling to Victoria, British Columbia.

Even though the hotel was very old, they had a very large nice room and they were located in a good location to walk around in the downtown area of Seattle. They spent time looking around in Seattle and had a nice time. When they were ready to leave for Victoria they packed only one small suitcase to take with them to Victoria and checked the rest of their luggage with the hotel's bellman, to pick up when they returned to Seattle and the hotel.

When they arrived in Victoria, their ship docked near the Fairmont Empress Hotel. They took their bag and checked into the hotel for two nights.

In Victoria they took a tour of the city and the island and saw some beautiful sights, and the next day they took a tour of Butchart Gardens.

Before they got to Butchart Gardens, Susan told Chance she wanted to show him how she wanted their backyard to look.

After Chance toured Butchart Gardens, he told Susan, "First, we will have to buy all the houses in our subdivision in order to make our backyard look like Butchart." Susan only smiled at him. Chance made a reservation for high tea at the Empress Hotel and it was quite impressive to both of them. It was a lot of fun and done very elegantly. Susan loved it, maybe not as much as Butchart

Gardens, but she loved it.

The next day they returned to Seattle and checking back into the Best Western Pioneer Square Hotel, they got their luggage back that they had left with the bellman.

The next morning they took a taxi to board their next train, the Coastal Starlight to Los Angeles scheduled to leave at 9:45 a.m. Their bedroom didn't improve any on this train, the same size and no better soundproofing of the walls between compartments.

They arrived in Los Angeles on Sunday, October 9, at 9:00 p.m., where they had reservations at the Kyoto Grand Hotel in downtown Los Angeles, where they would be staying for next three nights.

The Kyoto Grand Hotel was a very beautiful hotel and had a really lovely garden, which Susan and Chance liked very much. Their room was large and the soundproofing between rooms was great.

The next day they picked up a Hertz rental car and drove to the Ronald Reagan Presidential Library and Ranch, as well as several other sites located in the north part of Los Angeles.

Chance and Susan were both fans of President Reagan and they enjoyed seeing his museum and ranch. They thought it had been very well done. They really enjoyed having the opportunity to have their picture taken getting out of President Reagan's Air Force One airplane. They pretended to wave just as the President would have done when he stepped out of the plane. It was hard to believe that the plane was located inside a building, but it was.

They checked out of the Kyoto Grand Hotel and moved to the Hyatt Regency Hotel in Garden Grove, where they would stay for three nights to be nearer to Disneyland and the Richard Nixon Presidential Museum.

Chance and Susan enjoyed their visit to the Richard Nixon Presidential Museum. Although Chance was not a big admirer of President Nixon, he was interested in all the things he had accomplished and seeing the home where he was born.

Chance did approve of at least two things President Nixon did as president. He had recognized China and had kept daylight savings time all year long for one year. Chance thought it was so wrong to go back to standard time after we had experienced DST all year long.

Their trip to Disneyland was fun, as always, and they had been looking forward to going to the new park called the California Experience but they were very disappointed in what little they saw. Apparently, a lot of other people felt the same way, as most of the park was closed and being changed to something else.

Chance had called his step-grandson Jerry Johnson and his girlfriend, Laura Darling, to invite them to dinner while they in the Los Angeles area, and they made a date to have dinner with them at the hotel the night of October 13.

Jerry and Laura were both graduates of Missouri State University, with degrees in Fine Arts, and were working and living near Hollywood hoping to get a chance to work in the film or TV industry.

Chance knew Jerry was an actor, because he was always "on" ever since he was a little boy. Chance had seen some of his work in the theater in Springfield, where he stole the show every time he was cast in a play.

Maybe it was only his grandfather's notion he stole the show, but Jerry always got the largest and loudest amount of applause when he was introduced at the end of the play, so other people must have agreed with him.

Because Jerry and Laura lived so far away from the hotel where Chance and Susan were staying, their guests showed up for dinner over two hours late. However, they all enjoyed getting together and had lots of laughs over a late dinner.

Chance and Susan returned to the Kyoto Grand Hotel the night before they would be boarding their train back to Kansas City.

They returned their rental car on Saturday, October 15, and went back to their hotel waiting for the time to go to the train depot.

When they checked out of the hotel, they had a hotel car drive them to the Los Angeles Train Station, where they boarded the Southwest Limited at 6:15 p.m.; it was the same train they left Kansas City on when traveling to Chicago.

By going from Los Angeles to Kansas City on this portion of their trip, it allowed them to complete the entire route of the Southwest Limited.

They returned to Kansas City and arrived at 7:24 a.m. on Monday, October 17.

Chance and Susan spent the night at the Hilton Garden Inn in Overland Park, Kansas, before driving back to Springfield on Tuesday, October 18.

Chance and Susan decided three long train rides was enough for them and they vowed never to do it again. The famous saying of "Been there! Done that!" was how they felt about doing another long train ride; three of them was enough for them!

25

2012, A Year of Changes

*I*n December 2011, Chance and Susan drove to Webster, Kansas, to see Chance's brother William and his wife, Betty, and stayed at the Holiday Inn Express for a couple of days visiting, and then drove to Wichita to see Chance's best friends, Doc and Susan Schmidt.

They planned to spend a couple of days in Wichita visiting with Doc and Susan. They checked into another Holiday Inn Express and after unloading their luggage they drove over to Doc and Susan's home. Chance had planned to take them out to dinner that evening but when they arrived at their home, they found Doc was really feeling ill.

Chance had talked on the phone with Doc and Susan the week before, and Doc told him he was getting along very well after having surgery and several treatments of radiation for brain cancer. Although Chance had kept in touch with Doc almost every week while he had been ill, after seeing him he was surprised how bad Doc looked and acted.

After they had been there for only a short time Doc said, "I'm sorry. I don't feel well enough to go out to dinner."

Chance replied, "That's not a problem. Maybe you'll be better tomorrow. Just take it easy and we'll see you tomorrow."

One of Doc's daughters was helping him up from his chair to get back to his bedroom where Doc then laid down on the bed to rest.

Chance and Susan spent a little more time talking with Susan. She told them Doc hadn't been doing very well all week and he had been looking forward to seeing them so much.

Chance and Susan went back to their hotel and later that evening, Susan Schmidt called Chance on his cell phone and told him they had to have an ambulance take Doc to the hospital. Susan said, "He was admitted and is in room South 4467 at Wesley Hospital."

Chance told her they would come to the hospital the next day and see her and Doc before they went back to Springfield. The next day Chance and Susan went to Wesley Hospital and made their way to Doc's room.

When they arrived at Doc's room, they found Susan and three of her daughters in the room with him.

After a round of hugs for each of Doc and Susan's daughters, Chance asked where daughter number four was and was told she had just left after staying with Susan and her dad all night.

Chance said, "Doc, you look a lot better today than when we saw you yesterday."

"Well, I feel a lot better today than I did yesterday."

Susan Schmidt and her daughters told them they were going to go to a nearby waiting room for a while so Chance and Susan could visit with Doc by themselves.

Susan Clark spoke a few minutes with Doc and then said she was going to go find Susan and the girls and talk with them for a few minutes to let Chance and Doc visit by themselves. Susan left to go down the hall to find Susan Schmidt and her girls.

Chance said, "Doc, I'm so sorry you are not doing very well and hope you start getting a lot better soon."

"Chance, I hope so. It's been a tough year with this brain cancer."

"Doc, I just want you to know that I love you and Susan.
You're my best friends."

"I know you do, and I love you, too. We've been through a lot together. I miss working and seeing you."

"Yeah, Doc, we had a pretty good run together. I think I better find my Susan and get on the road to home. I'll call your Susan and check up on you every day so get better soon. I still owe you a dinner."

With tears in his eyes, Chance turned and walked down the long hallway to find his Susan for the long drive home. Before he got to the family waiting area, Chance took a Kleenex and wiped away the tears.

He gave each of the Schmidt daughters a hug and his friend Susan a bigger hug and kissed her and told them, "Susan and I have to get started back to Springfield, because Susan has to be at work with her dad in the morning."

Chance said to Susan, as they were walking to the car, "I don't think Doc's going to make it. I sure hope I'm wrong."

Chance called Susan Schmidt almost every day to see how Doc was doing and after being in the hospital for week Doc was released to go home.

Chance called Doc and Susan on Christmas day and talked with both of them. Doc sounded a little bit better than when they saw him earlier in the month.

Chance called them again on New Year's Day and talked with both of them again and although Doc didn't sound as good as he did on Christmas he sounded better than when they saw him.

January 10, Chance answered the phone and Susan Schmidt said, "Chance, Doc died this morning here at home. He'd been back in the hospital for a couple of days, but they couldn't do any more for him, so they sent him home. Chance, he told me he was ready to go."

"Susan, I'm so sorry. Is there anything I can do?"

"No, I think between my daughters and their husbands we can take care of everything."

"OK, then I will see you soon."

Chance knew exactly what Susan was going through having been there not long ago when he lost Annie. The pain is unbearable and the loss of your spouse is overwhelming to every fiber in your body.

To be able to function at all after losing your loving spouse is one of the hardest things you will ever have to do in your life.

Your mind and body just wants to shut down, but somehow you just can't let it. You don't know why you can't, because you want it to.

Chance's saying all his life had been, "The only sure thing in life is change" but why do so many of the changes have to be such bad changes?

Chance knew his Susan never went to funerals, so he planned to go by himself to Wichita the following day to be there for Susan Schmidt. He didn't know what he could do for her, but he knew he had to be there if she needed him for comfort or for any other help. Chance and Susan Schmidt had been friends before all but one of her daughters were born and the oldest one was only about eighteen months old when the four of them became best friends: Doc, Ann, Susan, and Chance. Now there were only two of them left.

Chance made reservations at the same Holiday Inn Express where he and Susan had stayed in December when they were in Wichita.

After Chance checked into the hotel, he drove over to Susan's house and when he rang the doorbell, Susan answered the door and when she saw Chance, she opened her arms and he held her tightly and told her how sorry he was about Doc.

They embraced for a long time and then Chance saw all of Susan's girls and gave each of them a hug and told them he was so sorry about their dad. Chance was like one of the family to them, having seen him and Ann all of their lives.

That evening they had visitation for Doc at the funeral home and Chance went back to the hotel to change clothes before going to the funeral home. When he arrived at the funeral home, he signed the guest book and went to the front of the chapel to see his best friend.

After standing there for a long time just looking at his friend's body, he took a seat in the second row and sat there just staring at his friend's body and thinking about all the fun and hard times they had had together.

He had gotten Doc into the parking meter business with him as a partner with his sales territory and later, when Chance was president of

Superior Parking Meter Company, Doc worked as the director of sales for him.

They had done everything together, from buying and rebuilding cars to starting several different businesses. They loved being together and working together and Chance was certainly going to miss him for the rest of his life.

The next day Doc's funeral was held at the Methodist Church, and while funerals are not noted for having very many funny moments, you could leave it to Doc to have a few.

During the service one of Doc's grandsons had made a very nice film depicting people and places in Doc's life, and Chance and Ann's pictures with Doc and Susan were flashed on the screen several times.

Later the minster conducting the service told about a funny thing one of Doc's grandsons said to him about his grandfather. He told him that when Doc took trips working overseas for several weeks, he knew Doc was really working for the CIA.

This statement caused everyone to laugh, hearing what Doc's grandson had said about his grandfather. The minster told his wife, who had actually worked at the CIA headquarters in Virginia, about what Doc's grandson said about Doc working for the CIA, so he asked her if she knew if Doc worked for them.

The minister said his wife told him, "If I told you, I would have to kill you."

This brought a bigger laugh from the mourners, and then the minster said he had met the man who got Doc into the parking meter business and asked him about the CIA and he said, "Sorry, I can't discuss things like that with you."

The last thing the minster had to say on the subject was he knew his wife and Doc always had a special relationship and now he guessed he knew why.

Chance went back to the house with the family after the service and stayed for several hours, and when he was ready to leave to go back to the hotel, he told Susan he would stop by in the morning to see her before going home to Springfield.

The next morning Chance drove to the cemetery to be sure he knew how to find his friend's grave and to say good-bye one more time to his lifelong best friend and to shed a few more tears.

True to his word, Chance stopped by to tell Susan good-bye and spent a few minutes with her and one of her daughters.

After having a cup of coffee and a little conversation with Susan, he said good-bye and gave her another kiss and hug and got into his car to go home to his Susan.

Six days later, Chance got a telephone call from a son of his best friend in high school, Don Smith, and Don's son told Chance, "Don passed away on January 16." Chance thanked

Don's son for calling him and told him he was so sorry for the loss of his father.

Life sometime doesn't feel very fair. Chance had lost the two best friends he had had in his lifetime just six days apart.

Chance guessed that was a major problem of getting older; your friends get older just like you, and sometimes they have medical problems and sometimes they just didn't recover from their illness. Chance didn't like it, but it was a fact of life, so it made his loving Susan so special and they intended to love and travel as much as they could while their health still allowed it.

Chance knew tomorrow was promised to no one, so you should make the best of every day you are given on this earth.

Susan was having her problems with her dad, as he had been in the hospital twice this year. He wasn't able to return to his duplex even with his twenty-four-hours-a-day care. His help was excellent, but they weren't qualified to handle medical emergencies.

Dad was not an easy one to look after, even when he hadn't been as ill as he was now. He didn't want to go to a nursing home, because he knew he could go back to his duplex and his people and Susan could look after him all right.

His doctor insisted he go somewhere where they had skilled nursing staff on duty all the time, since on this last visit to the hospital, they found he had a large cyst on his pancreas.

Mr. Christenson's family had a long history of dying with pancreatic cancer so hearing this was very bad news. Susan finally got her dad to agree to go a nursing home for a few days before going back to his duplex.

Susan's daughter Christy was a registered nurse and she knew her grandfather was in a really bad condition and didn't think he would last very long.

Since he was ninety-five years old and suffered with Inclusion Body Myositis, or IBM for short, which is an autoimmune disease that weakens the muscles. The disease had left him unable to stand, walk, or grip things with his hands over the twenty-year period of time he had the disease.

Mr. Christenson was transferred by ambulance from the hospital to the Manor at Elfindale nursing home, where Susan had made arrangements for a room for him. Susan and Chance were waiting at the nursing home when the ambulance arrived and they went with the ambulance attendants as they took her dad to his room.

As soon as the staff got him settled in, Mr. Christenson began telling Susan what he wanted brought from his duplex and the list was long, starting with his power wheelchair, and although he had a TV in his room, he needed his VCR and his recliner chair, plus various other pieces of medical equipment.

Susan told her dad that she and Chance would get all the things and bring them from his duplex. They left his room to go to his duplex, which was located in the same compound as the nursing home, and on the way Susan called her brother Jacob Christenson on Chance's cell phone, since she wouldn't have a cell phone of her own.

She called to tell her brother about their dad's condition and asked him to come to Springfield. Jacob told Susan that he and his wife, Cathy, would drive over from Oklahoma City the next day to see Dad.

Chance got the keys for Dad's handicap van and began loading up the things her dad wanted brought over to the nursing home, as Susan was gathering up the various pieces of medical equipment her dad wanted.

Susan called the three people who normally stayed with her dad to let them know that he was now in the nursing home and they were to come there to stay with him just as they had been doing at his duplex for the past few years.

As Chance and Susan arrived back at the nursing home, one of the employees helped Chance bring in the recliner chair to her dad's room from the van. Soon, Susan and Chance had everything her dad asked them to bring over in his room.

After Chance and Susan finished bringing everything into her dad's room, Ellen, one of her dad's ladies that stayed with him, arrived at his room.

A short time later the nursing home director came in to see how her dad was getting settled in.

Susan told her dad she and Chance were going to go home for a while since Ellen was there with him.

That night, Susan's brother Jacob called to tell her he and Cathy would meet them for breakfast at Perkins at nine thirty the next morning. Susan agreed and told Jacob to drive carefully.

The next morning Chance and Susan arrived at Perkins a few minutes before nine thirty to be certain they were there waiting for Jacob and Cathy. They asked to be seated in a large booth, since there would be four of them for breakfast.

They hadn't been seated very long, not even long enough for their waitress to pour them decaf coffee, when Susan's oldest niece, Jane, came up to the booth where they were sitting and said, "Hello, Aunt Susan."

Susan was so surprised to see Jane come up to their booth since she lived in Chicago and Susan said, "Jane, what are you doing here?"

"Dad told me about Grandpa and I thought I better come to see him."

"How did you get here?"

"I flew in this morning and Dad and Cathy picked me up at the airport."

By that time Susan's brother Jacob and his wife, Cathy, arrived at the booth.

After Susan and Chance greeted all of them and the five of them sat down in the booth, Jacob asked, "How is Dad doing?"

Susan replied, "He's not doing well. They found a large cyst on his pancreas on the day they sent him to the nursing home. Part of the time he doesn't seem to understand what's going on and other times he seems just like Dad."

Cathy asked, "Susan, do you think he's ever going to be able to go back to his duplex?"

"I don't think so, but it *is* Dad, so who knows?"

Cathy continued, "When you talked to Jacob yesterday, he thought Dad wasn't going to make it very long."

Susan replied, "I don't know how long he's going to make it.

I don't think anyone knows. He's made it to ninety-five."

They ordered their breakfast and after everyone had their order in, Jane said, "My sisters are coming later today. They are arriving at around four o'clock this afternoon."

Susan asked, "You mean Judy and Anita are flying in to see Grandpa, too?"

"Yes, with your kids, Christy and William, all of Grandpa's grandkids will be here today to see him."

Susan said, "That will be great. I'm sure he will be glad to see all of you."

Susan continued, "I think it will be best if Jacob, Cathy, and Jane go up to see Grandpa, so we don't have too many people there at one time, and Chance and I will come up later this afternoon."

Jacob agreed and after they finished breakfast, Chance and Susan returned home and Jacob, Cathy, and Jane went to the nursing home.

When Chance and Susan arrived at the house, Susan called her daughter Christy and son William to tell them all of their cousins would be here today to see Grandpa, and she thought it would be good if they made a point of going to the nursing home, so Grandpa could see all of his grandkids together.

They agreed, and that afternoon Chance and Susan went to the nursing home, after they knew the other family members had left and before the other two granddaughters arrived, to see how her dad was doing.

They were shocked at how alert her dad was after the way he had been in the hospital and how he was when he first arrived at the nursing home.

All the grandchildren were with their grandfather later Saturday afternoon and the following morning, and they were all pleased he was talking and doing so well.

Jacob's girls left Sunday evening to return to their homes, two of them from Chicago and one from Kentucky.

Susan's son and daughter lived in Springfield, where they both had moved after Susan moved to Springfield, so they would be able to see their grandfather again later.

It was remarkable the way her dad had rallied on Saturday and Sunday to be able to visit with all of his family.

Monday morning, Chance, Susan, Jacob, and Cathy met again for breakfast at Perkins before Jacob and Cathy left to go back to Oklahoma City.

By Monday afternoon, her dad was not doing well at all; he was going in and out of sleep or a coma, Susan wasn't sure which.

Christy came to the nursing home and checked on her grandfather and told her mother he was failing fast.

As Susan was leaving the nursing home to come home for a while, she was stopped by a lady at the front desk who told Susan the nursing home director wanted to talk with her.

Susan had to wait for a few minutes since the director had someone in her office but she was soon free and asked her to come in because she needed to talk with her about her father.

She told Susan, "We need to call in hospice to help with your dad since he needs someone that has nursing training with him all the time now, because we don't have enough people to stay with him all the time."

Susan asked, "Do you think he needs hospice at this time?"

The director replied, "We don't think your dad will be with us very long and hospice has the people to help with his last few days."

"OK, do you have someone you recommend?"

"We work with several firms and you can choose any one of them yourself, but we do a lot of work with American Hospice Care. They have been very good to work with."

Susan said, "Since I don't have any idea about hospice care companies and you have worked with American Hospice Care and think they do well, we should contact them."

The director replied, "I can call them for you and set up an appointment with them for you in the morning."

"Thank you. I would appreciate that."

Ten o'clock the next morning Chance and Susan met with two women from American Hospice Care.

The meeting lasted about thirty minutes and Susan provided all the information they needed to sign her dad up for hospice care and signed all the forms for them.

They told Susan they would start that afternoon; in fact, one of the women who met with them would be the first one with her dad this afternoon.

Christy had been with her grandfather, while Chance and Susan were at the meeting with the folks from hospice. When Chance and Susan went into her dad's room, he was in a coma and having difficulty breathing.

Christy showed them Grandpa's legs had turned black already. Christy told her mother, "Grandpa isn't going to live much longer. All we can do is to try to keep him as comfortable as possible."

Susan encouraged Chance to go home, and Christy and she would stay with her dad. Susan knew Chance had work to do on the magazine for Branson so he could get the book to the printers soon.

Chance returned home and about three hours later, Susan called and told him her father had died a couple of hours after the lady from hospice came to be with him.

Arrangements had been made with a local funeral home over a year ago to have them pick up her dad's body when he passed away and do cremation. The nursing home or the lady from hospice would call the funeral home.

Susan and Chance's families had far different traditions when it came to what happened to the body of a deceased loved one.

Susan's family, with their Norwegian heritage, didn't have funerals and their loved ones' bodies were always cremated. Susan's grandfather's ashes were even sent to Norway to be scattered after he passed away.

Chance's family, with an English heritage, always had funerals and buried their loved ones' bodies.

Before Chance and Susan were married, they had agreed that Susan would be cremated and her ashes placed in the Buffalo River near the little town of Ponca, Arkansas, where her first husband's ashes were scattered.

If they had a service for Susan, it would be a memorial service. Chance would have a funeral, and his body would be entombed in the mausoleum next to Ann in Big Springs, Arkansas.

They both agreed they would see that their wishes would be carried out when they died.

Susan and Jacob decided they would take their dad's ashes, along with their mother's ashes, which Susan had stored until their father passed away, and scatter both of their ashes in Lake Michigan, as their mother had asked Susan to do.

Their dad passed on February 21, 2012, but they wouldn't put his and their mother's ashes into Lake Michigan until May 4, 2012, which would have been their seventy-fourth wedding anniversary.

Chance made arrangements for a Spirit Cruise ship for the entire family to be able to be present for the scattering of Susan and Jacob's mother and father's ashes into Lake Michigan.

To make the occasion as pleasant as possible for all the family members, since there were several young great-grandchildren, Susan had Chance make arrangements for a meal to be catered during the trip.

Susan had found special heart-shaped boxes on the Internet to place loved ones' ashes in that could be used to put the ashes into Lake Michigan.

After being in the water for a while, the boxes would dissolve releasing the ashes into the water without the problem of having ashes blow back on any of the family members. Chance thought that was a very good idea.

After Susan received the special boxes, Susan and Chance transferred the ashes from the containers they received from the funeral home into the special boxes. Of course, Susan's dad's ashes gave them trouble fitting into the special box, but they finally were able to keep working the ashes down into the box until they were able to close the box. Susan said, "Dad never did what you wanted him to do, ever."

May 4 was a cool, windy day in Chicago and all the family met at the right pier at the right time for the ceremony for Susan and Jacob's parents.

The captain of the ship told them he was going to have to find as calm a place as he could for them to be able to place the special boxes into the lake since the wind was blowing very hard from the east, which hindered them from trying to throw the special boxes into the lake from the stern of the ship.

Susan had been hopeful they could venture farther away from the shoreline to commit the special boxes into Lake Michigan, but it was not to be; the lake was too rough and the wind was too strong. Finally, the captain told them he was in the calmest water he could find for them to put their boxes into the water. Susan took her mother's ashes and threw the special box into the water and it began to sink as soon as it hit the water. Next, Jacob threw the container with their dad's ashes into the water and it, too, sunk as soon as it hit the water.

As part of the ceremony, Susan had brought enough roses for everyone to be able to tear petals off and toss them into the lake near where the boxes had been placed.

Jacob offered a prayer for their parents and all the family members, and then everyone returned inside the ship to get out of the cold and wind.

Susan and Jacob had another surprise for the five grandchildren. Susan gave each of them a sizable check, which was money their grandmother had left to them but their grandfather had never given it to them after she had died.

It was the same for Susan and Jacob; their mother had left them an amount of money which their father had never given to them either. Their dad had kept all of their money in a trust until he passed away, and no one else could distribute these funds until then.

Susan had heard her father say many times about her mother's funds, "It's my money!" Despite her dad's quirks, he was a remarkable man; he was a successful inventor, as was his father and grandfather.

He could fix or repair anything and could devise all types of gadgets to help him after he lost his ability to use his hands to operate little things after developing IBM, like using toaster tongs to remove VHS tapes from his VCR, or a way to unscrew the top off a bottle of Vicks, gluing half of a tongue depressor on the lid, and using things he could find at home to solve his other problems; they were just plain ingenious.

With all of his success, his greatest ambition was to be a farmer. He had bought and operated two different farms in Virginia, sold them, and went back to working as an engineer- inventor when he couldn't make the farms successful. Later in his life he bought a farm in Hawaii, which he never operated.

If you asked him what he did in his life, he would tell you he was a farmer; he loved the idea of being a farmer.

The day ended with each member of the family sharing lots of hugs and kisses while saying good-bye to each other, as they left with their families going back to their homes in Illinois, Oklahoma, Missouri, and Kentucky.

26

So You Want to Travel

Not long after they returned from Chicago from putting Susan's parents' ashes into Lake Michigan, Susan said, "Chance, I plan to travel as much as I can, since I don't have to take care of my dad anymore, and I would like for you to travel with me, but I don't see how you can if you continue doing the magazine for the Branson tourists."

"That's not a problem! As soon as we deliver the 2012 edition of the books to the hotels and motels, we'll stop producing the book. We've lost enough money doing the book these past five years.

"I thought you liked doing the book with your son Shane."

"I did. I loved working with Shane on the book, but it doesn't look like we can ever get enough support from the Branson merchants to keep printing it."

Susan said she wanted to travel, and asking Chance if he wanted to travel with her was like asking a person who was addicted to heroin if he wanted heroin. Chance loved to travel. It was what he had been doing in his work for almost all of his life.

So in 2012, they started traveling and had no plans to stop as long as their health allowed them to keep going.

In late May and early June, they took a driving trip to visit Chance's brother Will and his family who lived in Hutchinson, Kansas. While they were in Hutchinson, they took a tour of the salt mines. It was fascinating, and they also stopped to see the Cosmosphere located on the Hutchinson Junior College campus. The Cosmosphere houses one of the largest collections of space hardware from both the USA and Russia in America.

Chance didn't know how the people in Hutchinson managed to acquire such a collection in the middle of Kansas, but found it was very well done. Good for them!

The next trip after that was Chance's first cruise and Susan's first riverboat cruise on the Snake and Columbia Rivers, following the trail used by the Lewis and Clark expedition when they were trying to find an inland passage to the Pacific Ocean.

Lewis and Clark never found an easy way to get from St. Louis to the Pacific Ocean, but what they did discover was an unbelievable amount of animals and native people living in an amazingly large country filled with mountains and plains.

To begin Chance and Susan's riverboat cruise, they flew into Spokane, Washington, where they would be picked up by bus and taken to Clarkston, Washington. There they would board their riverboat.

They found Spokane to be a beautiful city, with its marvelous waterfalls in the middle of the city and pretty little parks all over the downtown area. They thoroughly enjoyed the time they spent in this charming city.

On Saturday, the bus picked them up from their hotel and took them on a winding, hilly road trip of almost three hours from Spokane to Clarkston.

Arriving in the small town of Clarkston, they boarded their riverboat and Susan was surprised that their cabin was larger than she expected it to be. They found their cabin to be very nice except for a high step up to go into their bathroom, which they certainly didn't like.

They both knew if they got up during the night, they would need to be very careful going into the bathroom. They would need to remember about the step up to prevent falling. Neither of them liked that single flaw to their room.

Overall, it was a wonderful trip and they enjoyed every minute of the trip. On one of the excursions, they had the chance to observe the unbelievable devastation caused by the eruption of Mount St. Helen, now so many years ago. Nature was doing her best to bring back life to the lava-covered hills, with a lot of help from man, who began planting trees as soon as the soil was cool enough. It was quite a sight seeing the results of having a million trees planted.

Reaching the Pacific Ocean, they visited a replica of Fort Clatsop, near Astoria, Oregon, where Lewis and Clark had stayed the winter, before starting their return back to St. Louis. William Clark had drawn the entire layout of the fort in great detail, allowing the National Park Service to recreate the fort exactly as it was originally built.

The last stop on the trip was in Portland, Oregon. There they took a tour of the city and one of the stops was at a city park, with the most beautiful rose garden they had ever seen. It was spectacular and Susan took picture after picture of the various types of roses from all around the world located in this city's park.

Susan took hundreds of pictures during their trips, because she made scrapbooks of their trips, and she wrote a journal of their daily activities that added so much to their travel experiences.

They returned home to Springfield on Sunday June 24, and left for a short two-day trip to St. Louis on June 28, to go to a Cardinals game and to see the special Chinese Lantern Festival constructed at the Missouri Botanical Gardens.

At the Missouri Botanical Gardens it was very interesting to see how the Chinese could use such common things as plates, cups, spoons, and other porcelain pieces like that to build such elaborate dragons and other objects. It was a fun show and Susan enjoyed it so much.

They stayed home after coming back from St. Louis on June 30, until leaving on another driving trip to Oklahoma and Texas on July 15. Their first stop was in Oklahoma City to visit the Alfred P. Murray

Federal Building Memorial and Museum dedicated to the people killed and injured in the senseless bombing of Americans by a former American soldier. Visiting the memorial was heartbreaking.

From Oklahoma City they drove to Groom, Texas, stopping at The Cross of Our Lord Jesus Christ; the cross stands 190 feet tall above the flat prairie. They also came to view the lifesize statues of the Way of the Cross. Viewing the statues was inspiring, and they were so well done. Except it was alongside Interstate 40, they were really in the middle of nowhere. The only thing you could see from the highway was the cross and there was no indication there was more to see.

Chance and Susan had seen the cross before as they had traveled on Interstate 40, but had no idea of the life-size statues at the base of the cross, until Susan saw pictures of them on the Internet. She had to see them for herself and get them in her camera.

Next stop was Amarillo, Texas, where they spent a couple of nights. The first night they went to see what some people called the Cadillac Ranch, where some nut with more money than sense bought a dozen or so old Cadillac cars and buried them nose down into the dusty, flat earth of Texas. Then he invited people to bring their cans of spray paint and decorate them. It was nuts, but they went to see them anyway!

The next day they went to find Palo Duro Canyon State Park. As Chance and Susan drove along the flat prairie of Texas, all at once they saw a deep canyon on the right side of the road and continued driving until they found a sign directing them to the entrance to the state park.

After they paid the entrance fee, they continued following the signs directing them to the State Park's visitor center, located about halfway down to the canyon floor. Occasionally they pulled off the road at overview sites to look into the canyon below them; it was wonderful.

Arriving at the State Park visitor center they found information telling them Palo Duro State Park was the second largest canyon in the United States, with only the Grand Canyon larger.

Palo Duro State Park has over 29,000 acres; it's big, it's Texas.

Palo Duro Canyon is over 120 miles long and in some places it is twenty miles wide and eight hundred feet deep. The canyon was beautiful and Chance couldn't believe he had never even heard of

Palo Duro Canyon before they decided to make a trip to Groom and Amarillo. He thought it was a jewel that a lot more people should see.

Before they left the visitor center, they bought a large painting by a local artist of three small, frolicking black horses at the top of the painting, with one large horse running in the opposite direction. His form was outlined in black and an unusual color of red with blue-green splashes on the body. There were hues of copper tones surrounding the horses and random small lines of the same unusual red color used in the horse's body throughout the copper background.

They knew exactly where this painting would be hung in their home, on the rock wall in their living room, directly across from Susan's collection of Painted Ponies, displayed in a glassfront, old- fashioned cabinet.

The next stop on their trip would be in Turkey, Texas. Bob Wills had grown up on a farm just outside of Turkey and the town had the Bob Wills Museum that Chance wanted to see. Chance had been a fan of Bob Wills from the time he was a little boy living in Oklahoma. For Chance's fifth birthday his aunts had written to the Bob Wills's radio show on KVOO in Tulsa and asked Bob to do a song for Chance, which he did. So Bob Wills was always special to him.

When they arrived in town at noon, the museum was closed till one in the afternoon, so they had time to have lunch in a small restaurant in downtown Turkey, which consisted of about five buildings.

Susan got a big laugh when a young, really fit, good-looking young cowboy came into the restaurant as they were waiting for their lunch to be served.

There were several young women in the restaurant at the time, including two waitresses, and when this young cowboy strolled across the restaurant in his scuffed cowboy boots and dusty hat, the eyes of every girl in the room were fixed on his every move. The first thing this cowboy did when he sat down was pull out his cell phone!

The girls looked like they were wishing he was on the menu! He certainly didn't have to wait long to be waited on, that was for sure.

After they finished their lunch, they drove back to the museum and spent about an hour there. Before they left, Chance bought a couple of Bob Wills's greatest hits CDs.

From Turkey they were headed to Fort Griffin, Texas.

Chance wanted to do some research at the fort because he was writing a western novel he called *Indian Leader Trail Boss* about a trail drive of Texas Longhorns to Dodge City. In his story the cattle drive passed Fort Griffin which was on The Great Western Trail.

The found out when they got to Fort Griffin State Park that the official state herd of longhorn cattle was located across the road from the fort, so Susan certainly wanted to see them and take pictures.

They drove to the area where the longhorns were supposed to be, but they didn't see even one longhorn.

After driving across the highway to go up to the fort's visitor center, Susan told the lady working there she was looking forward to seeing the longhorn herd. Susan told her they drove all around the area where the longhorns were supposed to be, but they didn't see any.

The very nice lady, by the name of Judy, was working there and she told Susan that at this time of the day because it's so hot, they were probably all up in the shade of the trees away from the area where they're fed. Judy said, "I'll call over there and see if the boys working there can get a few of the longhorns down, so you can see them. They're quite a sight to see."

Susan replied, "That would be wonderful. I sure wanted to see them and take pictures of them."

Judy called over to the cowboys working at the cattle pens and one of them told her to have the folks come over in about fifteen minutes, and they would try to get some of the longhorns out of the trees so she could see them and take their pictures.

Judy told them what the cowboy told her, and Chance and Susan looked around the visitor center for a few more minutes and then drove back over to the longhorns' pens.

Chance parked their car as close to the holding pens as possible and when they arrived they began hearing honking and after a while the honking got louder and louder and then they could see a pickup slowly winding down a hill coming out of the trees. Behind the pickup they could see longhorn cattle sauntering; the driver continued honking his horn and then Chance and Susan could see more and more longhorns coming out of the trees following the truck.

The pickup stopped just across the fence from where Chance had parked.

Three cowboys began throwing what looked like corn pellets out of buckets to the longhorns as they slowly arrived at the holding pens.

Susan got lots of pictures and they were both were surprised at the length of the horns and now really understood why these cattle were called longhorns. Each animal's horns were as different as people's fingerprints: some were straight, some turned up, some down, and some even had one of each.

Chance and Susan were very appreciative for the cowboys bringing the longhorns down from the hills, and to their new friend, Judy at the visitor center, for her helping them to having the opportunity to see the longhorns up close and personal.

After leaving the fort, they were on their way to Dallas.

In Dallas they would visit with Lee and her family. Chance hadn't seen her for some time and would be really glad to see her again, since she came to Big Springs so often to be with her sister Ann. He had really missed seeing her.

During their time in Dallas, Lee drove them around and took them to see the famous glass-blowing artist Dale Chihuly's exhibition at the Dallas Arboretum and the museum of the infamous sixth floor, where Lee Harvey Oswald shot President Kennedy.

Summer in Texas is hot and the temperature on this day was 105 degrees and during their visit there the temperature varied from 103 to 106. It was not good timing to be in Texas in July.

Leaving Dallas, their next stop would be Austin, where they planned to visit Lyndon B. Johnson's Library and Museum, located on the campus of the University of Texas. Only one problem for their visit at this facility was that most of it was closed for renovation.

The next day, they drove to Johnson City, Texas, to visit the national park visitor center where President Johnson's boyhood home and his Summer White House were located on his ranch.

Chance and Susan enjoyed seeing the ranch and the home of President Johnson, who was born there, and where his and Lady Bird Johnson's gravesites are located very near to where he was born.

Chance and Susan intended to eventually visit every presidential library and museum. Their next stop was President George H. W. Bush's Library and Museum, located at College Station on the grounds of Texas A& M University.

George H. W. Bush was probably one of the most qualified, by experience, of any president in recent history to serve as president having served as a congressman, delegate to the United Nations, ambassador to China, head of the RNC, CIA director, and eight years as vice president of the United States.

The scenery changed dramatically in Northeast Texas driving through the Piney to Carthage, Texas, to visit the Texas Country Music Hall of Fame. Chance certainly enjoyed going there and before they left the area they visited the Jim Reeves Memorial, which was just east of town, where he and his dog Cheyenne are buried.

Their last stop in Texas was in Paris, Texas, so Susan could see a smaller version of the Eiffel Tower; the one in Paris, France, Susan claimed now belonged to her because she loved seeing it.

Because this smaller version of the Eiffel Tower is in Paris, Texas, it has a large red Stetson hat on the top of it. Susan just had to have a picture of it in her camera. She got it.

The very last stop they made before returning home to Springfield was in Tahlequah, Oklahoma, to go to the Cherokee Heritage Center, which is built on the site of the 1850 Cherokee Female Seminary, the first institution for higher learning for women west of the Mississippi; there are now only three tall columns remaining of the original structure.

Most of the museum was devoted to the Trail of Tears, a disgraceful period of time in America's history for the treatment of America's native people.

After seeing the pictures of people on the Trail of Tears, Chance felt ashamed of being a white person because the ones who forced this march had literally stolen the property of the Cherokee people and caused many of them to die making the trip.

Chance and Susan returned home on July 25 and left on a trip to Tampa, Florida, on Sunday, August 12, to visit with Susan's accountant in Sarasota and then drove to the Orlando area to go to Universal Studios, Disney World, EPCOT, Sea World, and back to Tampa to see Busch Gardens. Then they flew back home.

After visiting with the accountant in Sarasota, Chance and Susan went to the Ringling Circus Museum and were delighted they took the time to go there, since they saw a miniature circus that took up 10,000 square feet called the Howard Brothers Circus. It was a three-fourth-inch-scale replica of a whole circus. It was incredible!

In addition, they toured the many buildings at the museum which displayed Ringling's collection of circus memorabilia, including such things as John Ringling's private train car, along with his beautiful home and art collection, which he had willed to the state of Florida to keep creditors from getting them after the stock market crash of 1929. A smart move because it was all there for people to enjoy.

Arriving at Universal Studios, they checked in at their hotel and then took a water ferry over to the entrance of Universal Studios Theme Park and headed directly to the *Wizarding World of Harry Potter*. First thing they tried was *Butter Beer*, which, of course, actually had nothing to do with real beer; they both really liked it and neither of them liked the real thing.

The ride through *Hogwarts,* called *the Forbidden Journey,* soars over the castle grounds and lets you get up close and personal during the *Quidditch Match.*

Chance was not a fan of roller coasters but as rough of a ride as this one was, he enjoyed it as it traveled through scenes they had seen in the *Harry Potter* movies. Altogether it was quite an adventure for Chance.

All and all, they enjoyed their time spent at Universal Studios; even if they were over seventy, they certainly didn't have to act it. Chance knew you would live longer if you didn't try to act too old.

The next stop was Disney World and when Chance went to check in at the Contemporary Hotel he couldn't believe the hundreds of people waiting to check in; it seemed they were having a global Tupperware convention and this was the main hotel for the event.

Chance had Susan take a seat as he waited and waited for an opportunity to check in; there was no use having of both of them standing in this long line.

Susan kept their hand luggage with her. Finally, Chance made it very close to the front of the line when a hotel employee asked his name and when he told her his name was Chance Clark, she asked him to come with her.

She said, "You have been upgraded. Come with me."

Chance said to Susan, "I don't know where we're going but this young lady said we've been upgraded and to come with her."

Susan replied, "OK."

Susan handed Chance's briefcase to him. She picked up her bag and they followed the lady to an elevator. The lady took them to the top floor of the hotel. Arriving there she took them to a desk attendant who took care of checking them in and then told them she would show them to their suite.

They got a great deal with their upgrade at the Disney World Contemporary Hotel. The attendant took them to their suite. Chance and Susan were surprised to find their suite had a full kitchen, dining area, living room, bedroom, two bathrooms, two large televisions, and three large private verandas. Wow, what an upgrade!

In addition, they were on a floor where they had a free breakfast and light dinner available in the evening. They didn't know what they did to get the upgrade, but it was wonderful: Thanks, Walt.

They were scheduled to stay at this hotel for a couple of nights then move to a hotel near Sea World. They would have been very happy to stay where they were, but they couldn't since their suite wasn't available, too bad.

They enjoyed Disney's Magic Kingdom and EPCOT as they had so many times before; they loved going there and would continue to try going there every year.

Checking into their next hotel they had a normal room with a king-size bed, with just one room and bathroom and only one TV. It was a nice enough Marriott Courtyard, but it seemed rather mundane after the Contemporary suite they just checked out of.

They went to Sea World the following day and made the three shows they wanted to see: the Dolphins, Sea Lions, and Shamu, the killer whale.

They visited the dolphin nursery, the stingray lagoon, Shark Encounter, and the stingray aquarium. After all this, they had had enough and caught a shuttle bus back to their hotel.

Their last stop before returning home was at Busch Gardens and they decided instead of walking all through the park they would take the Stanley Steamer Railroad around the park in the awful August heat in Florida. Good move.

Chance and Susan had one more trip to make in the USA and that was to Boston to visit with Susan's dad's broker, and then they would spend some time traveling around New England.

They returned home from Florida on August 18 and left for Boston on September 4.

On their trip to Boston, Chance and Susan met with the broker; visited the JFK Library, toured Boston, visited Paul Revere House, boarded *Old Ironsides*, the oldest ship in the US Navy, saw Bunker Hill, stopped at Plymouth Rock, boarded the replica of the *Mayflower*, drove the length of Cape Cod, took a ferry from Hyannis to Martha's Vineyard and stayed overnight and toured the island, drove to Lexington and Concord, visited Walden Pond, visited Louisa May Alcott's home, visited the Salem Witch Museum and the House of the Seven Gables, made famous by the book of the same name, written by Nathaniel Hawthorne in Salem, stayed two nights in the wonderful Bass Rock Ocean Resort in Gloucester, Massachusetts, and saw the statue of the Gloucester Fishermen's Memorial and a memorial for Fishermen's Wives.

In addition to seeing all these sights Susan had told Chance she wanted to go to New York City to see the play *Wicked* so before they left Springfield he made arrangements for tickets to the play and the train tickets to travel from Boston to New York and back in one day.

They had a very early train ride and arrived in New York City by ten thirty in the morning and had breakfast then spent the day visiting several sites in the city.

They had an early dinner and then went to the theater to see *Wicked;* it was the first Broadway play for both of them and they loved it. Susan had read the book and loved it and she thought the play was as good as the book. One thing they learned from seeing the play was it was hard growing up green!

After the show they managed to get an earlier train back to Boston than their schedule but by the time they made it back to their hotel it was still almost one o'clock in the morning. They were very tired but very happy to have attended their first Broadway play and planned to see more of them in the future.

Susan wanted to go back to the Bass Rock Ocean Resort and stay a lot longer and just spend time sitting and looking out on the ocean. Chance and Susan loved that for the short amount of time they spent there, it was wonderful.

Years ago Susan had promised to take her daughter Christy on a cruise of the Greek Isles if she would stop smoking for a year, but as long as Susan's father lived, either she or Christy had to be in Springfield to be sure there was someone there to look after Mr. Christenson.

Life had changed a lot for Susan after she made Christy this promise; she and Chance got married, and now, she didn't want to be away from Chance for two weeks. Susan knew she now would also have to ask Christy's husband, Steve, to go with them. So instead of Susan and Christy going on the trip by themselves there would be four of them going.

Christy hadn't smoked for over seven years, so Susan asked Chance to put together a trip around the Greek Isles for the four of them, since she had turned over trip planning to him some time ago. In the past, Susan did all the planning for any family trips, so she was happy to leave the job up to Chance now.

Chance set about planning a trip and found a nice trip on a Greek cruise ship, the *Louis Olympia,* for a week.

They would leave Springfield on Friday, September 28, 2012, and then he added a stop on the way home in London for a week.

Susan hadn't been to England before and Chance wanted to take her there and show her his city; he thought of it as his city because he had been there so many times it felt like home to him. He also wanted to show Christy and Steve one of his favorite places in the world.

Steve was an ardent Beatles' fan, so he was thrilled to be stopping in London and to take a walk on Abbey Road and have his picture taken there.

Susan wanted to ride on the London Eye and Christy was up for whatever they were able to do in Greece and England.

Chance and Susan returned to Springfield from Boston on Sunday, September 16, and Chance, Susan, Christy, and Steve left for Athens on Friday, September 28, arriving in Athens, Greece, late Saturday afternoon, September 29, and checked into the Ledra Marriott Hotel.

After a few short hours of sleep, the four of them boarded a Gray Line tour bus at 8:00 a.m. on Sunday morning to visit The Tomb of (the Greek) Unknown Soldier, Olympia Stadium, the Temple of Zeus, the Presidential Palace, the Acropolis, in addition to visiting the new Acropolis Museum, and, of course, the Parthenon.

Four-and-a-half hours later, they all had been thoroughly impressed by the glory of Greece from centuries ago. Two of them for the first time and two of them again, since both Chance and Susan had seen them all before, except for the new Acropolis Museum, but they were still impressed with what they saw all over again.

Monday, October 1, they were taken by a van from their hotel to the *Louis Olympia* cruise ship. Once on board they settled into their cabins, where they would spend the next five days. The ship sailed at 11 a.m. that day.

The ship made a short stop at the island of Mykonos and Christy and Steve boarded a tender, which took them to tour the island. Chance and Susan stayed on board because the sea was very choppy and they didn't feel comfortable enough to get on and off the tender.

The ship traveled through the night and the following morning, the ship docked at Kusadasi, Turkey. They had to be ready to leave the ship at 7:15 a.m. to travel by bus through the city of Kusadasi, Turkey, and on to the ancient city of Ephesus, where now only the ruins of this magnificent city is left.

Before arriving in Ephesus, they stopped at the Shrine of the Virgin Mary, located on Mount Koressos. The shrine was built where legend says Apostle John took Mary, the mother of Jesus, after her son was crucified and she lived there the rest of her life.

Both Chance and Susan had been to Ephesus before and they both loved it. Chance thought it was one of the most interesting places in the world and he had been to a lot of places around the world.

Ephesus was one of the largest cities in the ancient world and was destroyed over the years by earthquakes. The excavation of Ephesus began as early as 1863 and is still ongoing. The people working on this project have to be very dedicated and be very good at putting together a huge puzzle, in order to be able to reconstruct the buildings the way they were originally built in this very large city.

The Romans controlled the city for many, many years and they had their typical Roman baths and public toilets. Many of the homes had their own toilet facilities complete with running water to carry away human waste. It was an outstanding engineering feat to be able to provide such a system considering it was done more than two thousand years ago. They had used running water in the home and had provided a sewer system to get rid of human waste from the home.

One of the most famous and favorite buildings in the city is the ruins of the Celsus library; it is probably the most photographed spot in Turkey. It is hard to imagine how beautiful this building was before the earthquakes, since what is still standing of the library building is so spectacular today.

The Temple of Diana in Ephesus counted as one of the Seven Wonders of the World and the huge amphitheater there has had performance in recent times by Elton John and Sting and still they say the acoustics are judged to be fantastic.

Ephesus is indeed one of the favorite places in Chance's world. The next port they visited on Tuesday, October 2, was Patmos. The island is only thirteen square miles and it is reported in the Bible as the place where Apostle John wrote the Book of Revelation.

Susan was very disappointed visiting here this time, since she had been there thirty years ago and was told John wrote Revelations *in* a small cave. Now, the cave is called the Convent of the Apocalypse and boasts a golden stand that they said John used to stand up after being supine for such a long a time. The cave has a cracked ceiling which was now said is the symbol of three parts of the Trinity through which God spoke to John.

Susan didn't buy any of this new information.

It was also some forty-five stairs down to the cave, so neither she nor Chance went down to see this new edition of the old story. The last stop on Patmos was in a tiny village of Chora, a beautiful whitewashed conclave of attached houses with narrow streets and steep stairs. After being served a drink of ouzo and cookies, they boarded a tender and returned to their ship.

On Wednesday, October 3, they visited Rhodes and their first stop was at an old monastery, the Acropolis of Rhodes, where the most interesting feature was a baptismal pool in the shape of a cross.

The monastery had twelve Stations of the Cross, instead of the usual ten. The eleventh Station of the Cross showed Jesus being taken from the cross and the twelfth Station of the Cross showed Jesus lying in the tomb with the word "Amen."

The next stop on the tour of Rhodes was the Palace of the Grand Masters surrounded by very high walls, which were from six feet in thickness and in some place forty feet wide. The facility was built mostly by the knights of St. John of Jerusalem where they cared for the poor and the sick from 1309 to 1522, until the Turks conquered the city.

From Rhodes, the knights fled to Malta where they remained for over two hundred years, until Napoleon took it over, and then they moved to Jerusalem where they still live and work.

Rhodes was noted in ancient history of having one of the Seven Wonders of the World, which was called the Colossus of Rhodes. It was built in 292-280 BC and it stood on a fifty-foot pedestal and was one-hundred-and-ten-feet tall, made of bronze plates, then mounted on a steel frame. The design was made to look like the Greek God Helios. An earthquake destroyed it only fifty-four years later in 226 BC. What was left of it remained on the shore for decades and was finally sold for scrap and it took over 900 camels to haul it away.

Their next stop on Thursday, October 4, was the island of Crete which claims to be the cradle of European civilization, since the Minoans ruled Crete 3,000 to 4,000 years ago and lived in richly frescoed palaces, with modern drainage and lavish entertainment. Their women wore makeup, jewels, and fashionable clothes, bared their breasts, and braided their hair.

It was amazing they lived in such luxury and modern surroundings centuries before the world even knew there was such a place as America.

The last stop on the cruise was on the island of Santorini, a fascinating volcanic island. The island is twenty-nine square miles in area and was formed from the rim of an ancient drowned volcano that exploded in about 1,500 BC. The island had a population of about ten thousand with four hundred churches; the guide said, "When you live in a volcano, you tend to talk to God a lot."

They drove to the top of the island, some thousand feet above sea level, for a spectacular view of the island and the beautiful ocean.

The cruise ended on Friday morning, October 5, and the group left the ship and returned to the Ledra Marriott Hotel in Athens and spent the day looking around in the central area of Athens.

The next morning Saturday, October 6, they checked out of the hotel and went directly to the airport for their flight to London and on arrival at London Heathrow Airport, they took a taxi directly to the Crowne Plaza Hotel in the Kensington area of London.

On Sunday they spent time resting and took a trip to King's Cross train station to buy tickets to go to the village of Selby in Yorkshire early on Monday morning.

Chance's mother was a Selby and she knew about an old abbey located in Selby, England, and since his mother had talked about the abbey and that was where her last name came from, Chance wanted to make the trip to see it.

From King's Cross station they took a taxi to Harrods department store and spent a couple of hours looking around there before going back to their hotel. It was fascinating to see all kinds of things they had for sale in this famous department store, from meat, candies, furs, veggies, fruits, wine, jewelry, shoes, fashion designer clothes, and toys from around the world.

Walmart may believe their saying "If we don't have it, you don't need it," but it certainly applies to Harrods.

The four of them met at seven the next morning to take a taxi to the King's Cross station for their train to Selby. They had breakfast at the station and boarded the train for the trip of about two hundred miles from London to Selby, which took just about two hours through the English countryside.

They had no trouble finding the Selby Abbey, since it sat right in the middle of the small town, which looked to be a very poor town since many of the stores were closed and empty. However old the exterior of the abbey looked, the inside was gorgeous.

The abbey was started in 1069 and on its nine hundredth anniversary in 1969 Queen Elizabeth came to distribute Maundy Thursday alms. Selby Abbey, although not a cathedral, is one of the largest abbey churches of the medieval times left in England.

Chance was surprised to find out George Washington's ancestors had been members of the abbey and that the abbey had a stained glass window with the Washington's family coat of arms in it. The coat of arms had three red stars and below the stars, it had two red bands separated by a white background. It is said the American flag used the Washington's coat of arms as its design and is the model of the city of Washington, D.C.'s flag.

Because the stained glass Washington window, with the coat of arms is located in the Selby Abbey, the abbey is on the American Heritage Trail.

The following day, Tuesday, October 9, they had a ten- hour tour of London including stops at St. Paul's Cathedral, the Changing of the

Horse Guard at Buckingham Palace, the Tower of London (where they saw the Crown Jewels), and the Changing of the Guards at the Tower of London, these are the guards who guard those precious jewels, and a ride on the Thames River.

The highlight of the day for the weary four was a trip on the London Eye. At 440 feet high, it's the tallest structure in London; it can carry eight hundred people at a time, which is equal to the number of passengers in eleven English double-decker buses. The London Eye moves slowly, at only ten inches per second, and it doesn't stop to load and unload passengers so you board as it's moving, but what a view!

Wednesday, October 10, they boarded another bus to tour several famous sites including the Salisbury Plain, and to the city of Salisbury to see the Salisbury Cathedral, home of one of the four copies of the original Magna Carta.

Chance was glad the people who originally had this copy could read it because he certainly couldn't read this document written in Olde English.

The cathedral also had the world's oldest working clock, which was very interesting, since it didn't have any hands and worked on a series of weights; it had no hands but it did sound the hour. Chance guessed each minute of the hour wasn't as important back in the days when that clock was made.

The next stop on this trip was at the mysterious Stonehenge, the huge monolithic circle of stones that no one knows why it was built or what it was for, even after all these years. These huge stones are standing in the middle of what seems like the middle of nowhere. The boulders, the size of cars, had been dragged or rolled by people for as much as three hundred miles from where they came from, to where they are now. These huge stones had been standing there for centuries, but why?

The one thing they do know is that at the vernal equinox, the sun shines through the circle of stones directly onto a center stone, which may have been some kind of an altar. Chance thought maybe these people worshiped the sun and the whole thing was built just to honor the sun, maybe his guess was just as good as anyone else's. The last stop on this trip was at the city of Bath, which had been a Roman city with its large Roman baths, which gave the city its name during the time when Rome ruled England. The beautiful bath complex is still very well preserved and is the only hot springs in England and these springs are still filling the baths with flowing water, although they are no longer used for bathing.

Bath, like every city they visited on this trip, had another magnificent cathedral, which they didn't even enter. After visiting a few of what now seemed like hundreds of cathedrals, they just didn't have the desire to look at one more!

As many of the tourists they traveled with had said, "ABC— *Another Bloody Cathedral.*"

Since they were flying home the next day, they thought the only way for Steve to take his walk on the Beatles' famous Abbey Road and to get his picture taken crossing it was to take a cab early the next morning on their way to the airport, even though it was in the opposite direction of the airport.

This is what they did, and Steve not only got his picture walking on Abbey Road, but also his picture going up the walkway into EMI Studio, where the Beatles had recorded their first record in studio two, before he saw the sign to "stay away from the studio."

When they arrived home everyone thought they had a wonderful trip and Susan had delivered the promised trip to Christy, even if it was delayed several years.

Thursday, November 15, Chance and Susan flew to San Diego to board a cruise ship for traveling to Hawaii. They would board the ship on November 17, 2012, which was the actual fifth anniversary of their wedding day. The trip would take them four- and-half days at sea to reach the Hawaiian Islands.

Chance had always wanted to take a trip around the world by ship. He thought it would be wonderful going by ship as he had made three trips around the world by plane when he was working for the parking meter company.

The first night they were out to sea, they were in a storm and the sea was so rough it emptied the swimming pool on the top deck of the ship.

They found out later during the trip, the voyage from San Diego to the Hawaiian Islands is considered the second roughest trip cruise ships make, at least according to one of the crew members they spoke with.

Chance had planned to work on a western novel he was writing during the cruise for the four-and-a-half days to and from San Diego, but made a huge mistake of allowing his computer bag to be loaded onto the ship with the rest of their luggage, the result being they broke the screen on his computer. So no writing was done on these nine days at sea.

Chance and Susan enjoyed the time they spent sightseeing on their stops at Hilo, Honolulu, Kauai, and Lahaina.

They enjoyed all the normal tourist spots during their stops and Chance thought the highlight of these tours was the submarine dive, their visit to Pearl Harbor, and boarding the battleship *Missouri* where Japan signed their unconditional surrender ending World War II. On the other hand, Susan was thrilled by seeing a live volcano, up close and personal on Thanksgiving Day.

When Chance and Susan finished their Hawaiian trip on December 2, Chance said, "Susan, I've decided I don't want to take a cruise around the world after spending nine days of seeing nothing but ocean. That was enough for me."

She laughed and replied, "I agree."

Their last trip of 2012 was one they hadn't planned to do at all. Susan was reading a story in the *Springfield News Leader* about an armistice for people who had taken items over the years from the Waldorf Astoria Hotel in New York City and she said, "Chance, I've never been to the Waldorf Astoria and there's a story in this morning's paper about all the things people have returned to hotel that had been taken over the years. They're getting things returned which had been taken from the hotel almost a hundred years ago."

"So, you want to go to the *Waldorf Astoria Hotel?*" "Yes, I would like to go."

"OK, then we could see New York with all of their Christmas decorations and go to a show or two."

"That sounds good."

Chance made reservations for flights to New York City and for two shows (the *Radio City Music Hall Rocketts* and *Jersey Boys*) and, of course, at the Waldorf Astoria, for December 16, and returning to Springfield on December 19.

Needless to say, on their trip the Clarks did New York City's Borough of Manhattan, Rockefeller Center Plaza, Saint Patrick's Cathedral, Fifth Avenue, the Memorial Site of the Twin Towers, the Empire State Building, NBC Studio, and thoroughly enjoyed their two shows, the *Rocketts* and the *Jersey Boys*.

After they returned to Springfield and the Christmas and New Year's festivities were over, Susan said, "Chance, I don't think we should go on so many trips next year."

27

2013-2014

*C*hance and Susan decided in 2013 they would cut back on the number of trips they took but would make some of the trips longer. Their first trip in 2013 would be a river cruise on Uniworld Cruise Line in Vietnam and Cambodia, where they would be gone for almost all of February, which suited Chance perfectly; he hated winter time after spending a lot of years working outside in the cold snow and ice.

This river and land tour would begin in Ho Chi Minh City (Saigon) then on to the Mekong River to Phnom Penh, Siem Reap, and Angkor Wat in Cambodia and then a flight from Siem Reap to Hanoi, Vietnam.

Susan was so excited about making this trip, and when people asked her where their next trip was to and they heard her say, "Vietnam," they all asked, "Why?" Susan always replied, "Because I want to see it and I understand the country is beautiful."

It was a wonderful trip and they met a wonderful couple from Australia, Geoff and Chris, and they would continue to be in contact with them and see them again in the USA and Australia.

In May, they took a trip called the Mid-Atlantic Inland Passage cruise on American Cruise Line from Charleston, South Carolina, to Baltimore, Maryland. The cruise included stops in: Myrtle Beach, South Carolina; Wilmington, Morehead, Oriental, and Kitty Hawk, North Carolina; Norfolk, Virginia; and Baltimore, Maryland.

The last of part of August they went on a cruise and land tour with Princess Cruise Line to Alaska. They flew from Springfield to Vancouver, British Columbia.

While in Vancouver, they took a side trip over to Victoria and spent the night at the Fairmont Empress Hotel, which they both loved, and while there, they took another tour of Butchart Gardens, which Susan kept telling Chance she wanted to use as a model for their backyard.

Chance continued to think they would first have to buy the entire subdivision they lived in to have enough space for her new garden.

On Susan's birthday, August 31, they traveled back to Vancouver and spent the night again before boarding the *Diamond Princess* on September 1.

The first port on their stop was Ketchikan, Alaska, where they went on a seaplane flight called *Misty Fjords Seaplane Exploration*. They loved the flight and saw such beautiful sights and with their first seaplane landing on one of the many lakes in the area.

Their next port was in Juneau, Alaska, and during this stop they visited Glacier Gardens and Mendenhall Glacier.

From Juneau, they traveled on to Skagway, Alaska, and took a tour called the Yukon Expedition& White Pass Scenic Railway.

This trip included a coach ride on the Klondike Highway over the White Pass and on the 1889 White Pass& Yukon Route Railroad, which was only three-feet wide and climbs from sea level to just shy of three thousand feet in twenty miles.

The next two days they were cruising and visited Glacier Bay and College Fjord before arriving at Whittier, Alaska. They boarded a train to Talkeenta, Alaska, transferred from the train and were taken by bus to McKinley Princess Lodge, located in Denali State Park, and much, much different than their elegant room on shipboard.

While at the very primitive McKinley Princess Lodge, they went on a really wild river cruise in a jet boat and up rapids that even the best kayakers in the world couldn't navigate. To say the least, it was a heart-pounding experience. *Wow!*

From McKinley Princess Lodge they were bused to Denali Princess Wilderness Lodge near the entrance to Denali National Park, and the next day they took the Tundra Wilderness Tour from eight in the morning to five in the afternoon.

Their last stop was in Fairbanks, Alaska, where they went on a riverboat cruise before going to their last hotel in Alaska, the Fairbanks Princess Riverside Lodge.

Their trip to Alaska was outstanding and they saw such beautiful sights, and the last one was the opportunity to see the aurora borealis from their airplane, just dancing across the sky; it was fantastic.

Chance and Susan's last trip in 2013 was the Enchanting Danube Cruise from November 7 to November 20. On this tripthey flew from Atlanta to Munich, Germany, and there they were taken by bus to Passau, Germany, to board a Uniworld riverboat, the *River Beatrice*.

In Passau they were scheduled to take a morning tour of the city except as they were getting ready to go to breakfast before the tour, Susan was in the bathroom combing her hair and Chance heard a loud pop. When he went into the bathroom to see what the noise was, he saw Susan was bent over holding her left wrist and she was having awful pain in her wrist.

Chance asked her what was the matter, and Susan said, "I think something in my left wrist broke." It was easy to see how much pain she was enduring, so Chance said, "We better take you to the hospital to see what's happened to your wrist."

They went to the front desk of the ship and told the young female concierge that Susan needed to go to the hospital and find out what had happened to her wrist. Chance said, "I heard a loud popping noise. It sounded like a bone must have broke in her wrist."

The concierge called a taxi and when it arrived, she accompanied them to the hospital. She could speak several languages, which would be a big help since Chance and Susan could only speak English.

The emergency room at the Passau Hospital was like all the ones in the world; it was busy.

However, they were able to see a doctor and he examined Susan's wrist and then asked another doctor to look at Susan's wrist. The second doctor said in a very broken English, "We should have an X-ray of your wrist so we could tell better

what's wrong with it, but it's expensive since you're not on our insurance."

Susan asked, "If it would help you, how much would it cost?" The doctor replied, "Probably as much as fifty euros."

Susan said, "OK, please take the X-ray."

After her X-ray was taken and the doctors had the opportunity to view them they told Susan they thought they should put her wrist in a soft cast and give her some pain medications. Then when she returned home, she should have her wrist checked by a doctor in America.

When they paid the bill with their credit card, the emergency room visit, two doctors, X-rays, a cast, and a large bottle of pain meds were all only eighty euros. So why does medical care cost so much more in America?

From that point on Susan had very special treatment by the ship's crew and they didn't take any of the tours. However, being a river cruise, they had lots to look at in their own stateroom or the captain's lounge located at the rear of the ship.

After Chance and Susan returned home to Springfield, Susan went to a doctor and after he had new X-rays taken of her wrist he told her that she didn't have a broken bone in her wrist but a tendon had broken and snapped and was now reattaching itself somewhere else. She didn't need surgery but the wrist was weak for a long time. In 2014 Chance and Susan took a tour called the South African Adventure. They left home on February 12 and returned home on March 14, 2014.

On this trip they met their tour group in Toronto, Canada, flew to Amsterdam, then on to Cape Town, South Africa, on February 14.

In Cape Town they rested up for a few days and toured the city and the surrounding area including Table Mountain, Cape Point, and the Kirstenbosch Gardens.

On Wednesday, February 19, they departed Cape Town, traveling by bus on the wine route where they made a stop at one of the private wine estates, then on to the town of Stellenbosch, the second oldest city in South Africa.

They stayed overnight in a one of the many wine estates before traveling on the following day on the garden route.

The garden route is the longest wine route in what is called the Western Cape in South Africa. They enjoyed beautiful scenery and stayed overnight in the city of Oudtshroon.

The following morning they toured the Cango Caves, a natural wonder of mysterious limestone caverns with cathedral of stalactite and stalagmite columns.

Then on to visit the Safari Ostrich Show Farm and for the next two nights they would be staying in a hotel on the banks of the Knysna Lagoon.

Saturday, February 22, they continued on the garden route, taking a cruise on the scenic Knysna Lagoon and visited the Monkeyland Primate Reserve and an adjacent Birds of Eden, the world's largest free-flight aviary housing more than three thousand and five hundred birds.

On Sunday, February 23, they traveled to Port Elizabeth for a flight to Durban, South Africa, the largest and busiest airport on the continent of Africa.

Monday, February 24, was a free day to rest and to take a bus tour of the city of Durban.

Tuesday, February 25, they traveled this afternoon to Zululand and had a chance to see a traditional Zulu dancing show. This was where the miniseries *Shaka Zulu* had been made; after the movie folks left, an enterprising millionaire had bought the site and turned it into a motel. Very novel, but no air-conditioning.

Wednesday, February 26, they took a boat cruise on the St. Lucia Estuary, a World Heritage Park. The number of hippos they saw was unbelievable. They saw plenty of crocodiles as well. The hippos and the crocodiles were the main attraction in the park.

Next, they continued their journey to Hluhluwe, a private game park. The accommodations for the night were supposed to be "luxury tented suites" with tiled floors and private wooden sun decks. Not very luxurious and, again, no air-conditioning. Don't they know this is Africa?

Thursday, February 27, was the day for a tour of the Hluhluwe Game Reserve known for its white rhino conservation and home to the "Big Five," the most sought after five large animals for the tourists to see: lion, elephant, rhino, buffalo, and leopard.

Next stop was in Swaziland, a small independent monarchy. Friday, February 28, after leaving Swaziland they reentered South Africa through the Malalane Gate and proceeded to a private concession located in the southeast corner of Kruger Park.

The only problem with that plan was the lodge they were to stay in had caught fire the night before and was too badly damaged for them to stay there.

So their tour guide had to find us other accommodations (for twenty-seven people) as they were en route to the lodge planned for that night. She did! She got them cabins inside Kruger National Park. Chance thought it helps to have the last name of Kruger and be a descendent of the founder of the park.

Kruger Park covers eight thousand square miles and is Africa's oldest, largest, and most famous game reserve established in 1898. Late in the afternoon they would have an open safari vehicle searching for the "Big Five" animals.

Saturday, March 1, early (4:00 a.m.) this morning they went again on another game drive with their expert guide. Generally, the game drives are early in the morning and at dusk when animal movement is most likely. Tourists move to their next location in the middle of the day.

Later in the day they moved to another private game preserve, where they would spend the night and take another game drive in the afternoon.

Sunday and Monday, they stayed in a private game park adjacent to Kruger Park where they made several more trips in the open safari vehicles looking for those elusive "Big Five" animals of Africa and had the opportunity to take more photos of them.

The morning of Tuesday, March 4, was their last game drive in South Africa. Then they traveled on the famous Panorama Route and saw the five thousand-feet-high Drakensberg Escarpment and the weathered rock formations of Bourke's Luck Potholes; it was an amazing system of cylindrical cavities sculpted by river erosion. Breathtaking scenery!

Then they traveled on a sixteen-mile trip along Blyde River Canyon, arriving at the historical town of Pilgrim's Rest, the site the oldest gold rush in South Africa.

On Wednesday, March 5, their trip continued to Pretoria. They had a tour of the city then moved on to the largest city in South Africa, Johannesburg, the center of the world's gold and diamond industries.

On March 6, they had a tour of Soweto, to visit Mandela House. However, they had so many school children visiting on a field trip that they didn't get to tour the house. The next stop was the Apartheid Museum. It was a very interesting and moving place to visit to have a better understanding about apartheid, truly a shameful part of South Africa's history.

Friday, March 7, Chance and Susan had an early morning flight to Botswana to go to the Chobe Game Park, known for its large herds of elephants, buffalo, hippos, and lions.

They went on a unique sunset river boat safari and were told to have their cameras ready to take some amazing pictures. Good advice for great photos!

Saturday, March 8, they went on another river safari in the Chobe Game Park. Of all the places they visited in Africa they liked the Chobe Game Park the best; all the places they had seen were great and very interesting but they liked the Chobe Game Park the most. Maybe because they had a chance to see several mother lions and their cubs made it so special.

Sunday, March 9, was a day Chance has been looking forward to ever since the trip began, traveling on to Zimbabwe to stay at the luxurious Victoria Falls Hotel and to see Victoria Falls.

That evening they were on a sunset cruise on the mighty Zambezi River. The sunset cruise turned into a terrible rainstorm and by the time they got back on the bus to go back to the hotel everyone was drenched.

Monday, March 10, Chance and Susan decided to take a scenic flight over Victoria Falls that was offered as an extra cost item to their trip. They took the trip but it was a bust; they had too many people on the flight to enjoy it. Susan was stuck in the middle between two people so she couldn't even raise her arms to hold her camera. Awful experience, never again would they be crowded into a helicopter.

Tuesday, March 11, they checked out of the hotel and began the long trip home flying from Victoria Falls, Zimbabwe, to Johannesburg, South Africa; then directly to Atlanta, a seventeen- hour-and-eighteen-minute flight; finally from Atlanta to Springfield, Missouri, on Wednesday, March 12.

The day before they were to fly home, Chance got an e-mail offering them a chance to sign up for a really low price, which included free airfare, on a river cruise in July and August in 2014 from Moscow to Saint Petersburg, in Russia.

After they spent time talking it over, they decided to take advantage of the offer so Chance signed them up. It would be one more place they both wanted to see and the trip included all the major sites they wanted to see in Russia.

Although the Russians were involved in a major dispute with Ukraine at the time, they thought their trip would be wonderful and because of where they would be, they didn't think they would be in any danger.

Chance and Susan were to leave on their trip to Russia on July 25, driving to Kansas City and staying at the Marriott Hotel at Kansas City International Airport.

Then on July 28, they would be flying to Washington; then to Vienna, and finally landing in Moscow's Domodedovo Airport at 2:45 p.m. on July 29, 2014.

On the afternoon of Thursday, July 17, Susan's son William came by to visit with his mother before she left on her trip to Russia since he hadn't seen her for a couple of weeks.

He had just come from having his hair cut, after not having it done for some time, and his mother thought he looked so handsome; she told him she wanted to have a picture taken of the two of them. Chance got Susan's camera and took their picture and it turned out to be a very good picture of both of them.

Then the three of them had a nice conversation, catching up with all the things going on with William and his family. His daughter Scarlett and son Skip had both graduated from high school in May and were both working at McDonald's.

After spending a little more than an hour visiting, William told his mother he needed to go back home.

Later that evening William telephoned and said he had forgotten to drop off a DVD when he was at the house earlier and was checking to see if they were going to be home so he could bring it back. He drove over to their house; Susan saw him drive up and went outside to get the DVD. They talked for only a few minutes and he left to return home.

A little after 6:00 a.m. the next morning July 18, the telephone rang and Chance answered the phone and he heard William's wife, Wanda, say, "William's dead."

Chance said in a puzzled way, "William's dead? Is that what you said?"

Susan was halfway out of bed and Wanda said, "Yes, William's dead."

Chance repeated to Susan, "William's dead."

Susan took the phone and said, "We will be right over."

They dressed as quickly as possible and drove to William's home and found Wanda, her daughter Scarlett, and son Skip sitting outside with a police officer with them.

Susan's daughter Christy and her husband, Steve, had gotten to William's house just before Chance and Susan arrived.

Susan asked as soon as she got out of the car, "What happened?"

Wanda answered, "Sometime about 3:00 a.m., William said his head was killing him and told me he was going to lie down on the floor for a while.

"I covered him up and went back to bed and when I woke up about five-something I got down on the floor to see how he was and he was cold and I couldn't wake him up so I called 911.

"When the police got here they confirmed William was dead. I don't know anymore."

Because William was only fifty-one years old and appeared to be in good health, they had to have someone from the coroner's office come to pronounce William's death. Then his body would have to be sent for an autopsy to Columbia, Missouri, to determine what had caused William's death.

They stayed and talked for a while and Chance said, "I'm going to go home and will be back in a few minutes."

They were all waiting for someone from the coroner's office to arrive before the police let anyone in the house.

Before Chance returned, the coroner came and pronounced William's death and made arrangements to have his body taken to Columbia for an autopsy.

Susan asked to see William before they took his body away and she was given permission to come into the house to see him before his body was removed.

One thing in life that is *never* supposed to happen is that you outlive your children.

Susan had been through so much already in life losing her husband, mother, father, and now her son. It was too much to ask of anyone.

Chance picked her up and brought her back home. Since William had looked so good the day before, they both wondered what had happened after he left them. They both had a horrible thought: Did William do something to cause him to die? He hadn't been the same since his grandfather passed away in 2012.

William and his grandfather had become so close in the last few years before his grandfather died. William talked to him every day while he was on the road driving his truck and came to see his grandfather every weekend.

Please don't let this be true.

Waiting to hear about what caused William's death for three days was pure torture for Susan.

While they were waiting to hear the cause of William's death, Wanda asked her mother-in-law, Susan, to help her take care of the arrangements for William's body to be cremated.

Susan told Wanda to meet her and Chance at the Walnut Lawn Funeral Home and she would help her make all the arrangements. The three of them met there a few minutes later and Susan helped make all the arrangements and paid for the service.

Keeping with the family tradition, there would be no funeral service and they would arrange to scatter William's ashes later.

The family decided to use the picture of William that Chance had taken less than twelve hours before William died, for his obituary, since it was the last very good picture taken of him. The funeral home managed to lift his picture from the original picture taken with his mother.

They got a report from the coroner late on Monday, July 21. William had died from a massive brain aneurysm and his heart was almost twice the size it should have been. The coroner told Wanda that due to the size of the aneurysm, William had been probably dead by the time he had laid down on the floor, so even if she had called 911 when he had laid down on the floor it would have been too late to help him.

Susan found out later that William had quit taking his high blood pressure medicine some time ago. He certainly hadn't been taking care of himself.

On Wednesday, July 23, Walnut Lawn Funeral Home called Wanda and told her William's ashes were ready to be picked up. Wanda called and asked Susan if she could possibly pick up William's ashes and, of course, she did.

Chance and Susan went to the funeral home and picked up William's ashes and took them over to Wanda's house. There was nothing more they could do since Wanda didn't know when or where they would spread William's ashes.

Chance and Susan didn't know what they should do about their trip to Russia; the trip had been paid for and there was nothing they could do for William or his family right now, so they decided to go ahead with the trip.

It turned out to be the best thing for Susan because she had something else to do and think about instead of the loss of her son.

They wouldn't see anyone they knew on this trip or anyone who knew about Susan losing her son while they were away.

She and William's sister Christy would have enough problems over losing William in the coming days, weeks, months, and years. When they returned from their wonderful trip to Russia they would be staying home for a while and Christy had been planning a wonderful seventy-fifth birthday party for her mother.

After Chance and Susan had been home for a few days, Wanda called Susan and asked her if she wanted to take William's ashes and spread them because she and her kids couldn't do it.

Susan said, yes, she would, and they would be put into the Buffalo River in Arkansas, in the same place she had put her husband Jack's ashes and where she wanted her ashes scattered. Wanda brought them over that same day and gave them to Susan.

Christy had made arrangements to have Susan's best friend from Chicago come down a few days before Susan's birthday, August 31, to be with Susan, without Susan knowing anything about her coming.

Christy picked Susan's friend Dodie up from the airport and brought her to her mother's house. When they arrived at the house, Chance opened the door and let them in while Susan was in her bedroom. When Christy asked her mother to come out and see her, she came out of her bedroom and saw Dodie. It was a very big surprise and Susan was so excited and happy to see her.

They spent a lot of time talking about everything that had been going on in their lives and Susan's loss of William. Dodie had been his babysitter when he was a very young child and Susan was working.

When they got up on Sunday morning, August 31, Chance told Susan to come and look at her front yard. Christy, Steve, and her grandchildren, Scarlett and Skip, had placed seventy-five small pink flamingos in their front yard sometime after midnight Saturday night.

Susan grabbed her camera and took pictures and said, "What a crazy surprise!"

Then Susan said, "I've loved flamingos ever since I saw a cartoon which showed a Mama flamingo saying to her awkward little one 'Stand tall and fluff your pink feathers.'"

Later that afternoon Chance took Susan and Dodie over to the Springfield Botanical Gardens. When they got there and found their way into a new building and a special room that Christy had rented for her mother's seventy-fifth birthday, the room had been decorated with flamingos and things from the movie *The Wizard of Oz,* which had come out in 1939, the year Susan was born. These were two of Susan's favorite things.

Susan got to see over forty friends and family including her three nieces, her brother and sister-in-law, and friends from Springfield.

After the party was over, Susan felt she had had a wonderful birthday party and day. Christy had done a great job of planning and having a really over-the-top birthday party for her mother.

The day after Susan's birthday, Chance, Susan, Dodie, Christy, and Steve took William's ashes to the same location on the Buffalo River where his father's ashes had been scattered and put his ashes into the river to make their way down to the Gulf of Mexico.

William's wife and children just couldn't take part in spreading William's ashes.

Chance had learned some time ago every person grieves the death of a loved one in their own way and in their own time.

Chance and Susan had one more trip scheduled for the year with the American Cruise Line: a cruise on the Hudson River in New York in October. It was going to be a beautiful cruise seeing the fall foliage along the Hudson River traveling through the Catskill Mountains and the Taconic and Berkshire Hills of New York.

On January 2, 2015, Chance and Susan would be going on a Princess Cruise through the Panama Canal and a tour along the west coast of South America with several stops, including a trip to Machu Picchu and Easter Island, then onto Bora Bora and Tahiti.

What else they would do in 2015 had not been decided; they would have to wait to see what new opportunities came their way and they would try to be ready to take advantage of them.

Chance and Susan knew they loved each other and they loved to travel and they would continue to do both as long as their health and God allowed. They enjoyed a wonderful life together and they were able to laugh at each other and at whatever came their way and comfort each other when things weren't going so well.

They had lived through the loss of their first loves and, somehow, the power of love had brought them together and let them love again.

As Chance and Susan slipped into bed at night, Chance would put out his left arm for Susan to lay her head on and snuggle up as close to him as possible. They tried to do this every night when they went to bed.

As they were lying together, Chance said, "Susan, do you know how much God loves us to have graced us once by having one love, then bringing us together with another such love? It's truly a gift from God."

THE END

About the Book

The Power of Love tells the story of how love can give you the ability to do things you never thought you were capable of doing. Chance and Ann married at sixteen and had been married for almost fifty years when Ann became paralyzed. Chance became her full-time caregiver. This story recounts their efforts to find a cure for her illness and the struggles to keep Ann alive. Chance learned to care for his paralyzed wife and did everything to take care of her—only the power of love could make that possible. Against all odds, they were able to celebrate their fiftieth wedding anniversary. They continued visiting doctor after doctor and hospital after hospital, searching for a way to keep Ann alive. Finally, they had success with Barnes Jewish Hospital and the doctors from Washington University in St. Louis, who were able to stabilize Ann's condition and stop her disease from progressing further.

Regardless of the challenges, they were able to maintain a somewhat normal life together. Then, without any warning, Ann suffered a cerebral hemorrhage and passed away, leaving Chance alone and lost. Chance and Ann's good friend, Susan O'Hara, had lost her husband over eighteen years before Ann passed away. After Susan lost her husband, she went to college, earned her degree, and graduated summa cum laude. Susan vowed never to get married again. This story tells how two people—who never expected to find love again—discovered that the power of love could let them love again and begin a new life together. Their story offers hope to everyone who has lost a loved one.

About the Author

CLARK SELBY was born in 1936 in Miami, Oklahoma, and attended school in Kansas and Oklahoma. He and his wife, Karen Serene Selby, live in Springfield, Missouri. He spent over forty-five years in the parking industry. Clark's work in the parking industry took him to over sixty countries on the six continents. During his years in the parking industry, he served as director of parking for the city of Hutchinson in Kansas: assistant director of transportation and parking for the University of Iowa: parking consultant with De Leuw Cather & Company, a transportation engineering company in Chicago; and project manager for a parking study in Perth, Western Australia. He worked for several years for Duncan Industries as a sales and service engineer, then director of manufacturing. Afterwards, he was promoted to vice president of International Sales and president of the company; During Clarks tenure as vice president of International Sales at Duncan, he was awarded the prestigious President of the United States Excellence in Exporting Award. Clark spent five years as publisher of the Eateries Restaurant and show guide for tourists in Branson, Missouri, publishing up to 100,000 books per year. Clark served in the Kansas Army and Air force National Guard for more than six years before he began traveling in the parking industry and was a sergeant in radio communications. Clark and his wife, Karen, spend as much time traveling and exploring places they haven't been and plan to keep doing it as long as their health allows them to. Clark loves writing new novels and plans to keep doing it, as he says, "I always hope my books tell a good story."

Author of:

- Indian Leader Trail Boss
- Together Forever
- Dangerous Journey Book One
- Dangerous Food Book Two
- Dangerous Cargo Book Three
- Dangerous Enemy Book Four
- Dangerous Mission Book Five
- Dangerous Ally Book Six
- Where's my Wife?